Praise for the novels of Natalie Caña

"This delightful mix of food, familia, and culture will leave readers hungry for more."
—*Publishers Weekly* (starred)

"An utterly charming romance that pays homage to the importance of culture, family, and friendship, *A Proposal They Can't Refuse* is a surefire winner!"
—Mia Sosa, *USA TODAY* bestselling author of *The Worst Best Man*

"Caña's characters leap off the page and into your heart. *A Proposal They Can't Refuse* delivers a happily ever after where familia, food, and finding what was under our nose the whole time are at the core of the story. Natalie Caña's debut will leave you smiling, hungry, and eager to read her next book!"
—Denise Williams, author of *How to Fail at Flirting*

"¡Wepa! Familia meddling, swoony friends-to-lovers angst, and quick-witted banter combine for a deliciously delightful debut!"
—Priscilla Oliveras, *USA TODAY* bestselling author of *Anchored Hearts*

A PROPOSAL THEY CAN'T REFUSE

NATALIE CAÑA

mira™

ISBN-13: 978-0-7783-8609-4

A Proposal They Can't Refuse

Copyright © 2022 by Natalie Caña

For questions and comments about the quality of this book, please contact us at
CustomerService@Harlequin.com.

Mira
22 Adelaide St. West, 41st Floor
Toronto, Ontario M5H 4E3, Canada
BookClubbish.com

Printed in U.S.A.

Para Abuela

Gracias por enseñarme que el amor se mida con hechos.

Dear reader,

I did my very best to write a story full of light and laughter, but—just like us—my characters have dark moments to overcome. Please know that this book deals with sensitive topics like childhood trauma and the loss of close loved ones. I hope I've treated these topics, my characters, and you with the care all deserve.

A PROPOSAL
THEY CAN'T
REFUSE

1

Kamilah Vega stomped up the short entryway and yanked the heavy glass door open with more force than necessary. A strong wind, the type only ever experienced in Chicago, grabbed a hold of the door and pushed it back so roughly that it made a loud bang. The front-desk secretary jumped and gave her a dirty look, but Kamilah barely noticed. Her attention went immediately to the two bodies slumped in the love seat outside the director's office.

She tried her best to keep the anger out of her voice because she already knew how the two troublemakers in front of her would react to it. "What did you do now?"

That garnered an immediate and very predictable response of "Nothing" from both occupants. It was a lie, of course. It always was whenever these two started claiming innocence in unison.

Kamilah rubbed both hands over her face and let out the type of deep and weary sigh that someone should let out at midnight after a hard and long day—not at eight thirty in the morning. She dropped her hands. "Don't you think it's time to stop with the shenanigans? You're eighty years old, Abuelo."

Her grandfather gasped in outrage at the mention of his age and scowled at her. His salt-and-pepper hair was sticking up all over the place like a fuzzy baby monkey, making him look adorable despite the baleful glare.

Looking decidedly more put together, even in his tattered denim overalls and faded flannel, Abuelo's roommate and best friend gave her his own version of the stink eye. "You're only as old as you feel," Killian replied in his deep Irish brogue.

"And that means what? That you two feel twelve?"

Before they could answer, the door to the office opened, and there stood Maria Lopez-Hermann, the director of Casa del Sol Senior Living. "Hello, Kamilah. I'm glad you were able to come on such short notice. I know you were probably in the middle of morning prep at the restaurant."

Kamilah didn't bother telling Maria that after closing the night before, she'd slept through her many alarms and was late to work. Now, thanks to the two hooligans next to her, she was going to be very, very late. Her employers wouldn't care about her excuses. It didn't matter that they were her parents. Kamilah was a Vega and an employee, so her main responsibility was to the family restaurant. Always.

Maria motioned for them to enter her office, and they filed in. Kamilah purposely let Abuelo and Killian sit in the two chairs in front of Maria's desk, while she stood behind them, a hand on each of their shoulders. It was the same stance her mami had taken the time she and her cousin Lucy had got in trouble for skipping gym class for two weeks.

Abuelo crossed one leg over the other and tucked his hands under his armpits, while Killian leaned back, spread his legs wide, and let his arms hang over the short back of the barrel chair. Kamilah once again marveled at their ability to look summarily unconcerned while she was sweating bullets, and she hadn't even done anything.

Maria took a seat behind her desk and interlocked her fingers, resting them on top of her desktop calendar. "I thought I had made myself clear after the bird incident that being banned from pet therapy would be the least of your worries if there were any more pranks pulled."

Kamilah closed her eyes and shook her head. It was a variation on what she'd said right before giving the Devious Duo a monthlong suspension from bingo for starting an illicit gambling ring; before that, there was a security-enforced curfew after the strip-poker fiasco. "What did they do now?" she asked, well aware that it was the third or fourth time she'd asked the question that morning and had yet to get a response.

"This morning we had two residents with high blood pressure show alarmingly high readings after breakfast. We did some investigating and found that Mr. Kane and Mr. Vega had snuck into the cafeteria last night and replaced the decaffeinated coffee grounds with fully caffeinated espresso."

"Abuelo!" Kamilah exclaimed.

"They don't have any proof it was us," Killian interjected. "They just want to blame us for everything that happens in this godforsaken prison."

"*Prison,*" Kamilah scoffed. "You two have more freedom than anyone else in here." It was true. Because of their relatively good physical health and stable mental health, Abuelo and Killian didn't require as much care as many of the other residents. It was more as if Casa del Sol were their college dorm rather than their senior-care facility. It didn't help that the two tended to view the senior-living center's strict rules as friendly suggestions.

"Your feelings aside," Maria continued, "we do have proof. The cameras that we installed in the cafeteria and kitchen caught very clear images of you both."

Abuelo softly damned the cameras. "Condenados cámaras."

But Killian had other concerns. "You hear that, Papo? Freedom," he harrumphed.

"They won't even let me drink café con leche," Abuelo added. "They give me light brown poop water and call it coffee."

"It's decaf with a splash of coconut milk, and your doctor says it's better for your heart," Kamilah pointed out. Abuelo's doctor also said his congestive heart failure was very treatable as long as he took his meds, stuck to a heart-healthy diet, and remained relatively active. Of course, Abuelo paid him no attention.

As if on cue, Abuelo made a noise of disdain. "Ese doctor no sabe na'. Cuando me duele el pecho, me pongo un poco de Vaporú y ya."

Kamilah sucked her teeth more at the claim that his doctor knew nothing than at the miraculous healing quality of Vicks VapoRub. All Latinx people knew Vaporú was the cure for everything from a common cold to heartbreak.

Abuelo looked at the director of the complex with petulance. "And when are you going to start serving carne frita con mofongo?" Abuelo continued, because apparently he was on a roll. "I'm sick of eating all these steamed vegetables like a damn rabbit."

Maria leaned forward. "Mr. Vega, if you are so unhappy with Casa del Sol, you are welcome to find another living facility to reside in."

Kamilah jumped in before her hardheaded grandfather could ruin the best thing he had going for him. "Maria, could I talk to these two alone for a few minutes before you lower the hammer?"

Used to their antics, Maria nodded her head and left the office.

Kamilah sank to her haunches between their chairs and waited until both men looked at her. "You guys have to stop this," she said in her *voice of reason* tone. She placed a hand on each of theirs. "I don't have time for you to be staging weekly high jinks like you're the Little Rascals. I can't be here all the time making sure that you don't get kicked out."

Abuelo turned his face away. "Nobody told you to come act like our mother."

Killian nodded. "We are grown men."

"Bullshite," a deep voice sneered from too damn close, startling Kamilah right as she felt a presence looming over her.

A girl who grew up on the West Side of Chicago and with four tormenting older brothers knew to strike first and ask questions later.

"Not today," Kamilah declared in her You-Messed-With-the-Wrong-Bitch voice, spinning around in her crouched position, morphing into famous Chicago heavyweight champion Ernie Terrell, and swinging her fist at her would-be attacker's crotch.

The moment her fist connected with the very sensitive part of the man's anatomy and she heard his pained "Son of a bitch," she knew she'd made a grave mistake.

Oh dear God, no. Not him. Please don't let him be here.

Meanwhile, Tweedledum and Tweedledee laughed their asses off like a pair of demented hyenas.

When he fell to his knees, Kamilah suddenly found herself face-to-face with the exact man she'd just prayed wasn't there.

Big, broad, and brooding, Killian's grandson didn't resemble him in the least. Where Killian had a round face and wide nose with a bit of a hook at the end, Liam looked like something conjured out of the *tie me up and spank me* books her sister-in-law was always reading. His face was all sharp angles, set off by dark stubble, a stern mouth, and cool eyes.

"What is wrong with you?" He wheezed. "You can't just go around dick-punching people."

The hyenas laughed harder.

Kamilah's jaw dropped. "What's wrong with me?" she asked, incredulous. "What's wrong with you, coming up on me like that? You don't sneak up on a woman and expect not to get junk-punched. Especially not a woman born and raised in Humboldt Park."

His French-blue eyes narrowed under dark brows. His nostrils flared while he inhaled deeply. That was Liam speak for *I'd really like to tell you off right now, but not going to engage.*

Kamilah saw that look often. Whatever. He pissed her off too.

"She has a point, lad," Killian said, the amusement still thick in his voice. "You deserved that whack to the wanker." He stood and pulled his grandson to his feet.

Kamilah found herself once again eye level with Liam's crotch. She quickly stood and turned away from him, her face flushing with embarrassment. She met Abuelo's gaze.

He arched his brows. "Nena, aren't you going to apologize to him?"

"Me? Apologize to him?" Kamilah let out an incredulous bark of laughter. "He should apologize for sneaking in here and scaring me."

"He didn't sneak. The door was open."

Kamilah didn't answer. She should own up to her part and apologize, but her pride wouldn't let her. Pride was the only thing protecting her from Liam. She couldn't let it go now.

Liam stared, expressionless. Then he ignored her comment completely. "Granda, what did you do now?"

Kamilah hated when he ignored her.

Killian opened his mouth, but Liam cut him off. "And don't say *nothing*, because I know you better than that."

Before Killian could come up with a story, Maria walked back into the office. "They threw away all of the decaf coffee and replaced it with Café Bustelo espresso."

"What the hell, Granda? You are willing to get kicked out of this place over coffee? Seriously?"

"It's not the coffee. It's the principle," Killian replied, his nose in the air.

Liam threw up his hands and let out a sound of exasperation. "What principle? That the people you pay to take care of you actually take care of you?"

Killian crossed his arms. "You don't get it because you're young."

"I don't get it because it's nonsense. Granda, where do you plan to go if you get kicked out? You sold your house to move in here with Papo."

At the mention of the house he once shared with the love of his life, Killian's face fell. That had been his wife's dream house, and Kamilah had always suspected that he hadn't really been ready to sell it.

"If you get thrown out, you can't live with me, Granda."

That was too much. Kamilah certainly wasn't in agreement with their troublemaking, but Liam didn't have the right to speak to his grandfather that way. Not after all Killian had done for him. "Because God forbid Super Loner Liam has to allow someone into his hermit cave."

He turned on her. "Excuse me?"

"I'm saying that if they did get asked to leave, which we don't know isn't going to happen, it wouldn't kill you to let your grandpa move in with you. That's what family does."

"I was referring to the fact that he can't walk that many stairs anymore, but I guess, as the almost thirty-year-old woman living with her parents, I should take your word on that other stuff."

Kamilah scowled. He didn't have to bring up her living situation like that. "It's interesting, isn't it? It's like it's not a big deal for us, because I'm not a miserable person who is extremely difficult to be around."

Liam scowled at her. "Don't you have somewhere to be? Like, off making someone else's day shitty?"

Rude. Her pulse sped up. "I usually would, but since I already started with you, I can check it off my to-do list and it's not even ten o'clock. Thanks a bunch." She added a sweet smile.

"Glad to be of service."

"Would you two just get a room already?" Killian said.

Liam turned his dark look on his grandfather, and she made a disgusted noise.

"What?" Killian shrugged. "All I'm saying is you two fight like a couple."

"Yeah." Abuelo added his two cents. "You should just get married already."

There was a beat of silence, and then both octogenarians' eyes lit with the same mischievousness. The kind that had no doubt led to all of them being in their current situation.

"You know what? Let's get back to the reason we are here." She faced Maria. "They may not look it, but I know Abuelo and Killian are sorry for the danger they put their fellow residents in, and next time they will think more about the consequences before they do something so incredibly stupid."

Maria let loose a world-weary sigh, much like the one Kamilah had released earlier. She gave a small eye roll while shaking her head because they both knew Kamilah was full of shit. "Their cafeteria privileges have been revoked for the next two weeks. Prepackaged paper-bag meals will be sent to their apartment, or their families will have to provide their meals for them."

"Is that supposed to be a punishment?" Abuelo asked. "With the stuff they serve here, it feels more like a rew—"

Kamilah covered his mouth with her hand. "That seems totally fair." In her head she was freaking out because she just knew she was going to be the one providing said meals, and she did not have the time for all that. "I'll make sure they get fed." She felt Abuelo's mouth curve behind her hand, and she saw Killian's pleased smile. "Don't get too happy," she warned. "You think they denied you? Just wait to see what I have in store. When I'm done with you, you are going to wish you *could* eat rabbit food."

They were completely unfazed by her threats. Probably because they knew Kamilah was a crème brûlée—right below a crackly hard surface, she was really just pudding.

Echoing her thoughts, Liam scoffed. "As if you aren't going to end up making them three-course meals complete with dessert."

Kamilah fought the urge to stick her tongue out at him like a six-year-old. Instead, she ignored him. "I have to go to work, but for the love of God, please behave yourselves today," she begged the duo of deviants.

She was almost positive she heard Killian mumble, "We make no promises."

★ ★ ★

A few minutes later, Kamilah was in the middle of the most changed part of Humboldt Park: the streets surrounding The 606. Snippets of the old, elevated railway recently converted into a greenway—officially known as the Bloomingdale Trail—peeked through the spaces between the historic homes and new condos. Kamilah couldn't help but scowl at the view no matter how beautiful it was. Everything about the trail had been carefully crafted by the public and non-profit sectors, but the real estate surrounding the attractive new amenity had been left to the marketplace. It was no surprise, then, when home values began to rise, making long-time residents unable to pay rents and property taxes. Since then, her tío Rico, who was the alderman, and other activists had fought hard to put measures in place to help mitigate the gentrification of the neighborhood, but as far as many of the original residents were concerned, it was too little, too late.

Kamilah didn't have a problem with other folks making their way into the neighborhood, especially if that meant new opportunities and an influx of money. Her issue was that a majority of the original residents were being denied access to those opportunities and the financial possibilities that came with the changes.

She pulled to a stop at a red light and shook her head at the direction of her thoughts. Something out of the corner of her eye caught her attention. It took her a few seconds to realize what it was. Kamilah sucked in a breath. The backlit sign from La Isla, a neighborhood Puerto Rican restaurant much like her own family's restaurant, was missing. The wooden sign in front of the restaurant now said *Swig*, and there was a patio that hadn't been there before. She knew the Rivera family struggled to pay their rent, but... La Isla? Closed?

Kamilah slowed and pulled up in front of the building. It was technically a no-parking zone, but she didn't plan to stay. She just wanted a closer look. Her hazard lights blinked with the touch of a finger. She unbuckled her seat belt and leaned over her middle console.

A list of the weekly specials decorated the sidewalk sign in chalky cursive. Everything listed was what her mami liked to call *bougie* food, what Kamilah called *modern American*, and what others called *hipster*. A colorful flyer sticking off the top corner caught her attention. Kamilah braced her hands on the console and twisted until she had a knee on the seat. She leaned closer.

This restaurant is a stop on the 3rd annual Fall Foodie Tour. Come join us every weekend this season as we hit the best restaurants in Humboldt Park.

Kamilah snorted. *Best restaurants,* her ass. She didn't have to be a genius to know there were no OG neighborhood restaurants on the docket. It never worked that way. It was clear from the beginning that the event was for these new supposedly cultured invaders to pat themselves on the back for ostensibly bringing enlightenment and class to the ignorant masses. The *caucasity,* as her best friend, Sofi, would say.

A tall blond man standing on the patio in chef's whites drew her eye. He was walking from table to table shaking hands and chitchatting with customers. Something about the way he stood reminded her of—

"No." She thumped her hand against the console beneath her. *It can't be.* Chase was supposed to be in LA, where he stayed after winning *American Chef Battle.* The selfish, treacherous jackass.

Kamilah leaned farther across the console to get a better

look. Her face was almost smooshed against the passenger-side window when the man threw back his head and laughed.

It *was* him.

"Son of a—" Kamilah's exclamation cut off when her sweaty palm slipped off the worn leather passenger seat, causing her to nearly fall to the floor. Her knee jerked, knocked into the steering wheel, and accidentally hit the horn. The horn that sounded like a drove of sickly donkeys and had the tendency to stick. Her 2003 Toyota Corolla—named Doña in an attempt to make it seem like a dignified old dame—was just plain old and janky as hell.

At the abrupt sound, Chase and everyone else on the patio turned, but Kamilah ignored them. Because the damn horn was still going. She flopped around like a panicked seal on the beach until she was back in her seat. She beat her fist against the steering wheel but only succeeded in causing a start-and-stop car-horn club remix. Finally, the sound of asses braying cut off, leaving only one ass.

An ass who turned and locked eyes with her ex-fiancé through the passenger-side window.

Chase's mouth formed her name in surprised confusion. He took a few steps in her direction.

"Shit." Kamilah jerked her car into Reverse, threw it into Drive, and peeled out of there.

She was reeling. After all the shit the Forest Glen born-and-raised jerk talked about Humboldt Park—namely, that it was a gang haven that would one day swallow her whole—Chase opened a restaurant barely two miles from her own. *How dare he?*

Humboldt Park was *hers.*

Kamilah's shoulders tightened even more as she turned

onto Division Street and saw yet another familiar business with boarded-up windows.

Division Street, particularly between Western and California Avenues, was the epicenter of Humboldt Park's Puerto Rican community. In its heyday, the area nearly resembled the neighborhoods of the island, many buildings imitating the Spanish colonial architecture found in Viejo San Juan. Colorful murals blurred by her window, paying homage to the culture and the walk of fame that honored prominent Puerto Ricans. Her lips curved as offices of local Puerto Rican politicians flew by, the storefronts dotted with local art galleries and dance academies.

But now? Now things were changing. Her brow furrowed.

Paseo Boricua was still a microcosm of Chicago's Puerto Rican community, but the miniature had begun to show cracks and chips just like an antique portrait painted on a porcelain pendant. Puerto Rican pride was still visible up and down the avenue, but it was no longer as loud or as vibrant as it had once been.

Her throat tightened as she drew closer to her work, her family, and their little restaurant.

Back when her grandparents had first opened it, El Coquí had fit right into the neighborhood. The Boricuas of Chicago flocked to El Coquí because no one did Puerto Rican food better than Abuela Rosa Luz. And because no one entertained more than Abuelo Papo and his salsa band, Los Rumberos.

But those regulars were gone now. Little by little, El Coquí had emptied until there was hardly anyone left. It reminded her of the scene at the end of her favorite movie, *The Sandlot*, when the kids playing baseball disappeared one at a time until the only kid left was Benny "The Jet" Rodriguez, still running the bases and doing his thing.

That was her family.

Still in the neighborhood doing their thing.

Kamilah pulled into her parking space on the left side of the building and climbed out of her car. She let herself into the back hallway, where a set of stairs greeted her. Instead of taking them up to her childhood—and current—home, she headed through the door that led to the restaurant kitchen.

Raised voices came from the dining area.

"I'm not going," Papi said.

"Oh yes you are," Mami returned. "You've put it off long enough. You were supposed to have a prostate exam two years ago."

Kamilah swallowed, pushing through the swinging doors. Papi was wiping down chairs, while her brother Leo cleaned glasses behind the bar and Mami bent over one of the tables. She scrubbed so hard the little ponytail on the top of her head, which Kamilah had warned her many times made her look like Pebbles from *The Flintstones*, flipped around like a tiny fan.

"No me importa," Papi said. "Ain't nobody sticking a finger in my butt." He lifted a wooden chair from the floor, slammed it onto the table, and wiped it down with unnecessary vigor.

Mami stopped scrubbing the tables, spun on her heel to face him, and placed both hands on her hips. "You didn't have a problem when I did it last week," she snipped in Spanish.

Kamilah's jaw dropped while the contents of her stomach rose. Her eyes met Leo's in mutual disgust and horror. If there was anything worse than listening to one's parents discuss anal play, she was positive neither one of them had yet to experience it. "Ay fo," she exclaimed at the same time Leo started loudly gagging into the sink behind the bar.

"Ay cállense." Mami told them both to shut up before she gave Kamilah a thorough once-over. "¿Y tu? You can't find pants without holes in them?" She paused and zeroed in on Kamilah's head. "Or a brush?" She shook her head and pursed her lips. "If you're going to show up late, the least you can do is fix your hair. I don't understand how you girls these days leave the house looking homeless." Mami was not a fan of the distressed look.

Sadly, everything about Kamilah screamed distressed, from her riotous curls and hastily done makeup to her perpetually wrinkled work shirt and scuffed tennis shoes. Poor Mami: she wanted so badly for her only girl to be a polished princess. Instead, she'd got a high-strung hot mess.

"No wonder you're single," Mami finished.

Kamilah grimaced.

At least Papi jumped in to defend her. "Ay, Valeria, déjala. She looks fine."

Mami turned on him again. "Don't you say anything to me unless it's about you going to the appointment I made for you."

"I'm perfectly fine."

"How do you know?" Mami asked. "Remember my cousin Jencarlos? One day he was fine, the next day he was dead."

"Wasn't he hit by a car crossing the street?" Leo asked, placing two glasses back on the shelf. Kamilah hid her laugh behind a cough.

Papi nodded.

"It doesn't matter," Mami exclaimed. "The point is you never know."

"I'm not going to die."

"You'd better hope not. I'm telling you right now, Santiago Vega. I'm too young and too pretty to be a widow."

Both of Papi's eyebrows went up, and he blinked. "What does that mean? Mujer, you better not be telling me that you'll marry someone else if I die first."

Out of the corner of her eye, Kamilah watched the youngest of her four older brothers slip on his Chicago Fire Department bomber jacket. He was getting ready to bail. "Tell them I got called into my shift early," he whispered to her as he slid past. "Oh and I forgot to restock the bar, so take care of that for me." He didn't wait for a response before he slunk out the door. He assumed she would do his bidding. Typical.

As much as her parents could annoy her, Kamilah wouldn't bail. Especially when she had the perfect idea to ensure that El Coquí—like Benny in *The Sandlot*—moved up to the big leagues instead of fading into nothingness.

2

The blonde in the crop top was one hundred percent over it. He'd guessed it a few minutes ago when she'd mouthed *Seriously?* to the girl next to her. But watching her mime shooting herself in the highly reflective pot of the five-hundred-and-fifty-gallon copper still definitely convinced him. Not that he blamed her.

In fact, Liam Kane was one hundred percent over it too. Unfortunately for them all, Liam's grandfather had taken off for some unknown errand, so this nightmare of a guided tour of Kane Distillery was up to him. Never mind that on his very best day, Liam would give his ability to deal with people a six out of ten. But after his run-in with Kamilah and her junk-punch that morning, he was currently at two...and falling.

Per usual, he'd been unprepared for Kamilah Vega. He tried his very best to build up immunity between their interactions. Like an athlete before a big game, he had to psych himself up before seeing her. *You won't stare at her. You won't* be an ass. *You'll act like a normal human being.* It never worked. *One day*, he told himself. One day she wouldn't affect him like this, and a brief interaction wouldn't completely throw him off his game for hours. Until that day came, he had a business to run and a tour to give.

"The first compounds released in the still as it heats up are the lower boiling-point compounds, which we call *the head*. These compounds include methanol, acetaldehyde, and lighter esters." He knew he sounded as bland and monotonous as that one actor from the "Clear Eyes is awesome" commercials, but he continued anyway. "Some of these compounds, particularly methanol, are poisonous to humans, which is why the head has to be separated from what we call *the heart* of the spirit, or the ethanol, used to create the finished product." He was sure there was some metaphor in there somewhere about keeping the head and the heart separate, but he didn't think about it for long because the blonde had finally had enough.

She raised her hand.

Liam contemplated acting like he hadn't seen it, but then she waved her arm all around, ensuring that everyone took note. "Yes?" Liam asked, even though he knew exactly what she was going to say.

"When is the tasting part of the tour?" Behind her was the mural that had taken him weeks to paint of the logo that had taken him months to design.

Along the top of the wall the words *Kane Distillery* were written in black calligraphy. Below was a detailed rendering of what looked like the Headless Horseman but was really the Irish faerie of death—the Dullahan—on a fierce-looking black stallion with glowing red eyes. The horseman was wearing gleaming spiked black armor and carrying a creepy, wide-smiling head in one hand and a long whip made of human spines in the other. The long tail of the whip wound through the air, where the end twisted, curled, and looped to create the *D* in *Distillery.*

The blonde stepped forward, causing him to refocus on her disgruntled face.

And that, right there, was why Liam hated giving tours. These people didn't give a shit about the level of craftsmanship that went into the process or the building. They couldn't care less about the endless years of hard work and dedication he and his grandfather had put into their distillery just to get to the point where they could even give tours. They only wanted to get tipsy for ten bucks and take cute pictures for their Instagram accounts. "The tasting is at the end of the tour."

She sighed deeply as if he were the one interrupting her busy day. "I know that but, like, how much longer?"

Liam tried to keep his annoyance from bleeding into his tone. "Well, I'm right in the middle of discussing the different cuts of distillation. After that we discuss the barreling and aging process and then bottling."

She actually rolled her eyes. "Can we just skip those parts?"

Wow, that's new. Liam's brows twitched, and he did a double blink. He'd never had someone ask that question aloud, although he suspected they thought it. He might've been impressed, were it not for the enormous sense of entitlement behind it.

"I'm not trying to be rude," she continued. A sure sign she was about to be *extremely* rude. "But, like, this tour definitely isn't as interesting as we were led to believe, and I'm not really looking to be on it for another—what?—forty minutes."

The other six people in the group had suddenly found the distillery around them extremely interesting. The blonde's friends were staring at the bottling station in the center of the room as if it held the secrets of the universe. And the older couple had stepped away and were taking pictures of the logo mural.

Liam was about to tell them all that they could leave, when something in one of the open garage doors caught his eye. He instantly recognized the familiar form of his grandfather, Killian, silhouetted by the sun.

Granda stepped through the door and into the large warehouse that housed their distillery. His eyes locked on Liam, standing among the dissatisfied group with his arms crossed. Granda's lips pursed. It was clear he wanted to know what was happening but wasn't about to interrupt the tour. He took a few steps in the direction of the office they shared.

Liam put a stop to that instantly. If anyone was going to escape to the office, it was going to be him. "Granda," he called, "these customers are unhappy with the Kane Distillery tour. This one in particular." He pointed at the rude blonde. "I was just about to suggest the Jeppson's Malört tour over at the CH Distillery instead."

Granda's thick, dark gray eyebrows rose over his wrinkled eyes. He knew that whenever Liam started suggesting that particular Chicago institution to customers things were bad. The Swedish bäsk liquor was arguably one of the most disgusting liquors ever sold. Made with wormwood, it was notoriously bitter with a foul aftertaste. The original label even called it brutal to the palate.

"There's no need for all that." Granda spread his arms like the Christ the Redeemer statue in Rio de Janeiro. "I'm here to give you all the *real* Kane Distillery tour."

"We want to get to the tasting," the blonde said with a flip of her long waves.

Granda smiled his trademark lopsided grin, the one that

never failed to charm the hell out of people, and if that didn't work, his Irish brogue would do the rest. "Oh 'course you do," he said as he ambled over. "A beautiful lass like yourself doesn't have time to wait around. She deserves to get what she wants when she wants it."

Now it was Liam's turn to roll his eyes. Granda was laying it on way too thick, but she ate it up. Liam saw the first smile of the day out of her.

"But, lass, I'm very proud of my life's work, so I hope you don't mind if I brag a wee bit first. I promise to keep it short." Like a pro, Granda didn't wait for her to give her permission: he looked at their place in front of the stills and jumped right in. "I see Liam was telling you all about our pot stills. It took me almost twenty years to save up for this beauty, but like you, lass—" he turned and gave the blonde a wink "—she was well worth the wait."

The blonde blew Granda a kiss.

"Now," Granda continued, "did he tell you about the cuts?"

"I just told them about the head," Liam informed him.

"The head," Granda exclaimed. "No wonder they were bored out of their minds when I walked in. How many times do I have to tell you, lad? It's all about the heart." He placed a hand over his. "And, if you're lucky, about the tail," he added with a waggle of his brows. The group laughed, and Liam took that as his cue to retreat.

He walked past the barrel room, which he knew was the next stop on the tour and where Granda would show off the most important barrel in the entire distillery. "This whiskey has been sitting in this barrel, turning into liquid gold, for almost twenty years. Soon it's gonna help us win the Best Craft Whiskey Distillery contest," he'd say. Then Granda would launch into a tale about his only son, Connor, and how he'd created this secret blend of whiskey shortly before he died heroically. He'd go on to tell perfect strangers that, in Connor's honor, he and Liam were making his dream of operating an award-winning distillery come true. Granda would say it with such pride that everyone in the room would beam in shared admiration of a man they'd never even met.

Just thinking of it all turned Liam's stomach. He trailed his fingers along the Kane Distillery mural Granda had made him design because he refused to use the Kane family crest. Yeah. The whole *family legacy* angle wasn't as sweet a sentiment as people thought. Once safely enclosed in the office, Liam pulled the shades to the large window overlooking the distillery floor and went to sit at his desk. He scanned his sticky-notes to-do list. Number one: call the bottle supplier. Over half of the glass bottles they'd received in the last shipment were weirdly cloudy and needed to be replaced. He also had to put in an order for more limestone-filtered water from Southern Illinois, call the repairman about their fermentor, and schedule a meeting with a local buyer. That was just one Post-it. There were four more full of things that required *his* attention.

Although Granda was his partner, as time passed and their business grew, more and more responsibility got placed on Liam's plate. That didn't even take into account how much their business would boom once they won Best Craft Whiskey Distillery. The fact was that they needed help. They couldn't go on just the two of them, no matter how much Granda argued that they could and should.

"The labels on these bottles say *Kane Distillery* because that's who runs this business—Kanes," Granda was apt to say whenever Liam brought up the topic. That and "We aren't bringing in a bunch of unskilled strangers to fuck up what I've spent my entire life building."

Already beset by the day and everything demanding his time, Liam scanned the adhesive notes for something he could handle, then smiled. He grabbed the accounting files spread across the top of his desk and stacked them in a corner before reaching into his top drawer and pulling out his sketchbook and canister of supplies. Setting the container on his desk, his fingers caressed the product sketches until he found a blank page. Their latest creation was a heavy, dark mahogany whiskey with a bit of bite, so Liam had named it Abhartach after the Irish folkloric vampire. Setting his pencil to the blank page, Liam began to sketch what would eventually become the label.

At first his lines were thick, bold, dark, and clumsy—a testament to his frustration with his inability to get and keep his shit together. As he continued to sketch, he tried to recall the story his grandmother had told him. With each scratch of the sharp pencil against the paper, his muscles began to loosen. His lines morphed into graceful, practiced strokes, and a detailed image began to emerge. He could almost hear her telling him about the tyrannical dwarf chieftain who was killed by a rival but came back as a vampire to feed on his subjects until he was finally vanquished with a yew sword through the heart. For the life of him, Liam couldn't figure out why she'd thought it a good story to tell a seven-year-old, but that had hardly been the first time she'd shared questionable folklore with him. Now Liam used those stories to name his whiskey. He was in the middle of adding long iron claws into his sketch when the door to the office shot open and banged against the wall.

"What the feck is wrong with you, lad?"

According to the therapist Liam was forced to see as a kid, the answer was *PTSD and depression*, but Liam knew Granda wasn't talking about that since he'd solely referred to Dr. Kofsky as "that self-important quack who doesn't know his arse from his elbow." Liam continued to sketch. "Could you be more specific?" He paused. The drawing was good, but perhaps a bit too creepy for a label.

"Stop fussing with that damn drawing, and look at me when I'm talking to you."

If only he had a dollar for every time he heard that specific phrase. Liam sighed deeply and looked up at his own small tyrant. He wasn't sure what he'd done, but—after living with his grandfather since the age of fifteen—he knew when he was about to receive a famous Killian Kane reaming.

"Care to explain the train wreck I walked into earlier?" Granda asked as he slowly lowered himself into the chair in front of Liam's desk.

"It seems pretty obvious." They both knew Liam hated giving tours. "You should've blacked out that time on the tour schedule if you knew you weren't going to be here."

"I have no idea how to work the damn computer program. You know that."

"I get it. I've only walked you through it approximately seven hundred and thirty times."

"Don't be a smart-ass, you little shite."

Again, if he had a dollar…

"What exactly are you mad about right now, Granda? You showed up at just the right moment and saved the day." Liam started to sketch again, focusing on the long dark scraggly hair. "When I walked away, you had everyone eating out of the palm of your hand, which is your favorite thing in the world."

"I shouldn't have to save the day." Granda leaned forward and plucked the pencil out of Liam's hand. "You should be able to get through a tour without acting like a complete eejit."

Liam leaned back in his chair and interlocked his fingers over his stomach. "That's not my thing."

"It should be. This is just as much your business as it is mine." Granda waved the pencil around in emphasis. "You should know it inside out and be able to do every single job that needs to be done."

Liam spread his arms wide to encompass their surroundings. "I do most of the jobs that need to get done, Granda. That's the problem. I don't have time to take over doing the tours too."

"Don't tell me you are going to start bitching about having a successful business now." Granda reached over and grabbed the pad Liam was sketching on. He snorted at the drawing and then tossed it back on the desk. "You should be busting your ass to grow it, not getting caught up in the details."

Liam could feel his patience slipping. Granda always had to push. He always wanted more. It wasn't enough that Liam bent over backward to try to be what he wanted. He needed to reinvent himself. Be something he wasn't capable of being. "If I don't worry about the details, who will? Running a successful business is more than schmoozing customers, Granda."

"You think I don't know that?" Granda slapped his palms on the desk. "I've been running this business since before you were a tadpole in your da's ball sack."

Liam grimaced. "Nice."

Granda threw his hands up. "All I'm saying is we're finalists in a national contest. We're one surprise visit away from being named the Best Craft Whiskey Distillery in the country.

You think we'll win with you giving shite tours and pissing off the customers? You have to do better, lad. We need to be operating at our prime."

It all came back to the contest. For over a decade they'd studied up on the American Spirit Distillers contests. When they announced contests for craft distilleries with categories for different spirits, they knew it was their chance to make Da's dream come true. All they had to do was wait for their secret weapon, Da's whiskey, to mature. This was the year. It was hard to believe that it had been two decades since his father created this special blend. Twenty years since he'd been gone.

Liam ran a hand over his face and sighed. "I know how important this is, Granda. I'm doing my best. Besides, you will be the one giving the tour when they come. Not me."

"If I'm here," Granda mumbled.

Liam frowned in confusion. "Where else would you be? Sipping piña coladas on some beach in Florida?" Liam always teased Granda about retiring to some tropical beach even though he hated heat, humidity, and sand.

"No. Dead."

Liam laughed. That was a new one. Usually when his grandpa wanted to guilt him into something, he just brought up the fact that he took Liam in when his mother moved to the East Coast with her new husband. "Yeah, well, how much do you think I could get if I sell your liver for research? Because it has to be some scientific anomaly that it's still functional."

"Funny you should mention my liver function."

"Why?" Liam smirked. "Because you've consumed more alcohol in your life than the majority of people have water?"

"No." Granda leaned back in his chair and stretched his

arms along the rests. His fingers curled around the ends and squeezed. "Because I have stage four liver cancer and will be dead before the end of the year."

Liam's wry smile fell, and he scowled. "That's not funny."

"It sure as hell isn't," his grandfather agreed.

"Granda, stop. I get it. One day you'll be gone, and I'll be running this place by myself, but to joke about having cancer is just wrong."

"I wish I were joking, but I'm not." He paused and looked Liam in the eyes. "I have cancer, and it's not the kind you live through."

There was an odd whirring in his ears, and the world seemed to swirl around him. Then he sucked in a quivering breath, and the world stabilized, but his body did not. There was a tingling sensation in his stomach.

"When I started shitting chalk, I figured I had something more serious than just stomach pain. They did a bunch of tests, and that's what they found."

Tests? When had they done tests, and how had Liam not known about them? Liam wanted to say something. The problem was he couldn't think of anything to say. Even if he could, he was pretty sure that if he opened his mouth he would throw up.

"Today they called me in to tell me all this shite about radiation and chemo injections or whatever, but I'm not doing any of that bullshite. I may be a miserable bastard, but I've never been a dumb one. I know when it's time to call it quits, and this is it. My time's up, lad."

He couldn't have possibly heard that right. There was absolutely no way that his grandfather, his partner, his rock, the only person who truly gave a shit about Liam, was telling him that he wasn't going to treat his cancer. There was no way he was telling his grandson that he was prepared to just die. That, just like everyone else in Liam's life, he was going to leave.

Liam did the only thing he could think of. The thing he'd been doing since he was old enough to discover the power play. Without even a glance at the man who'd just betrayed him, Liam left first.

3

So far Kamilah's proposition to enter El Coquí into the Fall Foodie Tour was going about as well as she had expected.

"I know what this is." Mami pointed an accusatory finger in Kamilah's face. "You think I'm stupid and that I can't cook."

Kamilah counted to five in her head because ten would take too long and Mami would just take the silence as affirmation of her guilt. "Mami—"

"No, no. Don't deny it," Mami interjected before Kamilah could even get a word out. "You think you're smarter than me and a better cook."

The restaurant, particularly the kitchen, was a constant spot of tension between them. After Abuela died, Mami had taken over the kitchen. In honor of her mother-in-law, Mami wanted to keep everything exactly as Abuela had it. Nothing in the kitchen was to be changed or upgraded unless it broke and couldn't be fixed. The recipes were followed step-by-step the exact way Abuela had drilled them into her head. The menu was the same laminated sheet Abuelo and Abuela had made up back when they'd first opened. It was all very traditional and comforting…but it was also stifling.

The first time Kamilah suggested a garlic Greek yogurt aioli instead of mayo ketchup, Mami had acted like her daughter had slapped her. When Kamilah made a light citrus-infused mojo instead of the typical garlic-and-butter one for their shrimp, Mami had literally cried at the betrayal. To this day, no one mentioned the couscous con gandules fiasco in their presence. Not her finest idea, she could admit.

As if on cue, Mami waved her off and headed toward the kitchen. "Miss Cucu always thinking she knows better because she went to culinary school." That was how Mami said *couscous*. Never mind it also meant something completely different. Her mother was well aware but chose to call her Miss Ass anyway.

Kamilah followed her parents through the swinging doors to their outdated but spacious kitchen. "Mami, we have to change. The customers are changing, and they're looking for different things. We have to adapt if we want to stay open."

"If we have to get rid of everything that makes us who we are, then what's the point?" Papi snapped. "My parents opened this place to celebrate us and our neighbors and the community. To show their pride and love of our culture. They didn't open this place to cater to a bunch of yuppies who want everything vegan and locally sourced."

Kamilah shook her head. "Abuelo Papo opened El Coquí because Killian convinced him that buying an abandoned ironsmith-and-masonry workshop would make them both rich. Plus, he wanted a place he could hang out and play music with his bandmates." Abuela was the one who had poured

her heart and soul into turning the old storefront into a restaurant, and she had always welcomed everyone with open
arms. When customers were in El Coquí, they were treated
like family. It was why the restaurant had been so popular
and the customers so loyal.

Kamilah knew they could be that way again. "It's not about
catering to any one group of people, Papi. It's about making
sure everyone who comes here feels welcome and valued and
that they leave feeling happy and satisfied. All we have to do is
update the menu and give the place a face-lift." Kamilah loved
the place more than anyone, but she knew it was a bit much.

El Coquí, named after Puerto Rico's beloved native frog
and mascot, leaned hard into the whole island vibe, complete with a neon sunset mural, palm-tree embedded walls,
beach huts over the tables, and hammocks hanging from the
ceiling. Not to mention the white Christmas lights (up and
on three hundred and sixty-five days a year), eight million
Puerto Rican flags, and coquí frogs in every available space.
The large group table was shaped like the island and painted
like the flag. Oh and the entire left side of the building's exterior was a mural of a cartoon coquí frog waving the Puerto
Rican flag, in case people weren't sure what they were.

Abuelo liked to call it *branding*, but they should be honest: it
was a brightly colored and tacky hodgepodge of kitsch. Back
in the day, customers had loved it, but those were also the
same people who'd put two huge metal Puerto Rican flags
across Division Street and named it Paseo Boricua. Subtlety
was not exactly their jam.

"All I'm saying is if we make some simple changes, things
to appeal to the changing community, we could bring in
more people. We could use the Fall Foodie Tour almost like
a reopening."

Mami scoffed. "You say that because ever since you went to culinary school, all you want to make is bougie food. And who's going to pay for these new fancy ingredients you want to use and the materials to redecorate?"

"You always do this," Papi said, following right on Mami's heels. "Come up with all these impractical ideas. Because, yeah, you went to culinary school, but you don't know how to run a restaurant."

Well, ouch. Kamilah winced.

Papi immediately looked contrite. He drew a deep breath. "Mila, I'm not trying to be hurtful, but we have to be realistic, and realistically…" He seemed at a loss for words. "You've always been a dreamer, mamita. Remember when you were a girl and thought you were going to marry the boy from the baseball movie? It didn't matter what anyone said, it didn't even matter he wasn't real, you planned a wedding."

"Umm, excuse me, I knew Benny wasn't a real person. I wanted to marry the actor who played Benny. It's called having a celebrity crush. You know, like your obsession with J.Lo or Mami's infatuation with Mario Lopez." She gave her parents a smart-ass look, all raised eyebrows, pursed lips, and tilted head. She should've known her superiority wouldn't last long. Not around her mother.

"What about Paris?" Mami added. "You had all these plans. Go to *that* school, become a famous chef. You watched all those videos and practiced all those recipes. You learned French. ¿Y para qué?" *And for what?* Wasn't that just the million-dollar question? "Aquí sigues," she added, as if Kamilah didn't know where she was. As if she weren't highly aware of the fact she'd never gone to Paris. "Maybe if you had tried as hard to get into that school as you do trying to run this place, you'd be a famous chef in Hollywood right now, like your ex."

"Basta," Papi said, calling an end to their shitting on Kamilah's life. "That has nothing to do with anything."

That wasn't exactly true. It had a lot to do with how they viewed her. She was their aimless daughter, who went through the motions but never really accomplished anything.

All talk and no follow-through.

Kamilah bit her lip. True, she hadn't followed through with some of her plans, but it wasn't because she lacked the drive, like they seemed to think.

Mami ignored Papi's command like always. "Yo na' mas digo, she's too dedicated to this place. How is she going to find a man when she's here all day every day and nights on the weekend? She doesn't see anybody but family or the same old drunks she serves here. Is that who you want her to marry, Santos? Un borrachón que no hace nada?" She gave him a look of disgust, as if he'd gift wrapped Kamilah for said lazy drunk. "She's getting too old to have babies, you know. Every day more and more of her eggs spoil."

If Mami had one talent, it was the ability to turn every conversation into a lamentation over Kamilah's single state.

"Hey." Kamilah waved her hands to get her parents' attention. "Hi, I'm standing right here, and we aren't talking about my love life. We're talking about El Coquí."

Mami spun on her. "I know what we're talking about," she said as her head bobbled. "We are talking about you being too busy trying to push us out the door to go out in the world and meet a man to marry."

Papi jumped in before Mami could really get started. "Kamilah, I know you want to help, but I've been giving this place my all since I was fifteen. My blood, sweat, and tears are soaked into the floorboards. I think I deserve the right to say what happens next, and I'd rather see it close how it opened, authentic and humble, than change completely into something I don't respect." He walked toward the back door. "I'm going to go take a walk."

Kamilah watched as his shoulders slumped right before he hit the doorway. Mami's hand came up to rub his back and she murmured something in a soothing tone.

"You need to give your father a break," Mami said as soon as Papi was out of sight. "This isn't easy for him."

"I know, Mami, but—"

"No. I don't want to hear it. The fact is that every day we fit in less and less in this neighborhood. It won't be long before we're pushed out like everyone else. You need to start thinking about what you're going to do next," she said, putting an end to the conversation.

That was what they didn't understand. There was no *next* for Kamilah. Her future was tied irrevocably to El Coquí. She had known that since the day Abuela's cancer had returned twelve years earlier. The day Kamilah gave up her dream school for her family.

No one ever knew the truth of Le Cordon Bleu. They thought it was another thing Kamilah had never followed through on. They thought she didn't want to be forced into making difficult choices about her future. They didn't know she'd already made those choices. She'd chosen to stay, and when Abuela had asked, she'd promised she'd do whatever it took to keep El Coquí open.

You are the only one who understands. Who knows that this place is more than just a restaurant. Fight for it.

Kamilah did know. El Coquí had been the hub of their family since its founding in 1979. Every holiday and almost every milestone was celebrated here. The restaurant had seen the most lively of parties to the most solemn of memorials. It

was the most stalwart family member: a pillar of kinship offering a sense of self and comfort and belonging to everyone
in the family. El Coquí was the glue that held them together
in Abuela's absence.

"Did you look at the plátanos before you signed?" Mami
asked, interrupting Kamilah's thoughts. She stood by the
stacked crates of produce next to the pantry.

"I didn't sign for them," Kamilah said. "Leo did."

Mami dug around in the crate of plantains. "No sirven para
nada." She bent and examined the other plantains through
the spaces in the crates. "Están todos maduros."

Jeez Louise, what were they supposed to do with three
crates of ripe plantains? They needed green ones for the tos-
tones and mofongo. Not to mention their specialty Jibarito
sandwiches. "I'll go get some plátanos verdes from the market."

"No, your papi and I will go. He needs to be away from
here for a little while."

Kamilah nodded.

"And throw out the garbage while we're gone," Mami told
her, gesturing to the full trash bags tied in neat little bows
by the back door. "Your brother must have forgotten about
it before he left."

Fucking Leo. He knew exactly what he was doing. He had
to have walked right past them. He couldn't have just taken
them out and tossed them in the dumpster? No, because her
brother loved to make Kamilah do all of his work. Grumbling in Spanish about inconsiderate older brothers who loved
getting on her damn nerves, Kamilah followed her mom out
the back door, heavy bags in hand.

Her mom turned right to go around the other side of the
building, where the distillery was and where she always parked

her car. She said that it was safer on that side since Liam and Killian could see it through their windows and usually open garage doors. Kamilah turned to the left and made her way around the corner where her own car was parked right next to the dumpster enclosure.

She backed into the small gap between the door and the gate, then booty-bumped it farther open. She turned to maneuver the bags through the entrance and jumped twenty feet when she saw someone standing there.

4

Liam knew who was behind him even before her startled scream grated his ears. He knew it was her because, of course, she'd be the first person he ran into after stalking away from Granda.

Could this fucking day get any worse?

Quickly, Liam wiped his eyes and cursed his lack of forethought. He should've grabbed his sunglasses. He should've known he'd run into one of the Vegas. Since his condo sat between the distillery and the restaurant kitchen, they were both his business and residential neighbors. He couldn't even walk out his door to grab the mail without seeing at least one of them.

"Why are you always lurking like some serial killer?"

Slowly, Liam turned to face Kamilah. He kept his gaze fixed firmly on the ground at her small feet. Her red, white, and blue retro Jordans were creased at the toes and spattered with oil. Although it was clear they were an old pair, he knew that had to be an irritant to her—the woman who loved her sneakers and spent as much on them as others did on their heels.

"Seriously, you—" She stopped midsentence. Her eyes fixed on his face. Specifically on his, no doubt, bloodshot eyes. "Are you crying?" The shocked disbelief in her tone caused the muscles in his neck and shoulders to tense even more. When he didn't answer or look up, she dropped the garbage bags in her hands.

He watched as she took a few steps closer.

"Are you okay?" Her hand lifted from her side, and he knew she was reaching out to him.

He stepped back into the wall and shook his head. It was as much an answer to her question as it was a rejection of her nearness. She absolutely could not touch him. He couldn't handle it right now.

Kamilah paused. "¿Qué pasa?"

He kept his mouth closed and tried to breathe through his nose—a deep breath in and a long one out. He shoved his shaking hands into his pockets and clenched them into fists.

"Liam, what's going on?" she tried again. Her voice was soft and full of concern.

He just shook his head again.

"Liam, you're scaring me. I'm about two seconds from calling in reinforcements."

Dear God, no. The last thing he wanted was more members of the Vega family witnessing his breakdown.

"Granda has cancer," he choked out in a strangled whisper. Then his throat closed, and he couldn't say anything else.

Suddenly, Kamilah's face filled his vision: she had bent at the waist and tilted her head so she could see his face. Usually staring at her big light brown eyes, high cheekbones, perfectly angled jaw, and overflowing lips caused Liam a sort of pleasure/pain, like poking at irritated gums or stretching a sore muscle. At the moment he felt none of that. He felt nothing but an encroaching sense of doom.

"What did you say?" she asked, grabbing on to his forearms with both hands. However, the widening of her eyes and the shock in her tone made it clear she had heard him perfectly. "When did he find out? What kind is it? What stage? Has it metastasized?"

He shrugged helplessly, unable to say it out loud, afraid it would make it more real. *Liver cancer. Stage four.*

"Well, what did the doctor say? What are they going to do? When?"

Liam thought back to what Granda had said to him right before he'd walked out. A spark of returning anger made it easier for Liam to speak. "He's not going to treat it."

Her already-wide eyes grew. She released his arms and used her hand to pull back her thick mane of curls as if they had prevented her from hearing him. "I'm sorry, but what?"

Liam couldn't look at her anymore. He couldn't watch as she came to the same painful realization he had. He turned his face away and stared at the fence of the enclosure. "He said that he's not treating it. He wants to just let it run its course."

Silence reigned for a few seconds before she burst out. "No! No. That's not happening. That's unacceptable. Where is he? In the distillery?" she asked, but she didn't wait for a response. She simply turned on her heel and started walking. Her steps were hard, and her stride purposeful. It was clear she was a woman on a mission, and while Liam usually resented the hell out of her controlling and meddlesome ways, he thought that she just might be the person to convince Granda to change his mind.

Liam followed her as she stomped right past the open back door to El Coquí without stopping. He quickly hit the lock on the doorknob and swung it closed and then continued after Kamilah. She rounded the corner of the distillery and stormed through the open garage doors.

Granda was sitting at a low table in the corner next to the warehouse entrance, playing dominoes with Papo Vega.

"Have you lost your damn mind?" she asked in lieu of a greeting.

Papo gave his granddaughter a chastising look. "Mira nena, respeta."

She turned on him. "Did you know about this? About the cancer and not treating it?"

Papo nodded his still salt-and-pepper head, and Liam gasped. For some reason it hadn't even occurred to him that Papo would know.

If there was one person in the world Liam respected more than Granda, it was Ricardo Vega, aka Papo. He was the type of person everyone admired and genuinely liked. The father of six, grandfather to eighteen, and great-grandfather to almost a dozen, he was the ringleader of a very large, boisterous circus, and he performed his duties with a stern but playful air.

His family absolutely adored him and would do anything for him. One of his many progeny would've definitely taken him into their homes if he wanted. However, Papo preferred to live with Granda just like Granda preferred living with Papo—the two were nothing if not loyal to one another. They had been since they met in the military at age twenty. They were more than best friends. They were brothers.

"You can't be okay with this," Liam told him. "He's going to let himself die."

Papo closed his eyes and rubbed at his chest as if it hurt.

"Of course I don't like it, but I can't do anything about it. It's his choice."

"I have no problem telling him he can't do that," Kamilah said. She looked again at Granda, who was looking at the dominoes in front of him with a frown of concentration. "If you can treat your cancer, you *are* going to do it."

Granda shook his head and smirked at her. "Nice try, lass, but this time you can't just shake your finger at me to make me do what you want." He chose a domino and put it at the right end. "Not even a wanker whack with that fist of yours is going to make me change my mind."

"Killian," she scolded, but the sheen over her eyes and thickness of her voice undermined her authority.

Granda glanced at her quickly, then looked away as if he couldn't stand the sight of her tears. "No, lass. Not even tears are going to work." Meanwhile, Papo studiously examined his own dominoes.

"But why?" Kamilah asked in a waterlogged voice. "It doesn't make any sense."

"Because I'm old and tired, and I just want to be with my wife," he said briskly. When Papo finally selected his domino and played it, Granda paused long enough to shoot him a dirty look. "Now, we have more important things to talk about."

"More important than your life?" Liam asked.

"Yes." Granda nodded. "We need to talk about *your* life."

Liam scrunched his forehead. "My life?" He wasn't the one with cancer.

Granda looked at his hand of dominoes, to the game, and back at his hand. "Actually, more like both of your lives."

"Me?" Kamilah asked. "*My* life is fine." The emphasis she placed on the first word made it clear that she thought Liam's was not.

"My life is fine too," Liam protested.

All three of them looked away and stayed silent.

"It *is*." He doubled down.

"It's not," Granda returned, picking a domino to play and smirking when Papo muttered a curse. "Neither one of your lives is what could be considered *fine*. You are both lonely workaholics who are focused on the wrong things."

"I am not," both he and Kamilah said at the same time. They shot each other the same disgruntled look. Liam reminded himself that he was a grown-ass man and could not tell her to stop copying him.

Papo finally looked up from his hand. "You are. You are both all about work, and it's making you lonely, especially you, Kamilah."

Kamilah barked out a fake laugh. "Ha! I spend every day in the company of my approximately seven hundred thousand family members. I *wish* I were lonely."

"And when was the last time you went on a date? My memory isn't the best, and even I remember that it's been years."

She scowled. "What is this, Shit on Kamilah's Love Life Day? Did you talk to my mami or something?"

"I did." He played a domino and then looked back at her. "She was leaving when I was walking up. She mentioned something about you pushing for us to do a restaurant tour."

"Did she also tell you that she and Papi are being hard-headed and don't want to enter it?"

"Funny you are asking their permission, when it's my restaurant." Although Kamilah's parents had taken over the day-to-day operations years ago, Papo was the owner of El Coquí. They still frequently consulted him about things, but it seemed like it was more to appease him than to seek his advice or approval.

Kamilah's eyes lit up. "You're going to let me do it?"

"I guess that depends," Papo said.

"Depends on what? Do you want to know what I have planned? I'm sure Mami told you. I want to update the menu and the decor."

Papo shot Liam a look that Liam did not like one bit. Warning bells began ringing in his head, and they only got louder when Granda turned to give them his full attention. Both grandfathers were wearing expressions Liam couldn't exactly describe. They were part stern, part sly, part amusement, but they were one hundred percent trouble.

Papo motioned between Liam and Kamilah. "It depends on you two."

"I have nothing to do with El Coquí," Liam hedged.

"But you have a great deal to do with Kane," Granda said.

Loud foghorns were going off now. "I fail to see what one has to do with the other, beyond the obvious." Liam motioned to the building around them. Beyond sharing the building the best friends had bought together in 1978, the two businesses were completely separate entities. Sure, El Coquí stocked Kane Whiskey at their bar, but that was about it.

"We *are* talking about the obvious," Papo said. At Kamilah's and Liam's blank looks, he continued. "You see, Killian and I are thinking about selling the building."

Liam must have woken up in some alternative universe where he was a boxer, because he'd taken so many damn one-two punches in less than twelve hours that he felt like he was in a ring getting his ass handed to him.

"No, we *will* sell the building," Granda corrected. "Unless the two of you get married."

And just like that, Liam was KO'd.

5

Last year, one of Kamilah's four nephews had his birthday party at a new indoor trampoline park that also featured a rock-climbing wall. Kamilah was goaded into racing Saint (her oldest brother and the ex–Special Forces soldier) to the top. Because she was woefully unprepared for the task, she lost her grip and her footing, fell fifteen feet, slammed into the rock wall, and knocked both the breath and wits out of herself. She'd walked around in a dumbfounded haze for days afterward.

She felt the same now. Like she'd just plummeted in free space only to crash into a wall and get knocked senseless.

She swung her gaze back and forth between Abuelo and Killian, both of them wearing the same expressions they'd worn that morning in the director's office: guilty but stubbornly determined to brazen their way through.

"You can't sell the building," Kamilah sputtered. She gestured between her chest and Liam's. "We live here." Liam, of course, lived in the gorgeous loft condo her uncle had renovated for him, while, after her breakup, Kamilah was forced to move back into her parents' small apartment above the restaurant. Now that she thought about it, her living at home was probably a large part of her parents' concern over her love life. She was cramping their style. "Your businesses are here." She tried to hit the heart of the problem.

"Let's be honest here, lass," Killian said. "Neither one of us actually runs our business, so we don't have much to lose on that front."

"We have more to gain, if you think about how much this building is probably worth now," Abuelo added. "You two are the ones with the most to lose."

That was undeniably true. Both she and Liam were totally dedicated to their grandfathers' businesses.

Liam glared at his grandfather. "The judges are due to show up any day now. We are one step away from winning the contest. You honestly expect me to believe that you're going to give up on the one thing we've been working toward for ten years, just to—what?—teach me a lesson or some shit?" Liam shook his head. "There's no way."

"You expect me to leave my business, my life's work, in your hands after I die, when you can't even give a fucking tour to some obnoxious millennials?"

"That's what you want?" Liam asked. "You want me to start giving tours? Okay. I'll do it. I'll even be happy about it. Just stop with this bullshite about not getting treatment."

"And us getting married," Kamilah added, since Liam had forgotten. "You two got away with this nonsense for my prom—"

"I only took you to your prom because you'd been dumped

by your boyfriend," Liam interjected. "Your only other option was Leo, which was just too pathetic for words."

"Um, excuse me." Kamilah folded her arms. "I dumped him." After Javier had told her that he was thinking about getting back with his ex, but still. *She'd* been the one to walk away. "And that's not the point right now. The point is, just because we agreed last time doesn't mean we will this time." She looked at Abuelo and Killian. "You can't just make two people get married because you want them to. That's not how this works. This is America. Land of the free."

Abuelo put a hand over his heart and closed his eyes. Then he opened his mouth and began belting out *And the home of the brave* as if he were Whitney Houston singing the national anthem at the Super Bowl. As soon as Kamilah tried to interrupt, he sang louder.

"Seriously?" she asked.

He began adding all kinds of runs and embellishments. His vibrato effortlessly caressed the word *brave*. Kamilah shook her head, rolled her eyes, and waited for Abuelo to run out of steam, which didn't take much longer.

Abuelo's voice faded out. He opened his eyes and looked around, as if waiting for a crowd to burst into applause like they used to. Instead, Kamilah and Liam, united for once, glared at him. "No one appreciates real talent these days," he grumbled.

"Nice distraction tactic," she huffed, "but it won't work. This is still wrong. Liam shouldn't have to get married simply because Killian wants him to, and neither one of you has any right to sell me like a high-class hooker."

"How dare you," Abuelo said, cutting off her rant, and shot her a serious scowl. "We would never sell a woman, especially you. My granddaughter. That's disgusting to even say. No seas mal pensada."

"Evil-minded? You literally just said that you expect me to marry Liam because Killian wants him to settle down. And neither one of you asked me if I wanted to be offered up like some kind of virgin sacrifice." Kamilah crossed her arms over her chest.

"We aren't offering you up as a sacrifice." He pouted. "You need to get married too. You need someone to take care of you."

"I don't need a man to take care of me, especially not Liam." A loud throat-clearing from behind reminded her Liam was in the room. She threw him an annoyed look. "No offense."

"Liam is young, smart, successful, and handsome." He paused and shook his head as if he didn't understand her. "¿Como no lo vas a querer como esposo?"

How could she not want him as a husband? Why *would* she? He was an antisocial ass most of the time. So what if the rest was true? Especially the handsome part. She swallowed, her throat dry. "Claro que no lo quiero. Es un amargado. I'd be all broody and emo within ten minutes of being married to him." Oops. She turned to glance at him. "No offense."

Liam's look told her offense had definitely been taken. "Bitter?"

"Pft." Abuelo waved away her comment. "Exagerada."

Maybe she was exaggerating, but not by much.

"Look," Kamilah started in her *let's be reasonable* voice. It was the same one she used when Abuelo refused to take his meds.

"Don't start with that tone." He pointed at her. "We already decided, and don't even think of going to your parents for help," he told Kamilah. "Because they've been asking me to sell for years." He paused and eyed them both. "You two will get married, or we will sell."

Kamilah looked to Liam for some assistance.

A red flush spread across his fair skin from the back of his neck to the bridge of his nose. The cords of muscle at the base of his neck stood out in stark white. Kamilah could almost hear his jaw creaking under the tension. He and Killian engaged in a silent standoff, and in the space of a few seconds, they had an entire conversation.

"Fuck it. Sell, then," he told Killian.

Kamilah's jaw dropped. *What?* Had he just seriously told them to sell? He stomped out the garage door. Liam was leaving? Just like that? Abuelo and Killian watched him walk away. Abuelo with a disturbed look on his face and Killian with a resolute one.

"He didn't mean that." Her hands twined together, shaky and unsure.

Killian's brow rose. "When have you ever known Liam to say something he didn't mean?"

She tilted her head. *That's true.* Liam didn't say much, but he meant what he said. However, that wasn't going to work for her. Not now. Not when his hardheaded, idiotic, and *selfish* decree ruined her future as well. She absolutely could not lose El Coquí.

"Wait right here," she told them. "I'll be right back with him, and then we can all discuss this like adults." Kamilah spun and took off after Liam before they could respond.

"Liam," she called as she jogged in the direction he'd disappeared. "Wait."

Liam had made it around the front of the building and was

passing the doors to El Coquí. "I'm done talking about this." His long legs ate up the sidewalk.

"I'd like to be done talking too, but we can't be." She chased after him, quickstepping it to catch up. Luckily, he'd reached the corner of their street and had to stop. Looking around, he turned and crossed the street. She could only assume it was so that she couldn't catch up to him. "Stop walking away from me."

"I'm not walking away from you," he said, continuing to walk away. "I'm leaving." He made it to the other side of the street and turned to keep going down Division Street.

She was on the brink of losing it all because of the stubborn hothead in front of her. "You can't just leave," she told him, hot on his heels. "We have to talk about this."

"What is there to talk about? You heard them. They aren't going to change their minds."

Kamilah full-on ran the last few steps and then grabbed on to his arm. She did her best to pull him to a stop, but he had six inches and around sixty pounds on her. The only way he was stopping was if he wanted to. It was obvious that he didn't, so Kamilah did her best to keep up with him as he passed under the Puerto Rican flag that marked the end of Paseo Boricua and stalked into the corner of Humboldt Park.

"Stop. Just stop and listen, will you?" She tugged harder, and he finally paused, an eyebrow arched, eyes flashing in anger. "My tía Flaca studied salsa, bomba y plena, and other bailes folkloricos at the academy." She pointed to her left. "Abuela was always a few blocks over at Don Isidoro's bodega, haggling for produce." He rolled his eyes, and she squeezed his arm. "My brothers and cousins grew up hanging out by that mural, trying to look hard, until Mami or one of my tías called them out and dragged them inside by their ears. My papi and his twin brother played cutthroat dominó tournaments on the sidewalk while salsa, merengue, bachata, and reggaeton played from the open windows and doors." She swallowed, suddenly choked up. Liam's eyes had softened only slightly, and here she was, about to cry. Everything about this street announced loudly and with pride that this was a Puerto Rican neighborhood where Boricuas could be Boricuas, even if they were on the mainland. Her family had always been a part of it.

"Obviously, us getting married is ridiculous," she added, when he stayed silent.

"I agree. I'd rather jump off the Sears Tower with no parachute."

"Rude." Why did he always manage to piss her off? He'd be lucky to be married to her. She was a fucking delight. *He* was the one who'd make someone want to run away screaming.

"It's the Willis Tower," she said, just to piss him off. Native Chicagoans would probably never call it anything but the Sears Tower.

He paused in his pacing and shot her a squinty glare.

Josefa, the owner of the nail salon next door—the biggest gossip on the block—stood by a nearby bench smoking a cigarette. Kamilah lowered her voice. "We still have to talk about this."

Liam threw his hands in the air. "Why? It's not like we're going to do it. They will eventually give up."

"You didn't see their faces when you walked away. They aren't going to let us ignore them, and they aren't going to give up. They're going to sell the building and our futures."

Liam shook his head. "Then I don't know what to tell you.

But if you go back in there and argue, all you're going to do is make them more determined."

"You telling them to do it made them even more determined. You should already know never to try and call their bluff." Her nostrils flared.

"You even engaging with them in the first place is what made them start. If you had just minded your own business, the conversation would've never happened."

"Me? Now this is my fault? You're the one who's so socially inept your grandpa is spending the last days of *his* life scheming ways to give you *any semblance of a life*." As soon as she said it, she wished she could take the words back. Dios, this man made her crazy.

Liam sucked in a breath.

"I didn't mean it." If anything, she'd made it worse.

"You did." The look he gave her was withering. "Own it." He glanced down Division Street.

How the hell was she supposed to apologize without sounding like an insincere asshole? He always brought out the worst in her. Maybe because he only let her see the worst of him.

He hadn't always been so disagreeable. He used to be a really sweet kid who went out of his way to make her smile. After that terrible boating accident, her best friend slowly became someone she didn't recognize and couldn't reach no matter how hard she tried. Eventually, Kamilah realized that he was never again going to be the best friend she'd loved. She'd stopped making an effort.

Now, as an adult, Kamilah could better comprehend the complexities of how Liam's trauma had altered him. However, she was still clueless as to what it was about her, specifically, that brought out his animosity. Liam treated Kamilah like a pimple on his ass—unwanted and painful to interact with.

And now their grandfathers wanted them to get married. It was ridiculous.

"Look." She pushed an unruly curl from her face. "Neither one of us can afford to lose what we want most right now. So give yourself a cootie shot or whatever, and let's figure something out."

Liam turned his attention back to her. He looked like he was contemplating pushing her into the pile of brightly colored leaves to their left.

"You're so hilarious," he deadpanned. "Why don't you have your own Netflix special yet?"

"I do. We're filming it right now. It's like *Punk'd*, but instead of playing pranks on celebrities, two old guys force rude and annoying hermits to marry me."

He smiled sardonically as he moved around her. "As always, it's been a real pleasure. Like lighting myself on fire and then trying to put it out with a screwdriver."

"Wait." Kamilah rushed around the front of him, placing two hands on his chest. Her eyes widened at the very defined pecs flexing under her palms. It was impossible not to notice that he'd grown taller and bulked up. But noticing it in passing and truly taking it in were two completely different things.

Two large hands wrapped around her wrists like manacles.

Kamilah realized she'd been pawing and kneading his chest like a leopard did before pouncing on its unsuspecting prey. She balled her hands and made to pull them back.

Liam's hands tightened in refusal.

Her gaze snapped up to his face.

She'd always thought his hooded eyes, sharp stubborn-set jaw, and mouth naturally downturned in the corners, paired with his short scruff and thick straight brows, gave him a distinct Grumpy Cat look. She'd thought wrong. His features were a mix of his father's rugged handsomeness and his mother's cool beauty. However, there was a tantalizing intensity that was undeniably unique to him. At some point Liam had turned into a whole snack, and she was feeling decidedly peckish.

Her eyes flared wide in surprise at her last thought. Peckish? For Liam? No. She'd put that all behind her after her prom night when he'd left her confused, hurt, and unfulfilled. Just like she had when she'd yanked the hem of her dress from around her hips and hopped down from the bed of his grandpa's truck, Kamilah pushed down all the emotions Liam Kane made her feel. She tugged at his hold on her wrists with enough force to let him know she was serious about being released, and Liam opened his hands instantly.

Liam's smoky-blue eyes were narrowed on her face, but for once it wasn't in annoyance. He looked like he was trying really hard to read her mind. Thank God he couldn't.

Kamilah floundered for a few seconds trying to get her mind back on track. They weren't there so Kamilah could awkwardly feel up his torso. They were there to discuss the ultimatum. They needed to figure out how to not only convince their grandpas to stop this whole *sell the building* thing but also get Killian to accept treatment. That was the most important part. The only problem was that for the life of her she couldn't think of how to get the two most iron-willed men she'd ever known to back down. It wasn't in their nature. They didn't concede. When they couldn't dominate outright, they charmed and manipulated. They loved to play games, and they loved to win. The only way Kamilah saw this working was to cheat.

"What if we did it?" The question burst from her mouth.

The smoke cleared from his gaze, and he regarded her with all the warmth of Lake Michigan during the Polar Plunge. "Did what, exactly? Got married?" A bark of incredulous laughter escaped him. He examined her face, then shook his head. "Fuck no to whatever buffoonery you're currently planning."

"Just listen for a second," she tried.

"Hell to the no." He used his shoulder to push her out of the way. "Now, move."

Usually, Kamilah would've retreated, but she couldn't. Not when everything was riding on this. She slipped the fingers of both hands through the belt loops at the back of his jeans and yanked hard.

Liam jerked and turned his head to glare at her.

She wouldn't be deterred. Not this time. "Look, I am not losing El Coquí. Especially not because you want to get in some pissing contest with our stubborn and troublesome grandpas, who you know damn well will do what they threatened. Do you not remember camping? They let us starve for two days because we refused to eat fish with the eyes still on them."

Liam scoffed. "Kamilah, we were seven and eight years old."

"Exactly. We were kids, and they starved us until we caved. Imagine what they would do now?"

He didn't have a response for that, but he did look to be mulling it over.

Good.

"I'm not saying that we give in. I'm saying that it's time to beat them at their own game."

He crossed his arms over his spectacular chest, completely

unimpressed with her declaration. "And how do you plan to do that?"

"We outfox them. We play dirty, just like they are."

Liam looked at her as if she'd just thrown up on his shoes, part astonishment but mostly disgust. "You want to scam our sickly eighty-year-old grandpas?"

Kamilah raised both her hands, palms up. "Aren't they trying to blackmail us?"

He gave a short nod. "True enough."

Kamilah's mind whirled with ideas. "What if we tell them that we will do it, but we just hold off."

Liam shook his head. "That will never work. They're as impatient as they are uncooperative."

"I mean, there is going to have to be some waiting involved. Unless they expect us to elope to Las Vegas." She snorted at the thought. "As if I would ever be forgiven for denying my parents a wedding for their only daughter." Kamilah gasped. "That's it. We'll tell them that we can't just suddenly get married because my parents would know something shady is going on and flip out. Instead, we have to be dating for a while, before we can even think about getting married. Of course, we aren't really going to be dating or get married. We just hold them off while we get done what we need to get done."

"That's nice, but I still don't think they would sell. We're on the verge of making my dad's dream come true."

Both Killian and Liam had worked with a single-minded focus for ten years—from the day Liam graduated from college—to get their distillery to a place where they could have a chance at winning the Best Craft Whiskey Distillery award in Connor Kane's honor. It probably meant a great deal more to Killian now, given his diagnosis...

"I got it." Kamilah clapped. "We will make Killian getting treatment a condition of our acceptance."

Liam's eyes widened the tiniest bit. He opened his mouth, closed it, tilted his head back, and looked into the branches of a tree while he thought.

Kamilah fought the urge to push her point. That wouldn't work with him. Eventually, he looked back at her.

"All I want is for Granda to see the winners get announced. He's worked his ass off for the last ten years for this, but if he doesn't treat this cancer..." Liam trailed off.

Her eyes narrowed. The consequence was clear. If Killian didn't get treatment, there was a good chance he wouldn't see whether their hard work paid off. He wouldn't get to finally put his son to rest, and Liam would have the expectations of yet another ghost to live up to. Her chest tightened at the thought.

She stepped close and wrapped both of his hands in her own. She pulled them up to her chest and held them there, so he could feel the steady beat of her heart against the back of his fingers. She stared into his eyes.

"We can fix this. My plan will work. We all get what we want," she said. Then she thought better and added, "Maybe not exactly what we want or in the way we wanted to get it, but no one is left empty-handed."

He shook his head. "This is a terrible idea."

"Liam, trust me." She smiled. "When have I ever steered you wrong?"

"My entire childhood." He paused, then blew out a deep breath of resignation. "Fine. We'll do it."

6

This is so Godfather-*ish*.

From the kingpin and his henchman sitting at a table in an empty restaurant, nonchalantly picking at a banquet of food, to an oddly solemn-faced Kamilah, who sat with her forearms resting on the table and her fingers interlocked as if in prayer. Liam assumed the posture was supposed to portray a sense that she was willing and not at all worried. However, from his spot next to her in the booth, Liam was all too aware of her body, and he could feel how stiff she was holding herself. Add in the fact that they were about to negotiate the shadiest of deals while looking out for their own interests and it was like a scene directed by Francis Ford Coppola.

Kamilah motioned to the large plate of rice and slow-roasted pork in front of Papo. "You know you shouldn't be eating any of that. It's too much salt."

Papo shrugged. "That's what makes it taste good." He took another bite of pernil.

"Abuelo," she started, but Liam jumped in before she could get any further. They had an understanding to reach, and they would never get there if Kamilah put them on the defensive from the get-go.

"We can't just get married," Liam told the grandfathers. "There are other people to consider here." Even though he was staring at his now-alert grandfather, he saw Kamilah's face swing in his direction from the corner of his eye.

"I didn't know you were seeing someone," Granda said to him. "I know you have your fun with the lasses who pick you up at your buddy's bar, but I didn't think any of them were serious. You haven't introduced any to me."

Liam ignored the dig about women having to pick him up because it was true. He never initiated anything, but he was approached by plenty of women. Sometimes he slept with them. Sometimes he didn't. The only constant was that eventually they would realize Liam wasn't a turtle or an oyster that they could coax out of his shell. He was more like a high-security safe, set deep in the bowels of the earth—extremely difficult to reach and basically impossible to open. "I'm not talking about relationships. I'm talking about the Vegas."

Now Papo looked at him alertly. "What about my family?" Dear God, by his tone one would think Liam had threatened to have them all sleeping with the fishes.

"What would they think if Kamilah and I just got married out of the blue? Everyone knows we can barely stand to be in the same room. There's no way they'd think we had the sudden urge to get married. So unless you plan to tell them what's up..." Liam trailed off.

Kamilah took his silence as her prompt to jump in. "Regardless of us having differing views of El Coquí, my parents do love me, and they would go postal if I just up and married someone. They would start to ask questions. If they found out about this blackmail scheme of yours," she said as she used her finger to motion between their grandpas, "they would quit and leave. Everyone else in the family would find out. People would start taking sides. It will be like Tía Flaca moving to New York with Eva and leaving her other girls all over again."

It was clear by the way his face fell at Kamilah's comment that he did not want to cause another rift in the family. "You're right," he told Kamilah. "They can't find out about this."

Kamilah pounced. "So you agree that this plan is stupid?"

Liam almost banged his head against the table. She had about as much finesse as a drunk at closing time. He had no idea how she ever planned to run a business when she tried to browbeat everyone around her.

As if on cue, Granda jumped in. "Our plan is still going to go on." He put down his fork. "It would be a shame for the family to find out about this," he said, wiping his face with a napkin, "because if they do, then we will be forced to act. And then? We all end up worse off." He let his threat hang in the air for a minute, before leaning back and resting his hands on his full stomach. "So really, it's in your best interest to make sure this goes off without a hitch. Isn't that right, Papo?"

Papo nodded. "Makes sense to me, Killian."

"As a matter of fact," Granda continued, "I think we should make that a rule. You keep your mouths shut about this, and so will we."

Liam swore. The only way this could get more farcical was if his grandpa started mumbling in a raspy voice and talking with his hands.

"All right, Marlon Brando, we'll keep our mouths shut." Liam leaned forward. "Now let's get to the important stuff. It's clear we can't just get married, but we can go on a few dates or something." Beside him, Kamilah inhaled. In his peripheral vision, he saw her mouth open. He quickly squeezed her thigh, a signal to zip it and let him handle this.

Her hand found his, her touch soft and warm before she knocked it away. Still, she settled back in her chair. He turned his attention back to the grandfathers, who were both shaking their heads.

"No," Papo said. "That's not good enough. The point is to prove you can balance work and personal life. Going on a few dates doesn't prove that."

"It has to be something that requires more commitment," Granda added.

Liam's gut told him that they had a fifty-fifty chance at getting them to settle for a fake relationship, when the big mouth next to him blew those odds to smithereens.

"Fine. We'll get engaged. Does that make you happy?"

Liam gave her a look he hoped conveyed his plan to kill her as soon as they were alone.

It must not have, because the look she gave him clearly said *What are you mad about? This is what we agreed to.*

Fine. If she thought she could do this any better than he could, let her try. Liam sat back in his chair, crossed his arms over his chest, and watched a bird land on the windowsill.

Scenting blood in the water, Granda leaned in. "How is that different from getting married? Your parents will still think something is up."

Liam felt her gaze on the side of his face, but he kept looking out the window. Doña Josefa's good-for-nothing younger boyfriend, Jonel, had pulled up in his brand-new Toyota

C-HR. Weird, considering the man didn't appear to have a job. Liam always saw him sitting in front of Josefa's nail salon smoking weed and catcalling customers.

"Well." Kamilah paused. "We can tell people that we've been dating on the down-low for a while."

Liam fought a snort. *Right, because that would be totally believable.*

"Tell me exactly what you plan to tell them," Papo said.

Across the street, Jonel opened his door to step out of his car, and Liam did a double take, confused at the odd way the sunlight played off of the neon-blue paint. It was almost as if he could see a head in the reflection.

"I plan to tell them that Liam and I spent a lot of time together when we were with you two, and then we started hanging out by ourselves. Things just sort of progressed from there, and now we're engaged."

"¿Qué qué?" a woman's voice yelled from directly behind them.

Suddenly everything became clear. It wasn't Jonel's car that had caused that optical illusion. It was the distorted reflection in the window of Kamilah's parents standing in the doorway. They'd just been completely played by the grandfathers.

"Mami," Kamilah shouted and spun in her seat, practically knocking Liam to the floor in the process. He was forced to get to his feet.

Kamilah quickly wiggled her way out of the booth. She stepped in to his side, grabbed his hand with one hand, and wrapped the other one around his arm. He ignored the way her breasts pillowed his bicep.

Behind him, Granda and Papo stood up as well.

Valeria's eyes were the size of bowling balls, her jaw was

in danger of coming in contact with the floor, and her hands were clenched in front of her chest.

"¡Ay Dios mío!" Valeria shouted. "¡Qué alegría!" She gave a series of quick claps to emphasize her happiness. She turned to her husband and reached for both of his hands. "God heard our prayers, Santos. Our only daughter is engaged. She's getting married. Finally. And not to some comemierda like the last one. I never thought this day would come. I thought she was going to give us nothing but grandcats."

Next to him, Kamilah huffed in offense.

Liam could feel Santiago's gaze on them, but he didn't look yet. He couldn't. Not when he was about to engage in the highest level of shenanigans with the man's only daughter.

Santiago shook his head. "Why are we just now hearing about you two?" Santiago continued with a skeptical frown.

"Did you want to be kept up-to-date on your daughter's sex life?" Papo asked.

"¡Abuelo!" Kamilah exclaimed, and at the same time her father said, "¡Ay, Papi. Ya!"

Papo was unfazed. "I'm just saying."

"We haven't been keeping it a secret, if that's what you think," Kamilah said. "There's just been a lot happening lately, and…" She trailed off.

"'A lot happening,'" Santiago repeated with a frown. "What's been happening? I swear, Kamilah, if you bring up the damn restaurant—"

"I have cancer," Granda announced.

Santiago fell silent.

Valeria's hands flew up to her mouth to stifle the pained sound she'd made. Her big light brown eyes, exactly like Kamilah's, instantly filled with tears.

"They didn't want anyone to find out about them like this,"

Granda continued, "but with things as they are, well, need-less to say, the timeline has moved up a bit."

Santiago looked from Granda to Papo to them and back again. "But why—"

This time Papo cut him off. "But nothing, m'ijo." He ges-tured to Liam and Kamilah. "They are together. They al-ready planned to do this. They are just doing it sooner than expected. That is all there is to it."

Amazement filled Liam at how Granda and Papo managed to tell the truth and lie at the same time.

Santiago's eyes were fixed on the way Kamilah squeezed the shit out of Liam's arm. "Where's your ring?" he asked.

Kamilah and Liam froze.

"I have it," Granda chimed in. He stepped forward, pulled a ring box out of his pocket, and flipped it open. The one-carat emerald was encircled by tiny diamonds that flashed in the light.

"That's Nana's ring," Liam said, surprise and confusion warring in his voice as he stared down at the gorgeous gold-filigree ring. Belatedly, he realized he wasn't supposed to feel either of those things. He hoped no one else caught on, but he was shocked that Granda wanted to use Nana's ring for this farce.

When they'd first married in Ireland, Granda hadn't been able to afford anything but a thin gold band for his teen-age sweetheart. It had taken him many years to upgrade it, but mostly because she'd liked it the way it was. Granda had eventually been forced to slip the thing off her finger while she slept. He'd taken it to Chicago's finest jeweler to have it melted down and made into a brand-new ring.

The last time Liam had seen the ring, it was being cut off

his grandmother's swollen finger at the hospital before they pulled the plug.

Kamilah dropped his hand and took a step back. "I can't wear Eimear's ring," she exclaimed.

"Why not?" Santiago asked with narrowed eyes.

"Because it's Eimear Kane's ring," Kamilah insisted.

"And?" Santiago pressed.

She looked at Liam for help, but he couldn't offer any, as this had quickly spun out of either of their control. She looked at Papo pleadingly, but he was unmoved. She turned to Granda, who was simply determined.

He had every intention of bullying her into wearing that ring. "Eimear told me long ago that this ring was for her grandson to give to his future wife. That's you."

Kamilah floundered. "But I'm n—"

Granda jumped in before she could put her foot in her mouth. "I know you're worried it won't fit, but I know it will. Liam got it sized."

Liam worked hard to keep his face carefully blank. It seemed like the Dynamic Doddering Duo had thought of everything. It was enough to make his blood run cold. What else was in store from them? Just how far was this going to go? Granda had no boundaries when it came to getting what he wanted. Liam could only hope Papo was more merciful. Then again, the fact he was blackmailing his own granddaughter proved he was willing to go pretty far.

"Well?" Valeria's voice broke into Liam's spiraling thoughts. "What are you waiting for, Liam? Put it on her." She held up her phone as if preparing to take pictures or, God forbid, a video of the moment.

Liam stared at Kamilah, who stared back at him. There was a kaleidoscope of emotions tumbling around her light brown eyes, but the most prominent was panic. She didn't have the right to panic. She was the one who'd put this whole thing into play by jumping headfirst into some half-cocked idea like always.

"Has it occurred to anyone that we might want to be alone for this?" Liam asked.

"I think you've had plenty of privacy, considering no one even knew you were together," Santiago commented. He straightened to his full height—which wasn't much over five-ten—and then crossed his arms over his chest. "The least you can do, since you proposed to my only daughter without asking for my blessing first, is let us see her get a ring."

When it became clear that no one in the room was going to argue that fact, not even Kamilah, Liam reached for the ring box in Granda's outstretched hand. Kamilah stood stock-still, doing her best statue impression. He suppressed an eye roll, then turned to Kamilah, grabbing her left hand to lift. And she tugged. Fighting against him. Was she for real? Liam stepped in close and dipped his head to whisper in her ear. "Don't act scared now. You're the one who came up with this idea."

That seemed to work. She unfroze enough to turn her head and whisper into his ear. "I—I—I'm sorry. I didn't mean… I mean, I didn't think," she stammered.

"No, you don't get to do that," Liam whispered back. "You talked me into doing this. Now, we're doing this, so lift your damn hand, unball your fist, and smile, for fuck's sake." That got him an annoyed huff of breath he felt all across his neck, but she did lift her trembling hand.

Liam tugged the ring out of its resting spot in the box. It slid on as if it were made for her. Something about it being on her finger fit in a way that didn't just have to do with circumference. The ring sat prettily right between the faded white line of a knife cut and a tiny oval-shaped scar from a burn. Without thinking, Liam brushed a calloused thumb over all three, her skin soft against his. Something tightened in his chest.

"I think it's too tight," Kamilah whispered.

"It fits perfectly," he told her with another unconscious brush of his thumb.

She shook her head. "It feels wrong," she told Liam. "This doesn't belong to me. It belongs to the woman you love as much as Killian loved your nana."

Liam met Granda's gaze from where he was standing close enough to hear their whispered conversation. The look on his face said *If only she knew, huh, lad?*

Liam dropped her hand and stepped back quickly. He lifted his gaze to the group, ready to make an excuse for his odd behavior, but they weren't paying him any attention.

"Ay, que romántico." Valeria rushed over to them and wrapped her arms around them both. Valeria squeezed them with all her might. She was really strong for a skinny woman who barely reached his chest. "I always knew you two would end up together," Valeria said. "Ever since you were little." She let them go suddenly and turned to Santiago. "Right, Santos? Didn't I always use to say they would get married one day?"

"No," Santiago replied with a foreboding scowl, but he grudgingly followed her lead and embraced them both.

"We will have to start planning the wedding right away," Valeria was saying. "We can't waste any time."

"Mami, wait a second. We haven't even talked about that yet."

But Valeria completely ignored her daughter and started going on about calling the family.

Granda appeared at his grandson's side, wearing a pleased smile. Liam snorted. "If I'm putting up with all this, then you are damn well going to try whatever fucking treatment the doctor says," he muttered. "I'm not going through this and watching you let yourself die at the same time. A man can only take so much."

Granda laughed outright and patted him on the back. "I won't promise you that, lad, but I'll go talk to him again and consider the options. Hell, I'll even let you come."

Liam released a deep breath and felt the muscles in his neck and back relax. For now that was enough.

7

Kamilah took a deep breath and knocked on the door of the apartment where Lucia and Eliza—Lucy and Liza to family and friends—lived. They had met in their sophomore year when Kamilah's cousin Lucy had gone on one of her trademark rants about the plight of Latinx women, and Liza had chimed in about the battles Black women face. Their conversation became a debate, the debate got heated, that heat eventually had them burning up between the sheets, and they'd been together ever since.

Both of Liza's eyebrows shot up at Kamilah, and her lips pursed as she hid a smile.

"It's that bad?" Kamilah asked.

In response Liza turned and yelled, "Babe, Mila's here."

To which Lucy responded forebodingly, "Good. Send her in."

Immediately another voice chimed in, "Yeah, so we can kick her ass."

Oh shit. Sofi had already arrived. Kamilah had hoped her best friend wouldn't get there until later, giving her the chance to get Lucy on her side first. When Sofia and Lucy banded together, things never worked out well for Kamilah.

"You know what, Lizzo?" Kamilah's nickname for Liza, given the similarity in name and resemblance to the famous singer. "I think I forgot something in my car." Kamilah took a few steps back from the door.

"Oh no," Liza said, grabbing on to Kamilah's wrist and pulling her forward. "I've been listening to them freak out for the last half hour about the video your mom posted." She tugged until Kamilah was firmly in the entryway to the apartment. She closed the door behind Kamilah, flipped the lock, and pushed her toward the living room. "You need to get in there and explain yourself."

Before Kamilah could even take a breath to steel herself, Sofi sashayed around the short wall that separated the entryway from the rest of the open-space apartment. She paused and hit her mark like a model at the end of a runway: head up, shoulders back, hip out, and hand at her waist. She'd spent her childhood and adolescence competing in pageants all over the country, so it was natural to her.

It was obvious she'd come straight from work, still wearing what she liked to call a Boss Bitch outfit. Today's consisted of a black leather pencil skirt that hugged her slender curves from waist to shins, a sheer white blouse, a fitted black-and-white herringbone blazer, and a pair of sky-high open-toed booties that made her already-long legs look even longer. Her lips were a velvety red that complemented her deep brown skin to perfection, and her tight black curls were pulled away from her face to better show off her überdefined cheekbones.

"Kamilah Lorena Vega Ramos," Sofi growled. "You have

two seconds to explain yourself, before I put my foot so far up your ass that when you open your mouth all you'll see is the red bottom of my Louboutin."

Lucy came up from behind Sofi. Barefoot and measuring five-three, Lucy just met Sofi's shoulder. Their heights were hardly their only differences. Where Sofi was a bona fide beauty queen, Lucy preferred not to subscribe to cisgender, heteronormative ideas of beauty. She wore no makeup, a pair of loose jeans, and a plain white T-shirt that had probably come out of a package. "You know them is bloody shoes," she quipped.

Kamilah shot her favorite cousin a look, but turned to Sofi quickly. "Sofia Maria Rosario Santana, I promise I have a good reason for this." She held up her left hand to show off her ring.

Standing between them all, Liza let out a whistle. "Damn. That's a nice ring." She looked at Sofi and Lucy. "You have to admit that ring is gorgeous."

"The issue at hand isn't whether or not the ring is nice," Lucy said, sounding an awful lot like her alderman father.

"It's about why the fuck it's there in the first place," Sofi finished.

Kamilah sighed. "Yeah, about that." She walked farther into the apartment and went straight to the cabinet she knew housed their wine. She pulled an already-opened bottle of red out of the cabinet, held it up to the light, noted that it was less than half-full, uncorked it, and drank straight from the bottle. After chugging the entire contents, Kamilah smacked her lips.

"You see, what had happened was…"

Then, over another bottle of wine, she told them everything, from waking up late to finalizing her deal with Abuelo and Killian after her parents left them alone.

Lucy was the one to break the prolonged silence that reigned after Kamilah stopped talking. She sat forward on the couch where she'd been snuggled into Liza's side.

"You're telling me that Abuelo, our sweet and goofy Abuelo, is blackmailing you?"

Kamilah laid her head back against the arm of the love seat she'd claimed for herself and thought about that for a second.

"I don't know that it can be considered blackmail now, since he has to support me with changing El Coquí and entering the Fall Foodie Tour." She turned her head and looked to Sofi, the marketing guru. "You're in business. What would you call it?"

From her spot curled on the armchair in front of the huge bay windows, Sofi snorted. "I'd call it the stupidest fucking thing I've ever heard and yet another example of you going extremely out of your way to avoid confronting your parents about how unsatisfied you feel."

Kamilah sat up. "I'm not unsatisfied."

Sofi sucked her teeth.

"I'm not," Kamilah insisted. "I'm determined to do whatever I have to do to make sure El Coquí stays in the family. That's something completely different." Her declaration was met with silence. "Plus," she said as she felt the need to continue defending herself, "Killian wasn't going to treat his cancer, and now he is." Technically, Liam said he'd agreed to look into his options, but Kamilah wasn't going to let it stop there.

"That sounds like more manipulation to me," Sofi said.

Kamilah wasn't surprised Sofi would think that. She was not the trusting sort where men were concerned. She'd been burned too many times since birth. However, Sofi didn't know Killian like Kamilah did. She didn't have long, meaningful conversations with him. She didn't notice how his eyes constantly held a depth of pain that became acute longing anytime he talked about his son or his wife. She didn't see the times his proud shoulders dropped in exhaustion when no one was watching. Kamilah was confident that, if it weren't for Liam, Killian would've given up on life a long time ago.

"I understand," Liza said. "You were backed into a corner, and you made the only choice you felt you could at the time."

"Exactly!" Kamilah exclaimed. "See? Lizzo gets it."

"Eliza," Lucy said, putting emphasis on her name since she hated Kamilah's nickname for her wife, "is a high-school principal. She spends *all day* talking to idiots who did something stupid and got themselves in way over their heads."

"Thanks, Lucy," Kamilah said with a grimace.

"I'm sorry, but you are, for all intents and purposes, engaged to Liam, for crying out loud." She threw up her hands with such force that her messy topknot flipped back and started coming loose. "Liam!"

"Yes. That." Sofi pointed at Lucy. "Let us not forget that after years of close friendship, he turned his back on you."

"He was a kid who'd been through trauma," Kamilah said.

Sofi ignored that. "Then he treated you like you had skunk mouth for years."

"Okay, but—"

Sofi was on a roll. "Then he took you to prom but bailed before it was even over."

Yeah, that was after their ill-fated make-out session in the back of Killian's truck, so she could understand why he'd wanted to get away. However, no one knew about that. Not even Sofi.

"Since then, he's been a cold, dismissive asshat, who doesn't appreciate any of the things you do to help him and his grandpa."

"I don't do it to get thank-you notes," Kamilah said, more than a touch defensive. She was surprised to note that most of her defensiveness was on Liam's behalf, not hers. She had no idea why, when Sofi wasn't saying anything she hadn't said herself. "Look, you and everyone else I know with social media have already seen the engagement video, so there is no going back."

"Not to be an asshole, but I wouldn't worry about the… let's say *persuasiveness* of the video," Lucy said.

"What does that mean?" Kamilah asked, even though she already knew. She couldn't act for shit. She'd known that since the third grade when she'd auditioned for the part of "Lead Wampanoag" in the Thanksgiving play and ended up as "Pilgrim Number Five."

"It means that neither one of you will be winning any Oscars anytime soon," Liza said.

At least Liza had the decency to look apologetic about it, unlike Sofi, who waved her near-empty wineglass in the air before saying, "Which is yet another reason why this whole thing is a terrible idea."

"I know that," Kamilah exclaimed. "Don't you think I know this is a horrible idea that will most likely blow up in my face? But it's too late to go back now, so what I need is for you all to help me get through this."

Sofi actually harrumphed. "Of course I'll help you, mensa." She threw the pillow in her lap at Kamilah. "We are ride or die. You know that."

Lucy and Liza nodded their agreement.

"All I'm saying," Sofi continued, "is that if you were doing this with anyone else, I'd say it was ill-advised. But with Liam? Girl, with or without our help, it's a damn catastrophe waiting to happen."

Kamilah had no response to that because she had the sneaking suspicion that it was true.

There was a whoop followed by "Suck on these nuts, beeech!"

Liam continued pulling beers and the ingredients for ham sandwiches out of his fridge, completely unfazed by the rude shout from his living room. In fact, he didn't pay any attention to the response, "At least you can catch a ball in the game, because you haven't caught shit on the field," or the ensuing argument until there was a booming crash.

"What the fuck?" a different voice shouted. "You spilled beer all over me!"

Liam sighed. Why had he invited these idiots over, again? Actually, he hadn't. He'd only invited Ben. Ben had invited his cousins, Devon and Roman. The big rough-and-tumble brothers were prone to wrestling like overgrown puppies whenever they fought. Never mind that Devon was thirty-two years old while Roman was twenty-five. Liam looked over his shoulder to his living room and saw Ben stalking away while taking off his expensive leather coat, the couch tipped over, and the brothers on the floor still grappling with each other. Wait, scratch that. The couch wasn't tipped over. It was backless. "Did you assholes break my couch?"

Dev stopped long enough for Roman to get the upper hand. Although he was smaller than his former defensive-end brother, as a still-active wide receiver, Rome was quick, good with his hands, and had crazy-strong legs. It only took him a matter of seconds to wrap Dev up in some kind of compli-cated cradle-like knot.

"To be fair," Rome told Liam while his brother's brown

skin took on a red hue, "you've had that thing since before I was even in high school."

"And he found it in the alley behind the dorm," Dev choked out from his pretzel position. "It's actual trash."

"You're talking a lot of shit for a guy pinned to my floor with your ass in the air and your legs behind your head," Liam pointed out.

Dev flipped him off with both hands, then double-tapped the floor next to him, signifying his submission.

Rome immediately let him go. Both brothers flopped onto their backs, panting.

"Your dumpster couch should've been set on fire years ago," Ben said as he reentered the room. "My jacket, on the other hand, is brand-new, and this is my favorite shirt." He gestured to the sopping wet T-shirt that clung to his chest.

Liam eyed it. "*Made in Taiwan*. Really, Benji?"

Ben smiled and shrugged. "I've been thinking about getting it tattooed on my forehead. Then maybe people will stop asking me what kind of Asian I am, like I'm some flavor of chip they were deciding whether or not to try."

"Try being Black and Asian," Dev said while climbing to his feet. "People literally ask me if I'm *Blackanese*." He reached down and offered a hand to Rome.

Rome grabbed on. "The worst part is that they think they're so clever." He got to his feet. "Like, bro, that shit was old in the nineties when Chris Tucker was saying it."

The trio of cousins shook their heads in unison.

"Oddly enough, I never seem to have that problem." Liam gestured to his basic white maleness.

Ben snorted at Liam's sarcasm. "No shit. Look at you with your black hair and blue eyes. You look like fucking Superman. You know, except disguised as a scrubby drifter instead of Clark Kent."

"Thanks?"

"You know what I mean." Ben waved him off with one hand. His sparkling gold watch, which definitely cost more than Liam's truck, jangled on his wrist. "You're lady catnip."

Oh perfect segue. "Speaking of ladies," Liam said and paused, unsure how to continue. He decided to jump right in. "I'm engaged to one." That sounded weird. "Not just, like, any lady. Kamilah, specifically." At their blank stares, he realized he probably should've started at the beginning, so he did.

By the time he was done, Rome's mouth was on the floor, Ben wouldn't meet his gaze, and Dev was shaking his head.

"Oh you fucking dumbass," he said a second later.

Liam threw up his hands. He looked at the brothers, who were clearly at a loss, so he turned his attention to Ben.

Ben had turned his entire upper body away, but the shaking of his shoulders announced exactly what he was doing. Ben let out a wheeze and immediately covered his mouth. He peeked at Liam over his shoulder and started laughing harder.

"Hey, at least they stopped talking about selling the building," Liam said, only to send Ben into all-out guffaws.

"What is so damn funny?" Liam asked.

Ben was laughing so hard now that he was wheezing. He didn't even have enough air to make noise. He toppled over the broken back of the couch.

Liam knew he wasn't going to get anything useful out of him, so he turned back to Dev and Rome.

Set off by Ben's antics, Dev had also started laughing. He at least had the decency to hide his in the collar of the shirt he'd pulled over his face.

For his part, Rome looked confused. Of course, he was

much younger than the rest of them, so he didn't really know Granda or much about Liam and Kamilah's history.

"You and Kamilah. Engaged. Old-man blackmail." Ben wheezed repeatedly in between bouts of silent laughter.

Liam cracked open his beer and took a long drink. He didn't know why he'd told them anything. His friends sucked.

Once he'd wiped his tears and regained his breath, Ben told him, "You are so fucked."

"What the fuck else was I supposed to do, Benji?" Liam stressed his friend's much-hated first name, just to watch his eyes narrow in annoyance. "My grandpa told me he was going to let himself die."

Ben crossed his arms over his chest and gave Liam the same look he'd given him back in college when Liam claimed he couldn't go out because he had to study for finals. "You're doing all this for Killian only. Right."

Liam's shoulders went back, and his chest puffed out. "What the fuck is that supposed to mean?"

"Dude, you've had it bad for Kamilah since you were kids. Don't act like you didn't jump at the chance to come to her rescue and win your way back into her life."

What utter bullshit. Ben took one Intro to Psychology course and thought himself a fucking therapist. "I had a childish crush. I got over that a long time ago."

Ben nodded, but the smirk on his face undercut his apparent agreement. "Then why did your grandpa choose her specifically to force you into a fake relationship with?"

"Because *he* loves Kamilah. He always tells her that he wishes she were his granddaughter. Plus, he probably figures she could manage me like she does everyone else."

"Mmm-hmm." That was Dev.

Liam swung to look at him. "Don't do that," he barked.

"I hate when you say *mmm-hmm*, all sarcastic and conde-scending."

Dev didn't say anything else, but the smirk on his face spoke volumes.

Ben dropped back onto the seat next to him. "Liam, all I'm saying is there were other options available to you, and yet you chose the one that includes faking an intimate rela-tionship with your childhood sweetheart."

"We weren't childhood sweethearts. We were friends, and then we grew up and grew apart like most childhood friends do. If I'm doing this now, it's only because I had no other option."

Ben gave Liam a disbelieving look and purposely drawn-out "Mmm-hmm."

"Whatever, man. I'm done talking about it. Help me carry this busted couch outside."

"Fine, but first just answer one question for me."

Liam sighed. "What?"

Ben gestured between himself and his cousins. "Which one of us gets to be the best man?"

All three of them busted up laughing, and Liam vowed to get himself new friends or, better yet, no friends at all. Friends were the worst.

8

"Peace be with you."

"And also with you," Kamilah responded to the elderly man in front of her. They shook hands, and Kamilah turned to make her way back to the pew with her family. Suddenly a hand reached out into the aisle and grabbed her wrist. Kamilah looked down into the face of Doña Cristina, Mami's oldest frenemy. They spoke constantly, but everything was clearly a competition. If Mami wore a new outfit to church, Doña Cristina had a fancier one the following week. If Doña Cristina's son, the deacon, gave a particularly good Gospel homily, Mami made sure that Leo—a long-standing but involuntary choir member— got a solo. It was a constant back-and-forth that Mami usually won. Except where Kamilah was concerned. Doña Cristina's daughter, Sonya, was Kamilah's age, and she was married with three beautiful kids.

As if on cue, Doña Cristina gave Kamilah a smug look and said, "Mira nena, y el novio?"

Ever since Kamilah's broken engagement to Chase, Doña Cristina relished asking Kamilah about her boyfriend every time she saw her. She did it specifically so she could follow up with some sort of rude comment like "In my day, we worked out, plus did all the hard housework. I used to go to the gym, then come home and scrub the floors on my hands and knees" or "I know all you girls want to look like the Kardashians, but there is a difference between curvy and chunky."

Today she was going to have to swallow her loose tongue.

"Peace be with you, Doña," Kamilah responded. She purposely used her left ring finger to swipe a curl off of her forehead and watched with relish as the woman's eyes rounded.

"Is that an engagement ring?" she asked.

Mami, who'd just walked up, jumped in before Kamilah could respond. "Sí, my Mila is engaged. Haven't you seen Facebook?"

"To who?"

"Her best friend since she was little," Mami said. "We all knew they'd end up married one day. That's why Santos and I didn't care when she broke up with that other one." That was a big fat lie. Mami had practically gone into mourning when Kamilah gave Chase his ring back.

"And where is this fiancé? Don't tell me he isn't a Christian," she added in a scandalized whisper. She made the sign of the cross on her front and kissed her fingers.

"Don't worry. He's a good and steady man with a job, and not some cheating bueno para nada." Mami flipped open her over-the-top Señorita fan with a flick of her wrist and waved her face as if it were not a blustery, cool fall day and she hadn't just shaded the hell out of Doña Cristina's *good-for-nothing* son-in-law. "Anyway, peace be with you." She grabbed Kamilah's arm and dragged her away.

Kamilah bit the inside of her lip to prevent herself from laughing at Mami's savagery. Mami was pretty funny when her barbs were directed at someone else.

"I thought you said you invited Liam," Mami whispered in her ear as they made their way back to the pew where their entire immediate family was waiting.

"He's busy," Kamilah whispered back.

"Too busy for church with his family?"

The judgment was strong, but Kamilah focused more on the last part of that sentence. It was weird how quickly Mami had taken to the idea of Liam and Kamilah as a couple. It had only been a week since they'd announced their sham engagement, and she'd already started referring to him as *mi yerno Liam* and telling everyone who'd listen about her handsome son-in-law. She'd even uploaded old pictures of Kamilah and Liam as kids to her phone. Her new pastime was showing them off to everyone.

Mami's favorite was of one-year-old Kamilah trying to swallow Liam's face, aka give him a birthday kiss, and two-year-old Liam looking absolutely disgusted while his birthday hat slid down his head and over his right eye. Mami had no idea how well that picture encapsulated their relationship. Kamilah was always making friendly overtures toward Liam, only to get rebuffed.

Case in point, he'd ignored her the entire first week of their engagement. Anytime she'd tried to engage him in any sort of discussion, he claimed to be busy and disappeared. His excuse for missing Mass? He had to work on preparing his dad's barrel for the contest. As if they would really be doing that at seven on a Sunday morning. He probably wasn't even awake yet. She, on the other hand, woke up at five to get a head start on kitchen prep.

"You should've convinced him to come," Mami was saying.

"And how was I supposed to do that?"

"You're a woman, aren't you? Use what you've got." Mami ran a hand down her still-trim but prominent curves proudly displayed in a navy blue sheath dress. "How do you think I get your papi to do anything?"

Kamilah frowned. Had her mother really just told her in the middle of Mass to manipulate Liam with sex?

Mami slid past Abuelo to stand next to Papi and pulled Kamilah so she was right next to her. "Santa Maria, Madre de Dios ruega por mi hija quien necesita de su ayuda." Mami finished her improvised version of the Hail Mary by making the sign of the cross.

Kamilah felt the need to defend herself. "It's not that serious."

Mami's eyebrows went up, and she raised her hands, palms out, in the universal Latinx mom shrug that usually accompanied some deep shade-throwing. "Bueno. Yo na' mas digo, if you can't even get your fiancé to spend time with you now, imagine after you've been married for thirty-five years."

Papi shushed them both, and for the rest of Mass, Kamilah didn't have to say anything besides what she was obliged to recite. However, the moment they were all out of the doors, it started all over again.

In a move that had to have been planned out beforehand, Kamilah suddenly found herself surrounded by all four of her older brothers. The twins, Cristian and Eddie, moved so they stood in front of her. The oldest, Saint, appeared at her right. From her left, Leo threw a muscular arm over her shoulder. It was not in brotherly affection. It was so she couldn't escape.

"Can I help you?" she asked them in the bratty tone reserved solely for brothers.

Leo exerted enough pressure on her neck to guide her down the stairs to follow the rest of the family on their four-block trek back to El Coquí. The other three moved with them. They were still with the rest of the family but had fallen a bit behind.

"What, we can't talk to our baby sister now that she's engaged?" Cris threw back at her over his shoulder. Of her four brothers, he'd always been a bit of a bully to the rest of them, with the exception of Saint, who they all knew better than to fuck with.

"Sure. I just don't know why you're surrounding me like a pack of vultures."

"A group of vultures is called a *committee*, not a *pack*." Eddie was annoyingly smart. And a smart-ass. "Or a *wake*, if they're feeding on a carcass."

"And just what are you four today, a committee or a wake?" Her lips thinned, and she had a feeling she knew the answer.

"A wake," Leo said. "We have a bone to pick with you." He smiled and waggled his eyebrows. "You see what I did there? Vultures—a bone to pick?" He laughed at his own dumb joke.

Usually, Kamilah relished going toe-to-toe with her brothers, but this was not one of those times. She glanced around for her sisters-in-law, Yasmeen and Summer, who were always on her side whenever the brothers got to be too much.

Unfortunately, both women were at the front of the merry band with all of the kids, who were headed to the small playground across the street. With a few words to Kamilah's parents behind them, they broke off and crossed over. Even Kamilah's fifteen-year-old nephew, Omar, went with them.

That left Kamilah with her brothers, Abuelo, and her parents. Her parents and Abuelo stopped so she and her brothers could catch up. *This cannot be good.*

They all walked quietly for a few minutes. They turned down the street that would take them past the left side of the building, where the Kane Distillery was housed.

"Papi mentioned renovations you want to make to El Coquí," Saint said into the silence. "Something about a food tour."

Kamilah furrowed her brow. What was this? An intervention or something? "Yes," she replied tentatively.

"Why?" Cristian asked in his typically brusque fashion.

"Why what?" Kamilah asked. "Why renovate, or why the Foodie Tour?"

"Both," Cristian replied.

The truth was that she'd already filed the application to enter and, since the application was technically late, had sent a long, detailed email to the coordinator about why El Coquí represented the best of the neighborhood. Per Lucy and Sofi's advice, she also added in the fact they had failed to feature original-neighborhood restaurants in previous years, which was discriminatory and offensive to a large population of residents. The coordinator had sent her a welcome email within a few hours. El Coquí would feature in Humboldt Park's Third Annual Fall Foodie Tour. Now she just had to make sure it was ready.

Not like that will be hard or anything.

She barely noticed when Abuelo broke away from the group and headed down the alley. It was barely eight thirty in the morning, and the parking lot was empty aside from her brothers' cars and Liam's truck. The huge, frosted-glass garage door that led to Kane Distillery was closed, and there were no lights on inside. Mami gave her a significant look, her lips pursed in irritation.

Stupid Liam lying about being busy when it could easily be discovered.

Time to refocus Mami's attention.

"I know you all think it's not worth it, but to me it is." Kamilah gestured to the small, faded El Coquí sign. "This is Abuela's legacy. I don't want to lose it."

"Mila, Abuela has been dead for like ten years," her brother pointed out. "She won't know what's happened to it." As a literal genius and engineer, Eddie dealt in facts and figures. Things like family members looking on from heaven didn't factor into his decisions.

"And so what? We just give up on her dream?" Kamilah returned. "She worked her whole life to make this place a reality, but we should let it close just because keeping it open is hard?"

Papi gave her a dark look over his shoulder but continued on to open the door in front of them.

"Abuelo's sick, and Mami and Papi are tired," Cristian shot back. "They're done with the long hours and the constant worry. Do you really think it's fair to make them keep going just because Abuela wanted it over a decade ago?" He followed Mami and Papi through the doors.

He had a point, but Kamilah was willing to step in to lighten the load. "If we just changed some things—"

Leo cut her off. "That's what this is really about," he told their brothers while crowding in behind her. "She wants to take over."

"It's not about taking over," Kamilah argued. They all spilled into the seating area of El Coquí and then spread out like spray from a nozzle. "It's about doing what needs to be done to make this place profitable."

Leo scoffed. "It's about your need to be the savior."

Kamilah spun and glared at her brother. "That's rich, coming from the guy who has to run into burning buildings just to feel important."

"At least I do something of value."

"Ya basta," Saint barked. As Papi's spitting image in looks and temperament, he was used to his younger siblings obeying his every command. Plus, he was using his commanding-officer voice. As a retired Green Beret, it was highly effective.

They both shut up.

"Leo, all you're doing is upsetting her," Saint said.

"Pobre princesita," Leo grumbled.

Kamilah's hackles went up. She hated being called a little princess, and he knew it.

"That's not why we're here." Saint grabbed a chair, turned it around, sat on it, and rested his forearms along the back.

Kamilah looked to her remaining family members. It wasn't lost on her that she stood with her back to the kitchen and facing them, as if defending her space, while they formed a conquering battalion in front of her.

"Look," she said. "I'm just trying to keep Abuela's dream going. I'm not trying to push anyone out. I want this place to stay open and be successful."

"We get that," Saint said. "But, Kamilah, renovating a business isn't some simple do-it-yourself Pinterest project, and, well, you don't really have a plan."

"I do have a plan," Kamilah countered. "Update the menu and the decor."

"We want specifics," Eddie pushed. "What exactly are you going to do, how are you going to do it, what is it going to cost, how long is it going to take, when would we see results, and where are you going to get the money?"

Kamilah stopped. *Specifics?* "Umm…"

"Exactly," Eddie said. "You have no real plans. Only a vague idea. You can't expect anyone with common sense to back that."

Ouch. And damn. *Double damn.* She hated when she inadvertently proved someone's point for them. Kamilah was so used to getting shut down at the idea level, she never got to the planning stage.

"I already got El Coquí into the Foodie Tour. We just have to make sure we put our best foot forward."

"You did what?" Mami screeched. "After we specifically said no?"

"Ay, Kamilah," Papi said with scorn. "You and your half-baked ideas."

"But—"

"Mila, you do this all the time," Cristian said. "You want to help, but a lot of the times you just end up making things worse. Remember when you babysat Omar and decided to help Yasmeen by making homemade baby food?" He paused for dramatic effect and then continued in Spanish. "El nene casi se muere."

"He didn't almost die," Kamilah shot back. "He got hives and puffed up like a balloon, but how was I supposed to know that babies aren't supposed to have cinnamon before six months? I was, like, fifteen. Also, I got that recipe from a baby website, so that's on them."

"Who was it on when you decided to help Mami save money and highlighted her hair?" Eddie asked as he pushed his thick black-rimmed glasses up the bridge of his nose. "She ended up looking like a leopard for a month until we could get it fixed."

"I told her to stop wiggling," Kamilah claimed.

"It was burning," Mami accused.

Kamilah crossed her arms. "That's because your developer was old."

"What about the time you helped Saint with his back patio and ended up knocking him off and into those prickly bushes?" Papi interjected. "That was last year."

Kamilah huffed. "I told him to duck."

"Oh! Oh!" Leo raised his hand like a little kid in school begging the teacher to pick him. "Remember the time she helped Doña Juana plant those," he said as he held up his fingers to make quotation marks, "*hybrid peas* in the community garden, and Tío Rico had to step in before she got arrested for growing weed?"

Her family busted up laughing over that, but Kamilah didn't find any of it funny. Her family was proving what they thought of her. She was nothing but a funny anecdote—the butt of a joke. She couldn't be taken seriously or trusted to complete a task the right way. She could argue her case until she was blue in the face, and they still wouldn't trust her with anything real.

That hurt. She felt like she had when Jessica Morales had got all the other girls to laugh at her for wearing Leo's hand-me-down pants and Jordans, like there was something wrong with her and she wasn't good enough. She swallowed the thickness in her throat and willed the tears forming in her eyes to disappear.

At that moment the kitchen doors swung open and knocked into her. She stumbled forward on her church heels and would've ended up face-planting if not for the hands that caught her at the elbows and pulled her into a familiar chest. Kamilah turned her head to verify her suspicion.

Liam was looking down at her. His gaze tracked over her face. When he got to her wet eyelashes he paused. He lifted a hand and touched the very tip of his finger to the corner of her eye. Then he pulled it back and stared at the moisture on his hand as if he'd never seen a tear before. His expression hardened in disapproval.

Kamilah shook off the fresh jab of pain and blinked rapidly to make sure no more liquid leaked out of her eyes. After all, Liam's expression was nothing new. He always looked at her as if displeased to find her breathing in his vicinity.

"I hope you aren't all ganging up on my soon-to-be grand-daughter," Killian said from Liam's side.

"I think we made our points," Eddie said.

"But let's talk about that," Cristian added, pointing at Killian. "I think we would all love to know how these two ended up engaged when none of us even knew they were together."

"I wouldn't," Leo threw out. "That seems like a story I don't want to hear about my little sister."

"Shut up, Leo," at least four people said at the same time.

Leo was unfazed. Dear God, he was so much like Abuelo that it was terrifying to contemplate.

"Last we knew, Kamilah was embarrassingly single," Cristian continued, pure savagery he'd inherited from Mami.

"You don't know my life," Kamilah burst out.

"Nor do you need to," Liam told Cristian.

Cristian's eyes narrowed at the evident challenge in Liam's tone. The two of them had never got along, even as kids. They both demonstrated too many qualities the other scorned. Cristian, the domineering, temperamental meathead, and Liam, the quiet, distant artist.

"I just think it's weird that they are never together," Papi said, drawing everyone's attention to him. "Not even after hours, and they both live and work right here."

"We don't have to be in each other's back pocket," Kamilah argued. "Plus, we've both been really busy lately."

"Too busy to spend time with the person you plan to marry?" Saint asked with a raised brow.

"That's why Kamilah is moving in with Liam," Abuelo said. "So they can spend more time together."

Both Kamilah's and Liam's heads whipped around at that pronouncement.

Abuelo put on a practiced look of remorse. "Oh I'm sorry. Was I not supposed to say anything yet?"

Kamilah felt her face turning hot. She knew others would probably think it was because she was embarrassed, but really she was pissed. All she wanted was to fix up El Coquí and put it on the track to success. That was all. Yet everyone and everything conspired against her. Why was it that she was expected to jump whenever anyone else wanted her to, but when she wanted to do something, everyone acted like she was being unreasonable? Now she had to play this stupid game with Abuelo and Killian just to do what her family should already be supporting her in doing.

Kamilah opened her mouth to object, but the look Abuelo and Killian gave her had her shutting it quickly. It was clear she and Liam had just received another term of their agreement.

9

Liam slowly swirled the ounce of cloudy, dark mahogany whiskey around his custom-made tumbler and watched it cling to the sides—a clear indication it was over the usual four to six years old. He held it up to the light and watched the sediments float around; he wasn't worried about that since the sediment would clear up once they filtered it. Liam was more worried about the taste.

The fact remained that he and Granda had no idea what all Da had used to make this whiskey, so they couldn't be sure the amount of time it had spent in the barrel hadn't turned it bitter or astringent. There was a fine balancing act when it came to the amount of time the alcohol stayed in the barrel, and it was even more delicate when dealing with a climate with harsh seasons. Places like Ireland and Scotland were able to mature whiskey for longer periods of time because of their temperate climes. Liam didn't think anyone would describe Chicago's climate as temperate.

He brought the glass close and took his first sniff, making sure to inhale through his mouth and his nose since the alcohol fumes would be high as he hadn't cut it with water. The first smell was intense but not overwhelming. He definitely picked up notes of dark fruit, which told him the barrel had housed another alcohol. He was inclined to think it had held a dry red wine, like a cabernet. Immediately thereafter he was hit with wheat, spice, and smoke—something like clove oatmeal cooked over a campfire.

"Do you smell that?" he asked Granda. "Is that peat?"

Sitting on a stool on the other side of their bottling-station table, Granda's head snapped back as if Liam had just punched him in the face.

"Fuck, no," he retorted before taking another sniff. "No son of mine would even *think* of adding peat to his Irish whiskey." His voice held conviction, but the doubt in his eyes gave him away.

"Granda, it's not Irish whiskey if it wasn't made in Ireland," Liam explained for the billionth time.

"It's Irish, because we're *Irishmen*, and that's why there is no fucking peat in there. That's for the Scots."

Liam didn't comment on that, because he wasn't sure he agreed. However, he wasn't going to argue with Granda about it. Not when they had other things on their minds. Namely, whether this whiskey was going to live up to their expectations. Their entire plan hinged on using it as their crowning glory in order to win the contest.

"Are you ready?" Granda asked him. He held up his own glass.

It was difficult not to ask him again whether he should be drinking at all, given the state of his liver, but Liam knew there was no way in hell Granda would refrain from trying this whiskey, and Liam would never dream of trying to stop him. They'd been waiting twenty years for this moment. All their hard work, all their sacrifices, all their hopes and dreams—it all came down to this.

Seeking something to ground him and calm his worries, Liam took a look around the distillery. There was nowhere he felt more at peace than among the copper stills and charred oak barrels. He'd taken his first steps in the barrel room. He'd ridden his bike without training wheels for the first time from the very spot he stood in. He'd sat on tall stools in front of the lauter tun for hours watching the rake arms turn. The back wall where he'd eventually painted their logo was the same wall he'd vandalized after his mother's abandonment. The distillery had always been Liam's place to simply be himself in whatever form he happened to be. It was his haven. His true home. A sense of serenity and belonging enveloped him.

He looked at his grandfather and nodded. It was time.

In tandem, they lifted their glasses. "Sláinte," they toasted each other, before taking a small sip.

Liam sank against the bottling-station table, bent his head, and squeezed his eyes shut. He felt the moisture build up in the corners of his eyes and eventually spill over, but he didn't wipe them away. For a few minutes he basked in the relief. Da's whiskey was everything they'd hoped it would be and more. There was no way it wouldn't hand them a win. Eventually, Liam opened his eyes and looked over at Granda.

Granda sat hunched over the table with his face in his hands. His shoulders jerked as he tried to silently stifle his sobs. His vision blurry, Liam reached out and put a hand on Killian's shoulder. The older man wrapped one hand around his grandson's wrist and held on tight, while Liam gripped his grandfather's shoulder hard and gave it a rough shake.

Granda then rested his head lightly on Liam's arm while he continued to cover his eyes with his other hand.

They sat like that for a while. The only two people on earth who were currently experiencing the same mix of sadness, regret, pain, relief, and hope. Granda and Liam were two sides of the same unlucky coin, two peas in the same pain-filled pod. They were the only two who could truly understand what the other one felt.

Liam was the one to break the silence.

"I promise I will play whatever game you want me to play," he said as he stared through the garage-door windows into the night. His voice was low and soft. It cut in and out as he continued. "I'll jump through whatever hoops you want me to jump through, but I need you to get treatment, Granda."

I need you to be here. I can't do this without you.

Granda was quiet for so long that Liam wasn't sure he'd answer, but then he croaked out one word that had Liam's eyes refilling and his heart restarting for the first time in two weeks. "Okay."

"Thank you," Liam told him.

Granda eventually released his wrist and patted his hand. "Enough of this," he said. He used both hands to grab his collar and pull his shirt over his face so he would wipe it.

Liam did the same.

Granda finished off the whiskey in his cup and stood from his stool. "I have a late-night game of poker to play." He motioned to the door between the barrel room and the mural wall that led directly to Liam's condo. "And you have a pretty fiancée waiting for you through that door."

Liam had not forgotten that fact. When he'd left his place a few hours ago, Kamilah had just begun unpacking her clothes.

It had taken a shockingly short amount of time to move

her things into his place. Barely two days between packing and hauling her stuff down one set of stairs and up the other. He'd expected more pushback from her family, considering their traditional views, but her parents were oddly eager to help her make the transition. They'd forgone prep, accounting, and cleaning both of the days the restaurant was closed to help get their baby girl moved out. It was almost alarming how eager they'd been to get rid of their only daughter.

"I might stick around here and get started on the design for the label," Liam said to his grandfather. He wasn't ready to see his place with her in it. There was too much change happening and too much that needed to be figured out.

Granda gave him a sharp look. "The hell you will." He grabbed Liam by the arm and started dragging him toward the door. "You're going to go into that apartment and check in with Kamilah. You're going to see if she needs help and make sure that she has everything she needs. Once you ensure she is fine, you are going to eat, shower, and get some sleep. Tomorrow we have a lot to do. Including a visit to my doctor." He pulled open the door and pushed Liam through. "Go on, lad. I'll lock up over here."

Since Liam had just promised Granda he'd jump through hoops, he closed the door to the distillery and made his way down the short hallway that opened up into his condo. He could hear Kamilah moving around in his kitchen, muttering to herself. He couldn't make out what she was saying exactly, but it sounded like a mix of English and Spanish. Conscious of not sneaking up on her again—his crotch hadn't forgotten the pain from the last time he'd surprised her—Liam called her name.

"Mila."

A mound of brown curls exploding from the top of a colorful printed scarf appeared around the corner. "I forgot that door was there." She leaned farther out and her face came into view. Her eyes zeroed in on the wall next to him. "Oh here's the thermostat." She came fully around the corner to fiddle with it.

Liam stopped dead in his tracks as if he'd just walked into a sliding glass door.

She was wearing more clothes than some of the women on the tours that afternoon, but the sight of Kamilah in a pair of black workout leggings and a gray sweatshirt affected him in a way the flirty sundresses and backless rompers had not.

Everything about her, from her lush figure and pouty mouth to her mass of dark springy curls and big bright eyes, brought to mind one word: *bountiful*. Kamilah was a bounty of beauty, energy, and affection, and to be in her presence was to desire to feast.

And I want to feast like a Las Vegas tourist at an all-you-can-eat buffet.

"I hope you don't mind," she was saying, "but I sort of re-arranged your kitchen. I didn't mean to. It just sort of happened while I was finding places for my kitchen supplies." She shifted nervously as if waiting for him to bite her head off. Her movement brought Liam's attention to her feet, which were clad in a tall pair of socks covered in cartoon cacti and the text *Can't touch this.*

Oh good, a well-timed reminder. He definitely could not feast— even though he'd been dying to ever since he'd discovered what it meant to be attracted to the opposite sex. He knew it would be so good, but the fact of the matter was that Kamilah was the type of woman who needed love and happily-ever-after. And sure, he'd loved Kamilah since they were kids, but it wasn't the right kind. His love was dark and resentful and needy. It was unhealthy, and the last thing he'd ever do was force it on her. She deserved better. She always had.

It took him a moment to realize she was staring at him, clearly waiting for his response to some comment or question. "Can you repeat that?" he said.

"Are you okay?" she asked. "You seem preoccupied."

"Yeah, sorry. It's been a long day." He moved around her and walked farther into the condo before turning the corner to check out his remodeled kitchen. Where there had once been nothing but a toaster and a Keurig, there was now a plethora of appliances on his counters. He didn't know what any of them were besides the yellow stand mixer and a gnarly-looking knife set. He could tell by the open cabinets that she'd been in the process of moving around his dishes and reorganizing his sparse food supply when he'd arrived.

"Do you need help?"

"Oh no." She came up behind him and slid around his side. She didn't touch him, but he felt an electric current anyway. "It looks bad, but I'll have it done in a few minutes. Did you eat? Are you hungry?"

"You don't have to take care of me." Liam shook his head. "I'm a big boy. I can take care of myself." He'd meant to reassure her that he wasn't going to add to her already-full plate of responsibilities, but by the slight jerk of her neck and the subsequent tightening of her jaw, he could see he'd only managed to insult her. He rubbed a hand over his face. He was always doing and saying the wrong thing. This whole thing was going to be a disaster. "Uh, I'm wiped out, so if you're sure you don't need help, I'm going to shower and go to bed."

"About that." She had her back to him and was putting stacks of plates in the upper cabinet to the right of the sink.

When she was done, she turned to look at him. "Where am I going to sleep?"

Liam frowned. "What do you mean? You're going to sleep in the bed, and I'll sleep on the cou—" He suddenly remembered that his couch was at the dump and his living room was outfitted with nothing but an armchair. "Fuck."

"Exactly," she responded. "If you'd told me that you have no couch and no furniture in the spare bedroom, I would've figured something out."

"You take the bed," he told her around a yawn. "I think I have an air mattress around here somewhere. I'll pull it out and put it in the spare room."

She rolled her eyes at him. "You're clearly exhausted. I'm not going to make you look for an air mattress that may or may not exist. Plus, I'd feel like an asshole taking your bed from you."

"Well, you spent the last two days moving all your belongings in here. I'm not going to make you look for a potentially fictional air mattress, nor would I ever let you sleep on it while I slept in the bed. I *am* an asshole, but even I have limits."

"You're not an asshole," she said. "Annoyingly self-sufficient yet socially incompetent, yes, but asshole? Not at all."

Liam ignored the warmth that spread through him at her faint praise. "So where does this leave us?" he asked.

"The way I see it, we can both sleep on the floor in some weird show of etiquette." She paused. "Or we can just share the bed."

He'd figured she was going to say that, and there were a million reasons why it was a terrible idea. He opened his mouth to give them, but she continued before he could get a word out.

"Look, we're both adults who know exactly what's up. It's

not like either of us is out to seduce the other one. We just need a place to sleep, and your bed is—what?—a California king? We can both sleep in it without even realizing the other one is there."

That was impossible. There was no way Liam could even be in the same room with her and not know she was there. He was too aware of her every movement. Her every breath. "I don't think—"

She spoke over him. "If it makes you feel better, we'll put a pillow wall down the middle of the bed like when we were kids."

Liam had to laugh at the image. "The pillow wall never worked when we were kids," he told her. "You always rolled over the barrier and took up all my space and my blanket."

"Well, I'm an adult now, and I have a weighted blanket, so I can barely move at all."

It was a horrible idea. But the temptation to sleep with her, even platonically, proved too strong to resist.

"Fine," he told her, careful to sound grudging instead of anticipatory. "But if you try to take my space or my blanket, I'm pushing you off the other side of the bed."

"Deal." Kamilah held out her hand, and Liam shook it.

In the end, it took less than two hours to regret it.

After helping Kamilah reorganize the kitchen, despite her protests, he'd taken a not-so-quick shower to—*ahem*—relieve his tension. By the time he'd come out, the pillow barrier was in place, and Kamilah was dead to the world.

As he'd expected, her claims to have matured into a calm and still sleeper were utter bullshit. She was as active in sleep as she was awake. Even her precious weighted blanket couldn't contain her energy and, based on the loud whoosh he'd heard five minutes after climbing into bed, was currently on the floor somewhere. True to form, Kamilah rolled right over the pillow barrier as if it didn't exist. Within forty-five minutes she was plastered all along his side with her arm thrown over his chest and her leg over his hips.

Now, approximately one hour and fifty-seven minutes into this torture, Liam stared at the dark clouds through the skylight above his bedroom loft and wished he could at least count stars or spots on the moon or something. Anything to help take his mind off Kamilah's breath brushing his chin and her soft thigh rubbing against his dick as she shifted repeatedly in her sleep. Unable to take any more, Liam flipped over onto his side facing the railing that overlooked his living room.

Kamilah jerked and for a moment he thought she might have woken up. He wished she would so he could send her back to her side of the bed. Instead, she snuggled up to his back and wrapped herself around him like a boa constrictor. It wouldn't have been that bad if not for her soft breasts pressed against his back. He shifted and swore he could feel her nipples hardening against his shoulder blades.

Son of a bitch.

He was going to spontaneously combust by morning.

10

Kamilah turned her head and buried her face in her pillow but was still unable to block out the bright light against her closed lids. Why was her bedroom suddenly as bright as the damn sun? And why did her pillow smell weird? Not funky or anything, but it didn't smell like her normal coconut oil mixed with Tide.

No, it smelled outdoorsy, like chopped wood or something—and a bit like dark liquor. And then Kamilah remembered she wasn't in her windowless childhood bedroom or in her bed. She was in Liam's huge loft bedroom and in his ginormous bed because she lived there now. She'd been living there for over a week.

When her warm-body pillow inhaled deeply and moved, Kamilah's eyes shot open. The bright sunlight streaming in through the skylights and the windows burned her retinas.

"Son of a whore," she cursed, closing her eyes again. This whole *being woken by rays of sun shooting her in the face like high-*

powered lasers was going to take a lot of adjustment. Unlike waking up snuggled against Liam's back with her leg hooked over his hip and an arm wrapped around his waist, which was all too easy to get used to.

She creaked one eye open a slit and stared at the back of Liam's neck in thought. She never would've taken him for the little-spoon type of guy. Many of the guys she knew considered it submissive and thus emasculating. However, in the few nights they'd been sharing the bed, she'd discovered that Liam liked it.

At least, he never complained about it.

She could see why the position worked for him. He got the benefits of snuggling without the work. He was able to receive a bit of affection without having to ask for it—or give it back. Wait a second. *Affection?* Since when did she have affection for Liam?

The scoff that sounded in her mind was a lot like Sofi's. She flopped onto her back. Okay, fine. She'd always had affection for Liam. It was impossible not to. They were best friends for their entire childhood. Just because their friendship ended, it didn't mean that those feelings had. Even on his part, she could tell that he still felt some sort of fondness for her. If Liam had felt absolutely nothing for her, there was no way he would've allowed her to invade his space, agreement or not. Sure, he barely talked to her, only allowed her close when they were sleeping, and just yesterday had spouted off at her for "shedding all over the damn shower like a husky," but she still knew he cared.

Kamilah lifted her hands in a stretch and was distracted by the wink of her engagement ring in the early-morning light. Looking at the ring on her left finger, a reminder of her en-

gagement to Liam, made her think of something her abuela
had told her long ago.

*Kamilah sat at the worktable in the kitchen watching Abuela
beat up a huge chunk of mallorca dough. Abuela was grumbling in
Spanish about Abuelo being too old to keep letting his party-animal
friends steer him down the wrong path. Kamilah was starting to get
worried because she'd never seen Abuela stay mad at Abuelo for so
long. Usually all he had to do was sing Abuela her favorite song,
and she'd get over whatever had her upset. He'd tried that two days
ago. Before he'd got through the first verse of "Amorcito Corazón,"
Abuela had called him "un viejo ridículo" and told him he could shut
it. They hadn't spoken since.*

*"Abuela, are you and Abuelo going to get a divorce?" Kamilah
asked.*

*Abuela stopped kneading the bread and looked at Kamilah in
alarm. "What? Why would you ask me that?"*

*"Because when you don't love each other anymore you're supposed
to get a divorce," Kamilah said as she watched Abuela's hands punch
the bread dough. "Ramiro Martinez's parents are getting a divorce
because they don't love each other anymore."*

*Abuela grabbed one end of the dough and folded it over the other.
"Well, that's not the same thing, because I do love your abuelo."*

"Then why won't you talk to him?"

*Abuela lifted the dough and slammed it onto the table with force.
"Porque me vuelve loca."*

*Kamilah nodded with all the wisdom her seven-year-old life experience
had given her. She frequently heard Mami telling one of her brothers to
leave her alone because they were driving her crazy. But Mami's desire to
be left alone never lasted long, only a few minutes, not days like Abuela's.
"You still love Abuelo, even though you don't want to talk to him, and
you're going to stay married," Kamilah concluded.*

"Claro." Abuela nodded. "Es mi mejor amigo."

Kamilah felt her eyes get big. "Abuelo is your best friend?"

"Sí."

"You married your best friend?" At Abuela's nod, Kamilah's jaw dropped, and she shook her head in disbelief. "Why would you want to marry your best friend?"

"¿Por qué no?"

"Because a best friend is one thing, and a person you marry is another," Kamilah explained.

Abuela smiled at her and shook her head. "No ojitos, son la misma persona. You should only marry your best friend. Remember that when you grow up." Then she went back to kneading the dough, but Kamilah could tell that she was doing it without anger now. Later when they pulled the sweet bread rolls out of the oven and dusted them with powdered sugar, Abuelo was the first one Abuela gave one to.

Kamilah sighed with nostalgia, suddenly missing her grandmother with a fierceness that brought tears to her eyes. She tried to envision what Abuela would think about the situation Kamilah had got herself into: blackmailed by two octogenarians, on the verge of making enemies of her parents, and playing house with Liam. Abuela would shake her head and warn Kamilah, "Antes caerá el mentiroso que el cojo." Kamilah knew she was stumbling along in her lies, about to trip and fall flat on her face, but she'd chosen this path. She'd gone too far along it to turn back. The only way left was through.

She suddenly had a strong hankering for some honesty and some mallorcas. Since she knew she wasn't going to be able to satisfy her first craving, she decided to satisfy the second. Careful to not wake up her bedmate, Kamilah slid out of the bed, took care of her morning ablutions, and then headed to the kitchen to get started on the three-hour process.

She descended the spiral stairs in the corner of the bedroom instead of the floating stairs at the other end of the second floor. Floating stairs freaked her out. On her way down, she let her fingers trail over the decorative railing. It was gorgeous, made out of wrought iron ivy vines and acanthus scrolls. So were the stairs under her feet. There were touches of artistry that spoke to the building's blacksmith-and-masonry past throughout the place. The huge wrought iron chandelier that matched the stairs and hung above the living room was the most obvious. Along with the antique Chicago common brick that turned his walls from a uniform smooth red or tan to a rough mosaic of buff yellows, salmon pinks, deep reds, and ashen blues.

Smaller features in other places demonstrated purposeful design flair too. Like how the imperfect reclaimed-wood flooring and arched windows added a whimsical warmth to the otherwise highly industrial-looking space. She turned to take it in from a different view.

Everything was a contrast, from the large farmhouse table with heavy iron chairs in the dining room to the boxy old metal vents juxtaposed with hanging-lantern light fixtures. Each aspect of Liam's home was a mix of cool strength and cozy craftsmanship. The only thing it was missing was a touch of Liam's personality. It was, in fact, almost barren-looking. It was as if he'd just moved in, when he'd been living there since he'd graduated college.

Kamilah shook her head and crossed the empty spot where the couch used to sit. She walked past the dining-room table and over to the now fully functional and plentifully stocked kitchen—since she'd made a grocery run the evening before while Liam was on his journey to pick up supplies for the distillery. She hadn't intended to, but she'd been working on her plans for El Coquí and feeling snacky. Once it became clear that Liam had nothing in his house but whiskey, cereal, milk, and frozen chicken tenders, Kamilah had decided to go pick up a few things. Her trip had cost her a couple hundred dollars, but it was worth it if it meant she had what she needed to cook whatever she wanted, like mallorcas.

She was singing, rapping, and dancing to a Bad Bunny song that was playing from her phone and coiling strips of dough into rolls when Liam finally came down the stairs. He still looked exhausted. She wondered what time he'd finally made it in.

"Buenos días," she said as he neared the counter.

"Buenos días," he murmured in the Puerto Rican accent he'd picked up from her family.

She'd only heard him speak Spanish a handful of times, but she knew Liam understood a great deal of the language, and it never failed to make her feel warm and fuzzy. She wasn't sure why, since it was mostly a testament to the frequency with which they'd been railed at by their elders, who tended to revert to their first language when excited or angry. They'd got into tons of trouble as kids—well, mainly she, her brothers, and cousins had. Liam usually ended up guilty by association, the poor, quiet observer. Yet he'd never complained or turned his back on her.

Now look at them: engaged yet barely friends.

"I'm making mallorcas," she told him while coiling yet another strip of dough. "Once I get them in the oven, they will be done in about fifteen minutes." She finished her last roll and lifted the tray to set them in the preheated oven.

Liam tilted his head to the side and eyed the baking sheet. "I don't think I've ever had those before."

Probably not. Abuela hadn't been a baker. She'd preferred cooking. Therefore, she'd only made mallorcas when she had a strong craving.

"You'll love them." She placed the sheet in the oven and shut the door. "They're soft, flaky, sweet rolls of deliciousness. The bakery down the street from Abuela Clara's house—my mom's mom—makes them fresh every morning." She walked to the cabinet at the far side of the kitchen to grab the bag of powdered sugar she'd bought on her grocery run. "Whenever we go to visit her, I gorge on them. I gorge on everything when we go to Puerto Rico." Kamilah walked over to another set of cabinets, bent, and began to rifle through the lower cabinet for the sifter she'd brought over from her parents'. "Actually, I gorge pretty much all the time, which you can see from my ass and thighs."

Shouldn't have said that.

She grabbed the sifter and straightened quickly. She spun to face Liam, expecting to see his eyebrow up in the air and the corner of his mouth curled in amusement. That was not the expression she found.

He was looking at her ass—at least, the spot her ass had just been—with a decidedly hungry look on his face. His eyes tracked up her body with only a brief but noted pause at her chest until he reached her face. When he saw her staring at him with an eyebrow quirk of her own, his expression went blank. He cleared his throat.

"I had all the stuff you needed to bake bread?" he asked.

Kamilah snorted. "God, no. Your kitchen was depressingly empty. I went grocery shopping yesterday while you were out."

"Let me know how much you spent," he told her. "I'll reimburse you."

"No way," she said. "I bought this stuff because I wanted it, not because you needed it."

"We'll split it in half, then," he said.

Knowing how stubborn Liam could be, Kamilah figured that was the best offer she was likely to get. "Fine," she agreed.

Liam walked around the counter and over to the fridge. He pulled it open and looked mildly overwhelmed to find it full. "Not to sound rude when you were down here baking bread at the crack of dawn," he said as he scanned the shelves and then ended up grabbing a coconut water, "but shouldn't you be at work?" He closed the door to the fridge, leaned against it, and opened the carton.

"Leo, Saint, and I rotate Saturday nights, so I don't have to be there until seven."

The sudden beeping of the alarm system had them both turning to the front door, where Killian was letting himself in with a key. Abuelo followed carrying a tray of coffees and two of the biggest pastelitos de coco Kamilah had ever seen. They'd obviously been down the street at Doña Álamo's bakery.

"Umm, hi?" Liam looked both confused and alarmed by his grandfather just walking into his house, so Kamilah figured it was not a regular occurrence.

That made her start to feel nervous. What were they doing there, and why had they shown up bearing gifts?

"That key is for emergencies only, you know," Liam told his grandfather.

Killian was offended. "You lived in my house for free for years, you ungrateful shite." He took the coffees from Abuelo and stomped over to the breakfast bar that separated the kitchen from the open-concept dining/living space. "In fact, considering this is in my half of the building, you still do." He set the coffees on the counter and then crossed his arms over his chest. "I guess I'll show up when I damn well please."

"Nice try, except we both know the payment for this place

was included when I bought into the distillery." A bunch of good-natured bickering followed.

Kamilah hadn't known Liam had purchased his partnership with Killian. She'd thought that, much like herself, he'd simply become enmeshed in the company through his efforts. The idea sent gears cranking in her own head. Maybe that was what she had to do in order to be heard and appreciated: buy her way into the restaurant. Of course, she was broke as hell, but she did have some money saved. Maybe that would be enough to get her parents fully on board instead of grudgingly following Abuelo's dictate that they let Kamilah try.

Her phone's timer went off, breaking her out of her reverie. She went over to the oven and pulled out the tray of mallorcas, using the new oven mitt she'd been forced to buy. She wondered how Liam had got all those chicken tenders out of the oven without one, then decided quickly she'd probably rather not know. Her own brothers had taught her that men could be amazingly innovative when it came to being lazy.

"You made mallorcas?" Abuelo asked in what could only be described as hopeful awe.

"I did," Kamilah replied as she began using the sifter to sprinkle powdered sugar on the tops of the buns. "Too bad you went and bought that pastelito you're not even supposed to have."

Sitting across the breakfast bar from where she stood at the island, Abuelo licked the remnants of his coconut cream puff pastry off his fingers. "Eso no fue na'," he said with a smack of his lips. "Algo pequeñito para endulzarme la vida."

"Right," Kamilah said with an eye roll. "Just a little something, except it was the size of your head."

"Are you saying that I have a big head?" Abuelo's face was stern, but his eyes were sparkling.

Kamilah's mouth worked to hide her smile before she rejoined, "If the pastelito fits." She walked over to the cabinet and grabbed four small plates.

"Just for that," Abuelo said while Kamilah started plating the buns, "I'm not giving you any café con leche, and Doña Álamo made it, so you know it's good."

"One more mallorca for me, I guess." Kamilah took the bun on the end of the spatula and added it to her plate, so she had two, and Abuelo's plate had none. Then she served Liam and Killian one each.

"Here." Abuelo shoved the coffee at her with one hand and made a gimme motion with the other.

Kamilah gave in with a laugh.

The next few minutes were quiet while they all thoroughly enjoyed their breakfast. She was pretty sure she'd heard Liam moan a few times, which caused her to squirm a little in her seat. These new and decidedly carnal reactions she was having to Liam were as distracting as they were unwanted. She didn't have time to pant after Liam like a cat in heat, no matter how long it'd been since she'd been…stroked until she purred. She had just spent the whole morning thinking about how complicated her life had become and all the things she had to still accomplish. Adding an ill-advised sex romp with Liam would only make everything worse. What she needed to do, now that she wasn't living with her parents in an apartment with paper-thin walls, was buy herself a sturdy vibrator and get herself off a few times, so she could focus on her goals. That was the smart thing to do.

"Are you two ever going to tell us why you're here?" Liam asked.

Killian and Abuelo looked at each other, and Kamilah felt her stomach cramp. Oh no. Oh no, no, no. They had another term to add to the agreement. "What is it?" she asked a bit frantically. "What do you want now?"

Killian reached a hand over and patted hers. "It's nothing that bad, lass. No need to hyperventilate."

"It's not bad at all," Abuelo said. "We thought of a way to help you both."

"Help us both what?" Liam asked.

"I don't want to leave you on your own with the judges' visit right around the corner, but I don't know how I'll be feeling after I get this surgery." They'd decided a few days ago that Killian would undergo treatment.

Liam, Killian, and the doctors were hopeful about the procedure. The only downside was that, given Killian's age and the intensity of the process, it would probably take two months for him to recover.

"The only thing you need to think about is recovery," Liam told him. "We're pretty much ready for the visit, and with Da's whiskey, there is no way we can't win."

"But the tour," Killian said.

"Don't worry about the tour," Liam interjected. "I can do it. I'll take a bunch of happy pills, dance an Irish jig, and shoot rainbows out of my ass if I have to."

Kamilah pressed her lips together to stifle her laughter because she could tell Liam was serious.

Killian had no such compunction. He laughed, and Abuelo followed suit. "As much as I'd like to see that, I don't think it's necessary," Killian said. "All you need is a tutor."

"As of next week, you're going to have chemo releasing beads in your liver, Granda. You aren't going to have the energy to tutor me."

Killian looked at her, and Kamilah's shoulders tensed. She did not like the look in his eyes or the smile on his face. It reminded her too much of the time he'd talked her into planning a surprise graduation party for Liam—who'd visibly hated every second of it.

"That's where Mila comes in," Killian said. He stood from his seat and walked over to get himself another mallorca. "She is just about the most social and likable person we know. She can help you with the tour."

Kamilah shook her head. "See, that's exactly what I thought you were going to say, and that won't work because—"

"You want to rebrand El Coquí, right?" Abuelo asked. He motioned with his empty plate toward Killian. "Fix it, change the menu, make it successful again."

Killian put another sweet bun on his plate and walked back to his seat.

"Yes," she replied.

Killian placed the extra on Abuelo's plate.

Abuelo nodded his thanks but continued his conversation with Kamilah. "Liam can help you with that. Look at what he's done for Kane."

Kamilah couldn't respond to that observation, because it was true. Liam was absolutely the best thing that had ever happened to Kane Distillery. He had the vision, talent, and knowledge to make his grandfather's tiny distillery into a real contender in a national competition.

"You want us to help each other with our projects," Liam said.

"Yes," Killian said around a bite. "You each have the skills the other one needs right now, so why not?"

"But this is another rule, right?" Kamilah asked. "You aren't really asking us if we want to do it. You're telling us this is what you expect."

Abuelo scratched at his eyebrow. "If you want to call it that."

She looked at Liam, who simply waved a hand in a sort of *Well, what are ya gonna do?* manner. He wasn't wrong. There really was nothing they could do. They'd already agreed to the charade. She wore his grandmother's ring like they were really engaged; her entire family thought they were engaged; they were living together like an engaged couple. Hell, they were sleeping in the same bed like a real couple. Helping each other like real partners wasn't too much of a stretch.

"Fine," she said. "I'll help you prepare for the judges' visit, and you'll help me make sure my plans will work."

"Fine," he replied.

"Great," she said. "Then I hope you don't have tons to do today, because my plan was to check out the competition this afternoon."

And her ex just happened to be the owner of the competition.

"If you two are going out together, take some pictures and put them on PichónChat and Caragram or whatever they're called," Abuelo said. "That way people will think that you actually like spending time together."

That was the problem right there. She did like spending time with Liam. She liked it too much. He just never seemed to like it as much as she did.

11

Liam was supposed to be helping Kamilah scope out the competition and create a game plan for El Coquí. Instead, he watched her scribble in a notebook with a watercolor pineapple on the cover with the words *I'm like a pineapple: spiky on the outside but sweet on the inside. Oh and I wear a crown like a f**king QUEEN.*

"The ramen is okay," Kamilah muttered to herself. "The sushi holds all the appeal." She looked up and studied the restaurant. "Contemporary and artsy. However, it's small, and there isn't a ton of natural light. The mural is really the only focal point." She looked at him. "You know about art and stuff. Why do you think this decorated wall works, but the one at El Coquí doesn't?" She pointed to the ancient East Asian–style mural of samurai warriors in the middle of a battle.

Because this mural was done by someone with actual artistic abilities. To Kamilah he said, "This one is like a mix of traditional art, street art, and a badass tattoo. It's edgy and cool. Plus, the colors complement each other and the space."

She smiled wryly. "You mean it isn't a clash of neon colors that looks like it would be in some drug dealer's Miami mansion in the seventies?"

Liam couldn't help but laugh at the apt description.

Kamilah's smile grew.

El Coquí could be better. It was too busy, too much. If they let the beautiful walnut bar speak for the space, it would feel much better in there. Of course, that would mean getting rid of all the flags and frog art.

"The whole frog motif isn't exactly appetizing either," he told her. "Have you ever thought of changing the name?"

"No," Kamilah said. "I would never change the name. It's too special."

"Look, I know how Puerto Ricans feel about coquís, but—"

"It's not just that," she interrupted. "Abuela picked the name because she loved the story behind it, and so do I."

"I thought coquís got their name because of the sound of their chirp."

"Yes, but there is more to it than that." She pushed her notebook to the side and leaned forward as if she were about to share a secret with him. She looked exactly like Papo did when he was about to tell what he considered a good story: eager and animated. "According to legend, there was a beautiful goddess who was infatuated with Coquí, the son of a great Taíno chief. She would protect him. In return, he would worship her. One evening, she changed herself into a Taíno maiden so she could go to him. They fell in love." Her eyes went soft and dreamy at the mention of love. "They made plans to see each other the next night, but instead the evil

and jealous Juracán arrived." Her voice lowered and deepened. "The sky blackened, and his winds howled. The goddess tried to protect Coquí, but Juracán snatched him away."
Her hands made a snatching motion, then folded over her
heart as she said, "The goddess didn't know how she could
go on without her love, so she created this tiny frog that will
forever call for him, just like her heart."

Liam shook his head. Leave it to Kamilah to be so enam-
ored with such a story. "I don't know how to tell you this,
but that story is depressing as fuck."

"If you look at the mere facts, yes. But you have to look
beyond. She created the coquí to call for him, because she
hoped in her heart of hearts that she would find him and they
could reunite. It's why the frog means so much to us. It represents the never-flagging hope for something better and the
resilience to keep fighting for it even when all seems lost. If
we call out to each other, then we are never alone."

It was beautiful in theory, but the whole thing smacked
of desperation and continued false hope. He knew Kamilah,
the eternal optimist, would never see it that way, though, so
he just told her, "I guess the name stays." Then he finished
his rainbow roll.

At the next restaurant, which Kamilah had described as
reimagined Americana served in an industrial farmhouse, she
made her notes and muttered observations while Liam sat
sipping a Bloody Mary and watching pedestrians walk past
their patio table. "What did you think of the duck tacos?"
she asked without looking up.

"Uhh…" Liam waffled. He thought they were delicious,
but he wasn't sure he was supposed to say that. Something
told him his response to this question was more important
than any of the rest he'd given.

She'd been giving off a very weird energy since they'd walked into the place. A mix of nervousness, defiance, and a bunch of other conflicting emotions rolled off her, although she was doing her best to look casual. From above the table she looked thoughtful and engrossed in her task, but below it her leg was shaking and bouncing so much he fought the urge to ask her if she had to go to the bathroom.

"Do you want me to be honest?" Liam eventually asked.

At that, Kamilah's leg stopped moving and she looked up. A ray of fading sunshine blanketed her face. It lit up her eyes until they were no longer the light brown of caramelized sugar but pure gold. They glittered with quizzical amusement. The sunlight brought out all the reddish-brown and dark blond highlights in her dark hair, even while the wind continued to make a mess of her curls. Despite the silky leopard-print scarf she was wearing like a headband, one springy curl was blown right across the bridge of her nose and down to her grinning lips before getting stuck in her lip gloss.

Liam had never wanted to kiss someone so badly in his life. He found himself leaning forward until she broke through his haze.

"Why would I want you to lie?" she asked while pulling the curl free of her lip gloss and tucking it behind her ear.

Liam sat back in his chair. "I don't know. You've been giving off a real cat-in-the-bathtub vibe since we walked in here." He took a drink of his Bloody Mary. It was okay. A little too watered down for his tastes. Another sip.

Kamilah sighed. "This is Chase's restaurant."

He swallowed wrong, coughing and sputtering as the name took him by surprise.

"Chase...as in your ex?" Liam hated that guy. He was a pretentious poser.

She nodded.

"I thought he was in Hollywood being a douche."

"Apparently not," she responded. "Apparently, he's buying old Puerto Rican restaurants in the neighborhood and turning them into hipster hangouts." She gestured around them and then picked up the menu on the table. "And he's made a fucking menu using recipes he stole from me."

That sounded on-brand for the douche. "I take it the duck tacos were your creation." Liam's hands fisted.

"Don't you see?" Her leg started moving faster as she got more and more worked up. "Ese hipócrita comemierda is trying to rub it in my face." Her palm met the table with every syllable she said. She was gaining the attention of the people around them, but she didn't seem to notice. "Why else come back to Chicago, and Humboldt Park specifically? Why else use my recipes?"

Liam ignored the little twinge of pleasure he got out of hearing Kamilah call her ex a hypocritical shit-eater. Her entire family used the phrase to refer to his snobbery, but something about hearing her say it pleased him irrationally.

"This is why you entered El Coquí into the Foodie Tour and why you are hell-bent on rebranding it. You want to stick it to your ex."

"No," she blurted immediately. Guiltily. His eyes narrowed.

Another thought materialized. "And that's why you brought me along," he continued. "You needed your new fiancé here in case you ran into your old fiancé." Here he was gazing at her all afternoon, fantasizing about kissing her…and she was using him.

Kamilah scoffed, but she didn't meet his gaze. "Our relationship is fake."

Liam just barely contained his flinch. "Yeah, but he won't know that." Liam let out a bark of incredulous laughter as something else occurred to him. "Is that why you had me waiting around for two and a half hours while you washed and styled your hair, did your makeup, and picked out that flirty outfit?"

And to think of how his eyes had nearly fallen out of his head when she'd come down the stairs in tan high-heel thigh-high boots, a pair of painted-on dark blue jeans, and an over-size sweater that looked innocent enough. Until she turned around, displaying swaths of smooth, beautiful skin.

"What are you talking about? I'm wearing jeans and a baggy sweater." She grabbed on to one side of it with her left hand and held it out as if presenting it for his inspection.

The emerald green sweater matched the engagement ring glinting on the same hand. *Oh she's good.* She was really good, and he was a fucking eejit for having enjoyed the sight of her bare shoulders every time the neckline of the sweater had slipped. Worse than a fucking eejit. He was an insanely jealous fucking eejit, because he wanted her to put that effort in for him.

He didn't care if she wore makeup or not. He didn't even care that he was about ninety percent sure she wasn't wearing a bra. *How could she, with such a sweater?* It was the thought that she wanted to look her best for some other guy that made him want to gnash his teeth. Not just any guy, but the douche in chef's whites who was currently weaving through tables when he should've been in the kitchen.

"I know you're used to seeing me in my work clothes," Kamilah was saying in a biting tone. "But I do own articles of clothing that aren't covered in grease stains." She glared at him fiercely, completely oblivious to the fact that Chase had caught sight of them and was making a beeline toward their table. "And guess what? I actually like to wear them. For myself. Not to impress anyone. As if I would flaunt myself for my ex." Chase was almost upon them, and Kamilah was still ripping Liam a new one. A fact he knew would embarrass her if her ex overheard.

Liam did the one thing he could think of to salvage their pride. He muttered a quick "Quiet." Then he pushed their dishes to the side, leaned forward, wrapped a hand around the back of her neck, and dragged her mouth to his.

The instant their lips touched, some part deep inside himself sighed as if relieved of endless torment. *Finally*, it seemed to say. He kept his mouth soft and light, coaxing and subduing her. He kissed her from one corner of her lips to the other, stopping only briefly to sweep the tip of his tongue down the crease at the center of her plump bottom lip.

Meanwhile, his brain yelled at him to stop. Warning signs flashed in his mind. *Danger! This way lies certain death.* Liam had known for a long time how dangerous Kamilah was. Already a flickering light bulb ready to burn out, adding Kamilah's insanely high voltage was a recipe for disaster. All that would be left of him was a jagged husk of broken glass, and poor Kamilah would be sliced to ribbons by the damage.

Liam started to pull away, but she reached up and pulled him closer. He forgot everything else, savoring her in the same way she'd savored different foods all day long—slowly, methodically, missing nothing, and enjoying everything.

A voice cut into Liam's absorption. "I hear congratulations are in order."

They broke apart, but when Kamilah tried to shove back, Liam refused to let her. She shot him a wide-eyed look of panic, like a kid caught in the act of stealing a cookie before dinner, but Liam kept a hold of her and used his thumb to slowly wipe her smeared lip gloss from the bottom curve of her lip to the corner of her mouth. He didn't let her go or sit back in his own seat until it was clear she'd pulled herself together. Only then did he turn and give his attention to the man standing next to their table.

Liam hadn't seen Chase Hastings in years, but his blond good looks were the same. Liam remembered thinking upon meeting him that he was as pretty as a Ken doll and just as fake. There was nothing authentic about him. He brought to mind the Gean Cánach. Liam's grandmother had told him about a male faerie who used his powers to learn a woman's deepest desires, turn himself into her ideal mate, enchant her with a sweet-smelling mist and his touch, use her shamefully, and disappear, leaving her addicted to him. That was Chase in a nutshell. Liam had watched him act the sophisticated, devoted, and supportive white knight to Kamilah and then play the role of all-American, aw-shucks golden boy for the cameras on *American Chef Battle*. Now he was playing the role of mildly amused and pleasantly surprised ex.

Kamilah gave him a confused look. "How do you know about us?"

"Your brother was here on a date a few nights ago," Chase answered. "I don't think he realized it was my restaurant until I did my rounds." His eyes lowered to her left hand, and he stared at her ring, which was pretty damn impressive. "He made it a point to mention your engagement."

Had to be Leo, since the twins were married and Saint dated as much as Liam—never.

Kamilah put her right hand over her heart and mouthed *Love you, Leo* to the ether.

"I'm glad you stopped in to check my place out," Chase

said to Kamilah. "It's not the same as staring at it from your car, is it?"

Kamilah gave a fake laugh. "What can I say? I was surprised, shocked—dumbfounded, really. It's not every day you find out your ex, who was reportedly across the country, had opened a restaurant less than two miles from your own."

"I would've sent you an invite to the grand opening, but I didn't think you still lived here." That was an obvious lie.

No one who truly knew Kamilah could envision her anywhere else. Sure, her family drove her nuts, but she would never be happy being far from them.

"Plus," Chase continued, "I doubted you or your family would want to hear from me."

Oh look, a bit of truth from the consummate liar. Liam scoffed.

Chase pretended to finally notice him. "Oh hi… Lionel."

"It's *Liam*," he corrected instantly.

Kamilah reached over and grabbed his hand. "Don't worry, Liam," she told him. "He knows your name." Then she turned to look back at Chase, whose face looked calm enough, except for the twitch in his eye. Some wordless conversation passed between them that left Chase's eye twitching more violently and Kamilah sporting a pleased air.

Liam's own eyes narrowed. He didn't like not knowing exactly what was going on here. "It's time to go," he told Kamilah, camouflaging an unspoken message of his own. He was done with whatever game she was playing.

She looked at him and evidently understood his communication, because she nodded. "Right," she said. "We don't want to be late." She started gathering her things.

Yeah, it would be terrible being late to an imaginary event. Liam pulled out his wallet and threw a hundred-dollar bill on the table as he stood. He knew their bill wasn't that much, but he didn't want to wait around for it. Plus, their waitress seemed like a nice kid, and he felt for her. It had to suck to work for this guy.

Kamilah brushed past Chase, her hip and shoulder grazing the other man's front.

Like some Neanderthal, Liam almost growled. He had to get out of there. He grabbed on to Kamilah's hand and pulled her closer to him.

"Next time you'll have to tell me what you think of the place," Chase said to her in a smart-ass way that made Liam want to punch him in the nose.

Liam answered as if the invite were directed at him. "I think it's exactly the kind of place that would be owned by un hipócrita comemierda."

Kamilah gasped.

Liam ignored it and started tugging them to the exit of the fenced-in outdoor seating. "Congratulations on figuring out how to feed off someone else's ideas for the last five years," he threw over his shoulder.

At his side, Kamilah burst into scandalized laughter.

Liam felt his annoyance fade away. And then he remembered the manipulative woman at his side had set him up.

12

For the second time in less than a month, Kamilah found herself chasing a pissed-off Liam down a Chicago sidewalk. The crisp fall wind rustled the trees lining the street and blew the sides of Liam's jacket open, making him look like an English lord storming through the streets of London. She eyed the way his hands flexed at his sides and wondered if he was imagining them wrapped around her throat.

She'd fucked up big-time. She could admit it. She should've told him beforehand that Chase's restaurant was on their list. She should've asked if their agreement extended to exes and if he were willing to back her up in front of hers. They were partners, and she'd just made a decision for him. If the shoe were on the other foot, she'd be pissed. Not that ex-stalking was even a possibility with Liam.

As far as she knew, Liam hadn't had a girlfriend since college, and that had ended badly for him. Something about him finding out he was the other man in an international open relationship. Since then, if he did have a partner, he'd kept it under the radar. That hadn't stopped Kamilah from envisioning her more times than she could count, especially after Killian had brought it up.

She could just picture the type of woman who approached Liam at his buddy's bar. She'd be casual and low-key because Liam didn't do high-maintenance. The type of girl who was effortlessly gorgeous while wearing little makeup, jeans she didn't have to jump in to get them up her thighs/hips/ass, old Chucks, and a T-shirt with an ironic saying on it. She probably had silky straight hair she didn't have to wrestle every day, but she wore it covered with a beanie or one of those cool wide-brimmed hats. She most likely had more than one tattoo and/or facial piercing, because she didn't let fear of her parents' or society's censure stop her from expressing herself. Her name was like Willow or Hazel or something and she rocked choker necklaces and designer tortoiseshell sunglasses. In short, she was a calm, cool, and confident badass who wasn't looking to settle down anytime soon and was game for some no-strings bed sport.

Kamilah was hard-pressed to figure out why she already hated Willow Hazel.

Liam's voice cut into her irrational dislike of an imagined woman. "I don't like being used," he said. "Especially without my knowledge or consent."

"I'm sorry," she told him. "I won't do it again."

She would've been perfectly happy to leave it at that, with her acknowledging her wrong, but then he had to catch an attitude.

"See that you don't," he said in the same tone she'd heard her brothers use when scolding their kids.

Now, wait a damn minute. Kamilah stopped walking and

forced him to stop too. "For the record," she said with as much attitude as him, "I brought you with me today because I really do value your honest input and your insight. I decided to go to Chase's place because I had you there to back me up as a friend. I didn't bring you to make you play the role of lovestruck, possessive fiancé. You took that upon yourself." Just like he'd taken it upon himself to give her the hottest, sweetest, most equally frustrating and satisfying kiss of her life.

Liam gave her a *get serious* look and crossed his arms over his chest. "If you'd simply wanted backup, you would've asked Sofi or Lucy. But no, you brought me."

Kamilah mirrored his pose and braced her legs. "I didn't ask Sofi or Lucy because they're likely to dick-punch him on sight. I'm not exaggerating. Sofi has literally stated that she will punch him in the penis the next time she sees him, and I've seen her do it before, so I know she has zero qualms."

"Right," he said with what could only be described as a partial eye roll. "Then what was that whole 'Don't worry. He knows your name' thing all about? Because that was obviously about me personally."

Shit. She'd been hoping he wouldn't read into that. The truth was that Liam had come up a lot during her seven-year relationship with Chase. Every time they'd got home after a get-together where Liam was present, there would be an argument. Chase would accuse Kamilah of harboring romantic feelings for Liam. He'd tell her, "You're like a child poking and teasing the boy you like." At which point Kamilah would have to remind him of Liam's all-around apathy toward her. Then the argument would start all over again with Chase accusing her of flaunting herself to get Liam's attention. Never mind that every time Mia, her tall and trim, blond-haired, blue-eyed cousin, was around, Chase salivated like a starving man.

"Well?" Liam asked, bringing her attention back to his question.

"Chase was always needlessly jealous of you," she told him.

In response to that, an eyebrow rose. *"Needlessly?"*

Kamilah realized how that sounded. "Not *needlessly* like he's better than you in any way. He's human trash, and you're obviously not," she clarified.

The eyebrow crept higher.

"I meant *needlessly* in that Chase created false narratives in his head. Like, he would say that I tried too hard around you or that you would stare at me when I wasn't looking. He always wanted to make it seem like there were secret feelings between us." Kamilah left out that she was starting to believe Chase might have been right. Two people who felt nothing for each other didn't kiss like that. "He was just using you, the only male nonrelative he ever saw me around, as a scapegoat to justify why he flirted with Mia all the time."

"Mia…your cousin Mia?"

"Yeah, you know, the Victoria's Secret model with a medical degree?" Kamilah tried to keep the cattiness out of her tone because she did love her cousin. The truth was they had never been close, not like Kamilah was with Lucy or her other female cousins. There had always been this sense of competition between her and Mia. A competition Kamilah perpetually lost. Mia was a beautiful and brilliant surgeon, worthy of being on one of those doctor TV shows, while Kamilah had frizzy hair, a culinary degree she wasn't using, and a minimum-wage job with her parents.

Once again proving that he could read her mind, Liam said,

"She's pretty, I guess, but she's about as interesting as those medical textbooks she was always studying."

Kamilah pursed her lips to keep from smiling. "Hey, that's my cousin you're talking about."

A small smile appeared in the corner of his lips, and he shrugged. "I'm just saying she'd never have the balls to take part in a Shakespearean farce directed by two troublesome octogenarians in order to make her dreams come true."

A strong and heady warmth wove its way from her heart through the rest of her body. She loved that he saw her as interesting and ballsy and not imprudent or immature. Her smile emerged full force. "I really am sorry for putting you in that position," she told him earnestly. "I promise to be honest and up-front with you about any and all tomfoolery from now on. Trust me."

Liam nodded his thanks and then took a look around them as if only just realizing that they were still standing on the sidewalk a few blocks from Swig. "So where to now?" he asked. "I have to tell you that I'm reaching the disgustingly full threshold."

She felt the same. "I think I'm done checking out places for now." Plus, she'd already taken enough notes to get the idea. Her plan for El Coquí was starting to take shape. She'd simplify the environment and amplify the food. There were already fragments of recipes running through her head. Shrimp, pork, Thai red chili peppers, pineapple, mango, yuca, plantains, lime.

Ways to let people know that El Coquí could play in the big leagues. When it came to the decor, she would go to the specialists, her cousins Gabi and Alex. They worked for their father's contracting company, and Kamilah knew they would help her come up with something beautiful. But simple, and most importantly, cost-effective.

"I was thinking," she told Liam, "maybe we should go on a distillery tour, so you can do the same thing. You know, scope out the competition, see how they run things and how they give their tours. Maybe seeing someone else do it will give you some ideas."

Liam shook his head. "I've been to almost all the distilleries in the area and most of the breweries. I know what a good tour looks like. I watch Granda do it almost every day. My issue is I can't do it because I don't like wasting my time and people are the worst."

Kamilah laughed. That was such a Liam thing to say. Only he would find engaging with his customers an annoying waste of time. "I swear, the things you and Killian say. Someone should write them down and put them on T-shirts." She paused. Her mouth opened in delighted surprise as an idea popped into her head. "You need to make T-shirts and sweatshirts to sell at the distillery. Shirts with the Kane logo, and images from your labels, and quotes from you and Killian. People would snatch them up. They love buying T-shirts from the places they go."

Liam had crossed one arm over his chest and rested the elbow of the other on it. He ran the backs of his fingers along his jaw while he stared into the distance with a slight frown.

Kamilah itched to run her own fingers along his jaw. She'd always loved scruff, and Liam's was top-notch. When they'd kissed earlier, it had scratched lightly at her palms and softly abraded her lips. They still felt warm and tight, as if they were swollen. She raised a hand to feel. That got her thinking about what Liam's stubble would do to the delicate skin between her legs. An image flashed in her mind of a dark head of hair and intense blue eyes framed between a pair of thighs. Her muscles clenched reflexively.

"It's a good idea," Liam said.

It's a very good idea. Kamilah fought the urge to moan.

"My only worry is that people would buy the shirts instead of the whiskey," he continued.

That brought her up short. "Huh?"

He gave her a *WTF is up with you?* look. "I said that I wouldn't want people to buy the shirts instead of buying the whiskey."

Having been violently pulled out of her dirty fantasy, Kamilah was slow to respond. "Uhh." She cleared her throat. "I would think that they'd buy both. They wouldn't buy the shirt if they didn't like the whiskey. If they like the whiskey, they're going to buy it. If they don't like the whiskey, they wouldn't buy it anyway. But there may be a few who don't like the whiskey, but do like the shirts—in which case, you'd get a sale that you wouldn't have otherwise gotten." She paused. "Did that make sense?" It was a legitimate question because her lust-fogged brain wasn't exactly firing on all cylinders.

Liam was trying to hide his amused smile behind his hand, but she could see it in the way his eyes crinkled.

"What?" she asked. "What's so funny?"

He shook his head and dropped his hand. "Nothing," he said, his smile still present in the corners of his mouth.

She gave him a speaking glance.

"It's just interesting to hear you think aloud. Your brain works exactly how I thought it would."

She couldn't be sure, but she didn't think that was a compliment. "Yeah, it's like dropping a box full of bouncy balls off a balcony."

He laughed out loud for the second time that day, an honest-to-God laugh. Genuine Liam smiles—with teeth and dimples—were rare enough, but a bona fide laugh? That was like spotting a rainbow with an actual leprechaun making it rain wealth by spinning on its head break-dance-style as gold coins shot out of its butt. "It's not that bad," he said once his laughter had subsided. "It's just energetic and a bit topsy-turvy. It's like in cartoons when they pop a cork and it goes ricocheting around the room until someone finally catches it."

She wasn't sure that was much better. "Those corks always do a lot of damage before they're stopped." That was her biggest fear. That her ideas or her efforts would ruin everything instead of help. She wanted to lighten burdens, not add to them. Change wasn't comfortable. It required getting in there and getting dirty.

But how much change was too much?

What if what she considered change was actually the destruction of everything her family wanted or believed in? What if she was just selling out and adding to the problems of her longtime neighbors? God, she wished there was some way to know for sure that she was on the right track. To know that this would all work out.

She was so lost in her own thoughts she barely noticed Liam studying her. She jumped when he said, "If you're done checking out restaurants, I have an idea about what to do next. I can give you a tour of Kane, and you can tell me what I need to fix."

Kamilah's eyebrows went up. She thought he'd be in a rush to get away from her.

Liam shifted his weight from one foot to another. Breaking eye contact, he pulled his phone out of his pocket and looked at the screen. "I mean, you have a few hours before you have to go to work, right?" He shoved his phone back in his jacket pocket and shifted his feet again. "Plus, we didn't take any pictures together like we were told," he rushed out.

"Yeah, no, I'm game," she said quickly in an attempt to soothe his nervousness. "I'm cool. I'm ready. I'm down to clown." She paused, realizing that she'd basically just expressed her willingness to fool around. She closed her eyes and scrunched her face. "That last one," she began, only to be cut off.

"I know," Liam said. "Let's just go." He placed a hand on the small of her back and gave her a little push forward.

13

As soon as they arrived back at the distillery, Granda had taken off, supposedly to run some errands. Liam was more than a little suspicious, but he didn't dwell on it for long, since Kamilah was waiting for him to give her a tour.

Right. A tour. It's nothing you haven't done tons of times. And yet, as he stood before her, he could only focus on the number of times he'd looked out into the crowd and seen glazed-over expressions.

"I need to write stuff down or something. Like a script." He glanced around as if a script would magically appear.

Kamilah appeared to bite back a smile. "You don't need a script, Liam. You know more about making whiskey than anyone I've ever met, including Killian."

That was the problem. He knew too much, so he shared too much, and people got bored and annoyed. "I bore people with what I know," he said.

At least she didn't laugh at him.

Kamilah gave his concern some thought. Eventually she said, "Think of it like a cooking show." She made her way over to the storage area where they kept their barley. "You start with the ingredients. Pull out some as visuals." She started walking along with her hand out in a Vanna White fashion, gesturing to the machines. "Then work your way through the process step-by-step until you have the finished product." She stopped at the tasting table. "Sprinkle in some history, fun facts, maybe a joke or two, finish the whole thing off with a tasting, and boom! You have a successful tour."

Liam crossed his arms over his chest. "They don't want to hear the step-by-step process. Trust me. They want to listen to me for about three minutes while I point at stuff and then drink."

Kamilah shook her head. "I refuse to believe that." She ran a finger along the surface of the table as she moved closer to him. "Brewery and distillery tours would not be so popular if all people wanted to do was drink. They can drink at a bar or in their homes. They go on tours for the same reasons they eat at restaurants. They want a handcrafted experience given to them by someone they consider an expert in that field. You're the expert. If you can give them that experience, they'll come, they'll come back, and they'll bring their friends."

Once again Liam was left staring at Kamilah in awe. She was so animated in almost everything she did that it was easy to mistake her passion for chaos and confusion. But she knew what she was doing and what she was talking about. Her brain simply worked faster than she could communicate calmly. The problem wasn't with her abilities but with people constantly trying to block or subdue her. Liam had seen it himself when he'd overheard her family arguing with her about entering El Coquí into the tour.

If he were honest, he'd been guilty of underestimating her too. But no more. Between listening to her think aloud as she broke down the pros and cons of neighborhood restaurants and the way she kept throwing out insightful ideas about his own business, Liam had come to realize that he could learn a few things from her.

"All right," he told her. "Teach me your ways."

Kamilah started walking toward the smaller entrance next to the garage doors. "Welcome them to Kane Distillery from the spot I'm standing in." She stopped in a spot diagonal to the door and motioned for him to stand in the spot in front of her. "Standing here shows off all of the coolest parts of the distillery without even having to say anything."

He saw instantly what she meant. His back was to the storage room, but the rest of the distillery—with its large painted logo, gleaming machinery, and arched, paneled windows—was creating a stimulating backdrop behind a smiling Kamilah, the most stimulating view in the whole place. His fingers twitched and flexed with the desire to sketch her exactly how and where she was at that moment.

"Have you ever thought of maybe putting another mural on that wall?" Kamilah pointed next to the storage room, where the wall that separated Kane and El Coquí started and ran the length of the distillery all the way to the door of the barrel room. Their big pot still was there along with the lauter tun, so he'd never thought to put anything on the wall.

"What do you have in mind?" he asked.

"I don't know," she said. "I was just thinking that when I was in school, I learned best when I had a visual. I loved when the teacher had a diagram or a chart I could refer to as she explained. It gave me something to fall back on if I got lost or didn't get what she was saying."

"So you want me to paint a diagram showing the steps of the distilling process on that wall."

She gave a one-shoulder shrug. "It's just an idea."

It was a good idea. They would be closed next week while Granda underwent his procedure and began the recovery process. In theory Liam could do it then.

Kamilah clapped her hands, and the sound echoed throughout the space. "Okay," she said with enthusiasm. "Let's switch spots and get started."

Liam led Kamilah to some large machines and stopped. "Kane Whiskey, like its truly Irish cousins, is made of three main ingredients: barley, water, and yeast," he said while ticking them off on his fingers. "This is different from many other American-made whiskeys, aka bourbon, which use corn in their mash."

"So even though you distill in America, your product isn't considered bourbon because you don't use corn?" Kamilah asked.

"Don't just interrupt," he grumbled. "You'll make me lose my train of thought."

"You'd better get used to it. People are always going to interrupt with questions, comments, smart-ass jokes, and demands to know when the tasting is. You can't let it throw you off your game, even if they're being rude and disruptive. Feel them out."

"Yeah," Liam drawled. "I'm not very good at reading people I don't know."

Kamilah tapped her fingers on her lips as she thought. "Pretend my brothers are here," she told him. "Eddie would ask a lot of questions because he's truly interested, so you'd be right to give him more information. Cristian, on the other hand, would ask questions in order to try to draw you into some sort of debate or make you trip up. In which case, your best bet is to answer his questions or respond to his comments quickly and succinctly without giving him an opening to start a dialogue. Which you already do with him, so you can take that and apply it to tour-goers."

Liam was starting to see where she was going. "Someone like Leo would make smart-ass comments because they want attention."

She nodded but added, "Or because they're bored. Leo always used to get in trouble for being a fidgety smart-ass."

"Used to?" Liam asked. Leo was still getting in trouble for it.

Kamilah smirked. "True, true. But the point is, once we realized he has ADHD, we understood that he usually seeks attention or acts like a smart-ass when he's bored, when he's confused, or when he wants to deflect."

"So if someone starts to make wisecracks, assume they are bored or don't get it?"

"Right. What should you do in that case?"

Usually he got annoyed and probably condescending, but he could see why that wasn't the right trail to go down. "Uh, maybe explain things better?"

"That's an option, but what does that even mean? How will you know? There's a lot of gray area there. I'd suggest that if you can tell someone or more than one person is getting bored, crack a joke or tell a funny anecdote and then just move on."

"But what if I'm not done explaining?"

"Then paraphrase the shit out of it and move on. Remember, you're giving them an experience. You're not giving them all the information they need to go home and start distilling whiskey out of their basements."

Liam nodded. He'd been looking at this whole thing the wrong way. He never thought to look at this as an entertainment-type experience; he'd looked at it like a teaching opportunity. Then he kept getting mad when people didn't want to listen to all the knowledge he was dropping on them.

No wonder customers always enjoyed Granda's tours. He didn't bog them down with information. He broke up chunks of information with stories. He created an experience for them. But Liam didn't want to talk about his dad the way Granda did. He wasn't capable of doing so nonchalantly, nor was he a charming jokester like Granda. "I don't think I can be funny like Granda or whatever."

Kamilah reached forward and grabbed his hand with both of hers. She pulled it up and held it to her chest. She usually did that whenever she thought he needed comfort. "You don't have to be Killian." She looked into his eyes. "You don't have to be your dad either."

Liam scowled and looked away.

She shook the hand she held and tilted her head until she was looking into his eyes. "You are Liam Alexander Kane, and you are your own man. A man who is incredibly smart, talented, creative, and more than capable. Own it. And run this shit like the badass you are."

Liam experienced something unlike anything he'd ever felt before. It wasn't a sexual desire. It wasn't *solely* sexual desire. It was the need to just be close to her. A need he couldn't resist. He stepped in close so their hands were sandwiched in between their chests. Then he bent his head until their foreheads touched. He saw her eyes widen and her mouth open in surprise, but he didn't answer. He closed his eyes and just luxuriated in being with her.

After a moment, Kamilah wrapped her arms around him and squeezed tight like she did when they were sleeping. Only this time Liam reciprocated and wrapped his arms around her. "Thank you," he said before dropping a kiss on her forehead. He left his lips there and just breathed in her coconut-and-sunshine smell.

Kamilah had always been the only person who never tried to change him. She'd seen him and accepted him exactly as he was. When they were little, she would defend him to anyone who dared criticize him, like a warrior princess. After the accident, she never tried to make him feel bad for his pain, anger, or depression. He was the one who hadn't been able to handle the idea of continually disappointing her like he did everyone else, so he'd pushed her away. Even after that she didn't try to change him. She let him be.

He didn't know how long they stood there, but eventually Liam became aware of the fact that she'd melted into him. Their bodies were touching all along the front while she rested her head on his shoulder, and he absentmindedly painted invisible swirls on her back where her sweater left her skin bare.

"I really missed you." Kamilah nuzzled into his neck. "I didn't realize how much until now."

At her whispered confession, Liam tightened his arms. He'd always been aware of how much he missed her. Like missing your own bed after traveling or fresh water while marooned on a desert island made up of nothing but rocks and sand.

"I've missed you too," he said, thinking of all the times she tried to reach out to him and he'd rebuffed her.

She reached up and pulled his head down, so she could give

him a forehead kiss of her own. She looked into his eyes for a few seconds and then let loose a blinding and charmingly crooked smile. "I knew my Liam was still in there. It's nice to see you, old friend."

My Liam. Holy shit, did he like the sound of that! As if he were something special she'd been waiting to see. He wanted to kiss her again. He wanted to do more than kiss her.

But she'd also said "old friend."

They were starting to rebuild their friendship. She'd just forgiven him. He didn't want to ruin all that like he had on her prom night, by rushing something that didn't need to happen. Her friendship was going to have to be enough. With a rueful smile and one last caress of her cheek, Liam stepped back and cleared his throat. "All right, back to the tour."

For the next hour he led her around the distillery, lecturing about the distillation process. She would interrupt with questions or give him suggestions after he finished his explanations. With her, the whole thing seemed so much easier and, dare he say, fun. He didn't struggle through trying to determine how much he should share or which words he should use. Hell, he even managed to make a joke or two.

"Is it time for the tasting now?"

Any other time that question would've pissed him off, but at the moment he was feeling himself too much to be bothered. "Yes," he replied without his normal derision. "It's time for the tasting."

"Yay!" Kamilah threw her arms up like a fan at a sporting event. "Let's go."

Liam shook his head with a smile and quickly set up three glasses for tasting and another glass of water. He picked up the first bottle. "First up we have our Kane traditional small-batch-blend whiskey. This is what I make the most of."

Kamilah laughed. "Why does this drunk leprechaun look like your grandpa?"

"That's a Clúricháun. They're kind of like leprechauns, except they love to drink and play mean pranks."

"Sounds just like Killian."

Liam couldn't help but chuckle. It was like Granda, which was why Liam picked it for the name. "This whiskey is Granda's specialty. He's been making it for sixty-five years. Since he brought the recipe with him from Ireland, this is the closest to a traditional Irish whiskey."

"Yum." Kamilah made a grab for the glass, but he pulled it away.

"Wait a second. I have to explain how to taste it the right way."

"Liam, I don't need your help with this. I was raised in a bar." Kamilah snatched it out of his hand, tossed her head back, and poured the whiskey sample down her throat. She grimaced.

"Well, step one is to not shoot it like a sorority girl, so you did that wrong."

"Fine, tell me what to do first."

Liam poured more whiskey in her glass. "The first thing you want to do is look at it. Is the color light or dark? Is it clear, hazy, or cloudy? Are there sediments in it? If you slowly swish it around the glass, does it cling to the sides?"

"It's sort of like wine tasting," Kamilah commented, following his instructions to the letter.

Where else would she follow his directions?

He swallowed the thought. "Yes, we experience most things with our eyes first, so the look of it is very important. Tell me what you notice."

"It looks similar to most whiskeys I've seen. Amber in

color, clear, with no sediments. It clings slightly to the glass, but not much."

"Good. Now you smell it."

She lifted the glass.

"No, don't just shove your nose in there like a blood-hound."

Kamilah growled. "Well, how else do you smell something besides with your nose?"

"You want to keep your mouth slightly open, so you aren't getting a straight-alcohol scent. Then you pass the glass under your nose from nostril to nostril." He usually had newbies smell it that way. Once they were experienced, they could do a more close-up smell, but at first it was best to waft as Kamilah was doing. "Good. While you inhale, think about whether or not the smell is delicate or intense. Think about what kind of grain you smell more of. Try to detect the smo-kiness, the spice, and the sweet notes. Being a chef, you have tons of experience with food-based aromas, so you should be able to pick up those notes fairly easily."

"It's a bit of an intense wood smell at first. I couldn't tell you which type of wood, since I'm not familiar with them, but I'm going to guess oak, based on the tour."

She glanced up at him with her nose still in the glass, and Liam's heart paused before it started pounding. She was so damn beautiful. One day those eyes of hers would kill him.

He cleared his throat and nodded.

"Under the wood scent, I get a definite aroma of vanilla. There's another sweetness too. It reminds me of sugarcane. There's spice there, but it's hard to tell exactly what it is."

"Once you taste it, you'll be able to identify it better."

"Yes." Kamilah nodded eagerly. "Tasting. Let's do that."

Yes. Let's taste.

He ran his knuckles along his jaw to hide the tug he gave his ear. *Focus, dammit.*

"The important thing to remember here is after you swallow, breathe out through your mouth right away to expel any alcohol fumes. Then you can mull over the flavors left behind. Got it?"

She held up a thumb. "I got it."

"I suggest you just drink it on the first sip. The first sip really is to activate the smells that enter the nasal cavity through the back of the throat instead of your nose. On the second and subsequent sips you can let them really coat your mouth. I'd also suggest another smell between sips. Each time you should be able to pick up more flavors and more aromas."

"Sounds good."

"Ready?"

"I'm ready."

"Go for it."

Kamilah tasted the blend and described it in perfect detail. Then she told him to record her while she did the same for the single malt, and the potín (which was basically moonshine). As he listened to her describe the rich fruit and cereal with a hint of spice of the potín, he decided the usual whiskeys weren't enough. There was one more she had to try. He wanted…he needed to see the way her lips wrapped around the glass, the way the delicate column of her throat bobbed as she swallowed. The way her eyes half closed in pleasure. He went to his office and grabbed an unmarked bottle from his personal stash.

"This last one is my favorite," he said upon his return.

"Is that your dad's?"

He shook his head. "No, we haven't bottled it yet. I'm still working on the label."

"So who made this one?" She gestured to the bottle in his hand.

"I did." He held it up. "This is the first whiskey I created on my own. Almost twelve years ago."

"Where's the label?"

"It doesn't have one. I don't sell this one."

"Why not?"

"I can't think of a name for it." That wasn't exactly true. The whiskey definitely had a name. It wasn't a name he wanted to share with the world or with anyone, really. Liam poured a small bit into her glass. "Here, try this and tell me what you smell and taste."

Kamilah stared at him for a moment. "Why do I suddenly feel like a kid handed a pop quiz on the first day of class?"

"It's not serious," he lied. "You've just done a good job so far, and I want to see if you can get this one."

"I want to watch you do it," she said. She picked up her phone and pointed it at him like she was recording. "Go ahead. Show me how it's really done."

"I don't know why you want to record me," he grumbled, but he picked up the bottle. "This specific blend is pretty sweet compared to most whiskeys I've made or even tried." He poured his own little bit into a glass for himself. Then he picked it up and nosed it. "It's soft and light on the nose—pleasant and understated notes of honey, coconut, and cinnamon. However, the taste is full and layered." Liam took a small drink, closed his eyes. He did it every time. He couldn't help it. "There are the sweet notes of vanilla, caramel, and butterscotch. This delicate interweaving of pink-peppercorn spice throughout adds to the warmth and almost emphasizes the sweetness." He took another smell and sip. "Then there's the slightest hint of black-coffee darkness to it that adds just enough antithesis to keep things interesting." He finished his glass and set it on the table. "It has a long, lingering finish that just rests on the tongue, tempting you to take another taste. One sip is never enough." To prove his point, he licked his lips. He always wanted more. "A man could happily get lost in the taste, if he's not careful."

When he was done, he opened his eyes and found Kamilah staring at him with a rosy hue to her cheeks. Her breathing seemed a little fast. She licked her own lips as if she'd just tasted what he had. She'd unconsciously lowered her phone, so he wondered how much of his description she'd actually got on video.

He hoped it wasn't much, because for some reason his own cheeks felt warm.

"I'm sorry," she said, trying to shake it off. "I have no idea why it affected me like this." She gave an awkward little laugh. "Your description was just... I don't know." She rolled her eyes at herself. "Too many samples, I guess."

Liam remained silent.

"Um, yeah. I should really get going. I have to get to work, but..." Kamilah paused as if contemplating whether she should say what she was thinking. She must've decided to just do it because she looked at him earnestly and said, "Can I just say something without you getting all cold and dismissive?"

Liam had a feeling he knew where this was going, but he nodded anyway.

"This, everything you've accomplished here," she said as she gestured all around them, "is amazing, Liam. You've taken everything you were taught and expanded it into something phenomenal."

Liam looked away. He cleared his throat. "It wasn't just me," he said in reference to Granda, his partner.

"I love Killian, you know I do, but this distillery would not exist if it weren't for you. He's the visionary, but you're the mastermind. Never forget that." Then after a quick kiss on the cheek, she was gone, and he was left to sit and wonder: Could he truly be enough?

14

It all started with bread pudding. Her intention had only been to have the treat Killian had requested ready for him to eat when he got released from his outpatient procedure. She'd decided to make Irish soda bread for the pudding instead of using an egg bread like brioche. Then she'd figured, *Why not go super Irish with it?* and used his favorite whiskey to make the sauce. After trying the whiskey sauce, she'd thought it would be delicious on flan de coco. She'd decided to make a coconut flan with the whiskey sauce to test her theory. Things had progressed quickly after that.

"Ooo, girl," Sofi said after letting herself in through the open front door. "This is bad."

Lucy, who'd come in behind her, let out a whistle.

"Oh good. You're here." Kamilah looked up briefly from the pan where she was frying up yuca, green plantain, and sweet yellow plantain for her trifongo. "I invited everyone over to eat, but now I'm falling behind. I need you guys to help me."

"Everyone who?" Lucy asked. She was still dressed for her nonprofit work at the community center in black slacks, a white T-shirt with the center's colorful logo under a black blazer, and black flats. It was about as dressed up as she ever got. Her wavy hair was down and brushing her shoulders.

"My parents, my brothers and their families, and your parents and brother. I invited Tío Luís and the girls because they've been helping me finalize a plan for the remodel." Kamilah turned the pieces of yuca to cook the other side. "I'm sure one of our dads mentioned it to Titi Iris, and you know she's always with Monica and her girls."

"So basically it's about to be a mini family reunion," Lucy said.

"Ya tu sabes," Kamilah responded.

Sofi came closer to the kitchen island and started looking around at the plethora of dishes. She must've gone home to change before picking up Lucy, because she was in jeans and a sweater. "And you did this why?" Sofi picked up a small piece of chicharrón and popped it in her mouth.

"I didn't plan this, if that's what you mean," Kamilah said. "I've been up since five, thinking about Killian and worrying." She'd got up early with the intention of going with them to the hospital, but Killian had made it very clear that he didn't want anyone to go with him besides Liam. In fact, poor Abuelo was over at El Coquí moping around, because Killian hadn't even wanted him there. Kamilah had to occupy her time, because she knew she was calling Liam for updates entirely too often. "You know how I get."

Whenever Kamilah was in a state of high emotion, she cooked. Cooking was her outlet, and big emotions meant that outlet needed to be able to handle higher voltage. Therefore, in times of need, the more complicated the recipe and intricate the techniques, the better. Which pretty much explained why, ten hours after she'd decided to make the flan, Liam's poor kitchen looked like a catering tent at a huge event.

"Are there any updates?" Lucy asked as she scooped a tiny bit of arroz con gandules into her hand, blew on it, and ate it.

"Liam texted me an hour or so ago. Killian's out of surgery, and it went well. However, he's having some not-great side effects from the anesthesia, so they're holding him a little longer for observation. Liam hasn't seen him yet." Kamilah had heard the disquiet in Liam's voice, which had caused her own concern to amplify. She'd asked him if he wanted her to go over there and sit with him, but he'd turned down her offer. So Kamilah had called Sofi and Lucy to tell them to come and eat. Then she'd started calling everyone else.

Sofi walked up to Kamilah and rested her chin on Kamilah's shoulder. "Anesthesia affects older people differently, and yes, sometimes it can be more dangerous, but usually it's that they just take a little longer to bounce back."

Since Sofi had planned on studying nursing before changing majors, Kamilah believed her. "He'll be home soon," Kamilah said as much to herself as to them.

"For sure," Lucy agreed. "And when he gets here, he'll have some bomb-ass food waiting for him."

If I ever finish it. Kamilah removed the pieces of yuca and plátano from the oil. "Leo's on the roof turning the spit. I need someone to go see if the lechón is done."

"Not it," Sofi said around a piece of grilled pineapple.

"Ugh. I hate the roof," Lucy whined. She looked at Kamilah. "Do you remember when we were playing tag up there for some unknown reason and Cristian pushed me so hard I almost went over the ledge? If Saint hadn't grabbed me, I would be dead. I've hated heights since then. I don't even go on our patio."

Kamilah threw some garlic, olive oil, and salt in her pilón and refrained from telling her cousin that the ledge itself was four feet high, so there was no way her child self would've gone over it. Even so, she'd been at least eight feet from the edge, and Saint had only caught her because she'd slammed right into him. Plus, Lucy's fear of heights stemmed from when she was a toddler and, anytime she was more than three inches off the ground, her overprotective mom screeched that she was going to fall and break her neck.

"Well…" Sofi popped another piece of pineapple in her mouth. "I hate Leo, so if I go up there, I'll probably end up pushing *him* over the side."

"That's okay, Sof. You can devein those jumbo shrimp for me." Kamilah nodded in the direction of a large bowl full of raw shrimp as she began smashing the garlic with the pestle.

Sofi followed the direction of Kamilah's nod and visibly gagged. She hated touching raw meat of any kind. Now they just had to wait for her to decide what she hated more: Leo or raw shrimp. "I'll go get the damn lechón, but I'm warning you now that Leo may end up the next pig that gets roasted." She stomped out of the condo.

Lucy smiled her thanks and then got to work on the shrimp while Kamilah went about adding the pork cracklings to the mortar and giving them a few good grinds to break them up a little bit. Once that was done, she'd add the plantains and cassava and mash it all together.

Their companionable silence only lasted for about a minute. As soon as they heard the familiar clarinet riff from one of their favorite Calle 13 songs, they squealed and started shimmying their shoulders at each other like that GIF of Shaq and the kitten. It wasn't long before they were rapping and dancing around the kitchen, Kamilah's anxiety successfully pushed to the background.

By the time Sofi walked back in carrying a baking pan full of roasted pork, Kamilah and Lucy had pretty much stopped cooking and were just booty-bumping along to Ivy Queen. "Aye!" Sofi cheered when she heard what song it was. Then she dropped it like it was hot while never losing grip on the pan like the badass she was.

Leo, who'd walked in behind her holding his own pan of lechón, watched Sofi back it up for a second before scoffing. "Of course you love this tease anthem."

They all froze as if the record had just scratched to a halt.

Kamilah's jaw dropped. "What? How dare you? Ivy Queen is, you know—" she paused "—well, a queen, and 'Quiero Bailar' is iconic."

Leo puffed out his chest and walked around Sofi. "The song is all about women getting men all worked up and then leaving them with blue balls."

"That's some misogynist bullshit," Sofi interjected, hot on his heels. "This song is about a woman's sexual agency. She's not playing a game." Sofi dropped the pan on the counter none too gently. "She's straight up saying, 'I can be in the club, acting how I want, dancing how I want, and we can even grind, but don't think it means I have to have sex with you.'" She advanced on him, but he stood his ground. "'I make the choice of how far I'm going to go, and I owe you nothing.'" Both hands came up, and the palms were pressed together as if she were praying for this poor idiot man. "And, Leo, the fact you even still think it's about a woman being a tease or playing some game is proof enough it's still relevant, and it's a muthafucking feminist anthem."

"Yas, Queen," Lucy cheered.

"Drag him," Kamilah said.

Leo's scowl deepened. "Whatever." He looked around Liam's kitchen and then looked back at Kamilah. "What is this?" he asked. "A tasting of the new bougie menu you're going to make us serve?"

She wasn't exactly sure at what point the idea occurred to her that she could kill two birds with one stone, but the answer to Leo's question was yes, it was a tasting of things she was thinking of putting on the menu. She'd been feeling inspired ever since Liam had given her the tour of the distillery and the whiskey tasting. That may have explained why every dish she'd made had whiskey in it somehow: from the Thai chili lime shrimp she was serving with the trifongo to the grilled pineapple slaw she was putting on top of her lechón sandwiches. Of course, there was also the flan de coco with the whiskey sauce.

She wasn't going to explain any of that to Leo, though, so instead she said, "I just felt the need to be with my family and cook for them." That wasn't untrue. Killian going in for surgery had made her want to hold her loved ones closer. Before Leo could make a smart-ass comment, people began arriving, and Kamilah was forced to focus on getting everyone fed.

In the end, it wasn't a huge family reunion. Eddie and Cristian showed up by themselves, as their families were busy with extracurriculars. Lucy's parents had come but not her brother, and neither Tío Luís nor Titi Iris and her crew had shown. Which left a group of sixteen, but their family had forty-six people in it. That wasn't even half. Still, it was enough, which was probably why Liam's eyes bugged out of his head when he walked in pushing Killian in a folding medical-transport chair.

"A party for me?" Killian exclaimed with a mix of sarcasm and genuine happiness. "I wasn't even gone for a day."

"Of course," Mami said with a smile. "You know we have to celebrate every day you are on this earth."

Killian held out his hands to Mami, and she walked up to give him a hug.

Soon everyone followed: the men giving him a handshake and a pat on the back, the women giving him hugs and kisses.

Liam made his way over to Kamilah looking drawn. *Oh shit*. She should've asked him first if it was okay.

"I'm sorry," she said when he was close enough to hear her. "You were probably looking forward to coming home to have some peace, and here I invited all these people into your house."

Liam looked around. "I expected more people, to be honest. I've been around your family long enough to know that you guys assemble anytime something happens. Like the Avengers."

"You're not mad?" Kamilah was surprised. Liam was the type of person who liked their space and required a lot of it.

He shook his head. "How can I be? Granda is eating this up like an ice cream sundae with extra whipped cream."

"Oh speaking of eating, let me make you a plate." Kamilah jumped to start putting together his meal.

Liam put a hand on her shoulder. "You don't have to serve me. I can get my own."

She really tried not to, but she ended up scowling at him anyway. "Liam, you've been at the hospital by yourself all day while your grandpa was getting cut open and pumped full of drugs." And it had just about killed her to not be there with him. "Just let me do something for you."

"You can do this." He used the hold he had on her shoulder to pull her to his chest. He enveloped her in his arms and just held on. Ever since their day in the distillery, Liam had become much more relaxed and even affectionate with her. He no longer froze when she touched him, and he would touch her as well. There were brushes of his hand when he walked past or quick squeezes here or there. At night she no longer had to chase him across the mattress. He met her right in the middle of the bed, sans pillow wall, and they would cuddle.

She wasn't exactly sure what was happening between them, but there was something. It was as if they were two statues that had spent years standing only a few feet apart, but then a thick vine started winding its way around them both. It pulled them closer and closer together until they were both precariously tilted on their sides, leaning deeply toward each other, with scant inches between them. That was where they were now: in a moment full of suspense, possibility, and anticipation. They were waiting to see who would tip over first and if the other one would hold up against the weight or if they would both end up crashing to the ground.

She wrapped her arms around his waist and tightened them as hard as she could. She placed a kiss between his pecs and then laid her cheek on his chest. She locked eyes with Sofi from across the room.

Sofi gave them both a thorough once-over. She pursed her lips and raised both perfectly microbladed eyebrows. Then she slowly and deliberately brushed one forefinger over the other. Everything about her expression and actions said one thing: *Shame, shame, I know your name.*

Kamilah gave her an eye roll that was equally slow and deliberate in return. Whatever. She knew she was getting too attached to Liam. One didn't have to be a genius to know this wasn't going to end well for her, but Kamilah had never been one to let things like common sense stop her. She wanted to hug, touch, and care for him, so she would. As soon as he gave her more of a hint about what he was feeling, she would probably do a lot more. No. She would definitely do a lot more.

Kamilah was frustrated. Sexually. Ever since she'd watched him, capable and intelligent in the distillery, proudly putting his skills on display in the hottest example of competence porn she'd ever witnessed, she wanted Liam with an intensity that was getting harder and harder not to act on.

He didn't seem to be feeling the same.

For all his touches, hugs, and cuddling, he hadn't made another move since that kiss at Chase's restaurant. She didn't know what to make of that. Had he really only kissed her to shut her up before she embarrassed them both in front of her ex? She found it hard to believe. There was too much desire, too much connection, in that kiss for it to have been only for show. If only she could work up the nerve to ask him.

"Nena, aren't you going to make your fiancé a plate?" Titi Elsa gave her a disappointed tsk. "You're just as bad as Lucy." She gestured to her daughter, who gave a *What did I do?* look in return.

"See now, how did I get brought into this? My wife isn't even here tonight," Lucy was telling her mom. "But if Liza weren't at a conference right now, she'd say that both she and Liam have two fully functional hands, so there is no reason why we should have to serve them."

Kamilah reluctantly let go of Liam and backed away. He looked ready to say something, so she shook her head. "It's no big deal. I'm going to warm up the bread pudding I made for Killian, anyway." No one paid her any attention.

Papi's voice joined the conversation. "Vez, esta es la mierda de millennial de qué hablo." He walked into the kitchen and began to expound on said millennial bullshit. "They don't do anything the right way anymore. They don't do anything for their significant others, they don't ask or think before they act, they just propose to your daughter without asking you for her hand."

"Santos, are you still on that? This isn't the fifties," Tío Rico interjected, thereby proving that he may be Papi's twin, but he was way more woke. "Liam didn't have to ask for your permission. Kamilah is an adult woman who can make her own choices." He looked at Lucy as if seeking her approval.

Lucy nodded and gave him a subtle thumbs-up.

Papi, however, sucked his teeth. "When a man wants to marry a woman, he needs to ask her father's permission to court her first, and then he asks for his blessing when he wants to propose," he grouched.

"Papi, you legitimately ran away with Mami and married her at the courthouse," Leo pointed out.

"That was different," Papi barked. "Her parents were about to put her on a plane back to Puerto Rico. And I did ask her father, but he said no. We had no choice."

The siblings looked at each other in the familiar bemused yet entertained way they always did when one of their parents said something nonsensical.

Cristian was the first to speak. "You're saying you basically did the same thing Liam did, except at least you asked first."

"Not even," Eddie put in. "Because Liam and Kamilah didn't run off and get married. They're only engaged."

"So really, Liam handled the situation better," Leo concluded with a smirk.

"Ay cállense ya todos." Mami told them all to shut up. She looked at Kamilah. "See what you did?"

Kamilah's mouth dropped open. "Me?" She would've thrown her hands up in exasperation, but she was currently piling pineapple slaw onto the sandwich she was building for Liam. "I didn't even say anything."

"She's legit in the kitchen making her man a sandwich," Sofi pointed out with a little too much emphasis on *her man.* "You want her to be barefoot and pregnant too?"

Kamilah's heart did a weird stop/flip/squeeze thing. For a split second, her imagination went wild: her standing in the kitchen, barefoot and completely at home, Liam standing behind her, and both of their hands resting on her beach-ball belly. Intense longing shot through her, tightening her chest. Beyond the assumption that it would happen one day, she'd honestly never really thought about having children before. Not when she and Chase were engaged, and not even when Saint had first brought Rosie home and Kamilah ended up being a stand-in mom to her for almost three years.

So why was her baby box suddenly standing at attention?

"If she is going to get pregnant, she should do it soon" came Eddie's unhelpful addition. "After thirty-five, it would be considered a geriatric pregnancy."

What the fuck? Were they really talking about this right now? She scooped a large spoonful of rice onto Liam's plate.

Lucy, Alex, and Gabi slowly backed away until they faded into the background. Her female cousins were obviously trying to avoid bringing attention to themselves and becoming the next ones put on blast.

"She's not even thirty yet," Cristian said.

"Yo na' mas digo, she'll be thirty in a few weeks," Mami said. "She needs to have all her babies in the next five years, before her eggs die." Mami gave both her and Liam a dirty look, as if to blame them for wasting Kamilah's eggs.

"Umm, can we not have a family discussion about my reproductive system?" Kamilah said, passing the plate to Liam but avoiding looking at him.

"Yeah," Leo called from the living room. "Some of us are trying to eat." For someone so reluctant to let Kamilah change El Coquí's menu, he had certainly been eating a lot of said *bougie* food.

Desperate to change the direction of the conversation, Kamilah threw out the one thing she knew would derail it completely. "I want to know what you all thought of the food, because these are a few of the items I'm thinking of putting on the menu for the Fall Foodie Tour."

Silence.

"I loved everything," Abuelo said, doing his part to honor their agreement. "I think people will like it."

"The hipster gentrifiers colonizing our neighborhood will certainly like it," Cristian said. "Maybe you should add some organic drinks in mason jars too. They love that shit."

"I hear it really helps them choke down that white guilt for stealing and destroying everyone's culture," Lucy said.

Kamilah shot her a look of betrayal. She'd thought Lucy would be on her side.

Lucy grimaced apologetically. "Sorry, prima, but I see the consequences of this every day. Papi's office is inundated with calls from longtime residents begging him to help them."

Tío Rico nodded. "We try to implement measures of protection for people, but rents are going up, and people can't afford it. They are being forced to adapt or leave."

"I mean, there is no doubt the food is amazing." Titi Elsa came and put a hand on Kamilah's shoulder. "You have always been incredibly talented, but it's not real Puerto Rican food anymore."

Kamilah sucked in a gasp. That one hurt.

Alex shoulder-checked Kamilah's overgrown brothers and pushed her way to the front of the circle surrounding the kitchen island. "You're all acting like El Coquí isn't in the exact same situation." Her cousin was barely five and a half feet tall, but Kamilah had seen Alex own men double her size. "If it's adapt or leave, then why not adapt?"

"I know that, as a white man running an incredibly hipster-esque business, I should just sit here and eat my food." Liam put his empty plate on the counter next to her and stood tall at her side. "But Kamilah is not to blame for the changes happening to Humboldt Park. Capitalism is to blame for that." He looked around at her family. "You are all looking at this from an ideological standpoint, but to Kamilah this isn't about the fucked-up system." He grabbed Kamilah's hand. "This is her life's calling, her heart and soul. This is her labor of love, and it's dedicated to you, her family. How can any one of you judge her for it? How can you not support her in trying to ensure it survives?"

His speech was met with more silence.

No one, not even Sofi, had ever understood her like Liam. For better or worse, he always knew exactly what she was thinking or feeling. It seemed years of distance hadn't broken that bond. Kamilah couldn't hold back. She was highly aware that everyone from their conniving grandpas and her hesitant best friend to her overprotective brothers and judgmental parents were staring at her, but that didn't stop her. She rose up on her toes, turned Liam's face to hers, and planted a kiss right on his lips. It wasn't as deep or as long as she wanted, but it was enough to get her heart pounding and her breath racing.

"Holy shit," Leo burst out.

Kamilah startled and stepped back.

Liam stared at her in confused surprise for a moment, before his gaze went hot. He looked ready to haul her back in his arms and give her the kiss they both wanted.

She almost hoped he would, but then Leo started talking again and reminded her that they were not alone.

"I've never heard Liam put together that many words in his life." Leo looked at Saint sitting next to him. "What about you? Do you have any monologues you'd like to perform?"

Saint just gave him a dirty look.

"*You* string together too many words," Sofi said to Leo. "You need to learn that shutting the fuck up is free, but constantly talking out of your neck can cost you."

Leo opened his mouth to no doubt say something rude and start an all-out argument with Sofi, but a quiet "Leo" from Papi had him closing it.

Papi turned his attention to Kamilah. He took in her expression and her hand engulfed in Liam's. Then he looked at the remnants of the evening's meal spread out in front of them. "We will do this," he eventually said. "We'll make the changes and do the tour. But if this doesn't work, if this doesn't drum up enough business to make and keep us profitable, then we're finally going to discuss closing and selling." He looked at Abuelo then, and Abuelo nodded.

It had just become more important than ever to make sure everything went off without a hitch.

15

From the middle of the distillery floor, Liam eyed the mural on the wall. He nodded to himself and then stirred a tad more black paint into the bowl of red at his feet. He wanted it to look more garnet than ruby. When he was done, he stood and made his way back to the mural. He passed Ben, who was looking at the smudge of brown paint on his white T-shirt.

He glared at Liam. "Great," he grouched. "Now it looks like I have shit on my shirt."

Liam eyed the smear. "It is a pretty poopish hue."

Dev's voice floated down from the ladder he was standing on. "I told you not to wear a new shirt. Now look at you. You look like you wiped your ass with your shirt."

Ben gave his cousin the middle finger but kept his attention on Liam. "This is what I get for offering to use my days off helping you. I should've stuck to my original plans."

Liam scoffed. "Plans? What plans? You're a textbook workaholic. Without me, your staycation would've lasted four hours, tops, so you're welcome."

Since Granda still wasn't feeling up to coming in, Liam had decided to keep the distillery closed for a few more days. In that time, he'd focused on finishing the labels for Da's whiskey, designing and ordering T-shirts, and painting the diagram Kamilah had suggested. The night he'd finished the outline of the mural and labeled the sections with the colors he'd chosen, Ben had offered to come in and help him fill it in. Ben had then coerced Dev into helping too.

He hadn't stopped complaining about it for the last three days.

"All I'm saying," Ben continued, "is that I was under the impression that this was a small painting and I would be done in an hour or two. Like when you go to one of those workshops to drink cheap wine and make a shitty still life of some dried-up flowers in a vase."

"When have you ever done that?" Dev asked. "And why wasn't I there to point and laugh?"

"I did it because I was on a date with the hot blonde who works in our legal department. I know it's been about eight years since you've been on one, but one doesn't usually bring their asshole cousin along for colorful commentary." A wet, paint-splattered rag just happened to fall right on Ben's head.

"Oops," Dev called. "My bad."

"Dick!" He ripped it off and tossed it at Dev's back.

Liam turned his face away before Ben saw his smile, which was why he saw the door to the condo open and Kamilah strut into the distillery holding a tray of food and one of those cooler bags. Dinnertime.

It was the only time he saw her anymore. He felt like he'd been living with an absent roommate since she and her family began remodeling El Coquí. She'd been up super early every day and knocked out by the time he went to bed. He was forced to start spooning her when she slept just to feel close to her. Sad, really.

His mouth went dry when he took her in.

In plaster-dusted boots, a paint-splattered tank top, and short denim cutoffs, she looked more like a member of a girl group filming a music video on the set of a remodel than someone remodeling. She had a bandanna covered in little Puerto Rican flags wrapped around her head and tied right above her forehead, her curls shooting out of the top like a plant in a pot. Actually, it was more like someone tried to stop the release of a streamer cannon after yanking the string— simply too much to be contained. He loved when she wore her hair that way. There was something so fundamentally Kamilah about it. She too wouldn't be contained.

"Mila," Ben shouted. He pushed Liam out of the way and practically ran to where she stood by the tasting table. "Goddess of food, keeper of my heart and stomach, what did you bring me today?"

Kamilah wrinkled her nose but laughed. "You're too easy, Ben. You just tried my food for the first time three days ago, and I'm already the keeper of your vital organs?" She held her cheek out, and Ben promptly placed a kiss on it.

A little too promptly and way too eagerly. Liam scowled.

"You won me over in one bite." Ben put his hands on his heart and batted his long eyelashes at Kamilah like a bad stage actor. "Now all I have to do is wait until the shenanigans with this fool are done, and then we can be together." He lifted her hand and pressed it to his scruffy cheek.

Kamilah rolled her eyes.

Liam smacked him on the back of his head with as much eagerness as Ben had shown kissing Kamilah.

"Oww!"

Liam wanted to pull her in for a real kiss, but she was unpacking the tray. He settled for placing a kiss on the back of her neck instead.

Her breath stopped for a second and she paused in pulling out something brick-sized and wrapped in aluminum foil.

There was a speculative sound from his side, and Liam looked up to find both Ben and Dev eyeing him. One with a look of contemplation (Dev), the other with one that fell just short of eyebrow-waggling (Ben).

Liam ignored both looks, grabbed a plate, and sat. "You don't have to cook for us," he told Kamilah for the third day in a row. "I know you're busy." He pulled out a chair and motioned for her to take it.

For the third day in a row, she pretended not to hear him. "The mural is looking good. You guys are almost done."

"Thank God," Ben said. He took a seat on one of the stools. "I thought this was never going to end."

Dev pulled out his own stool. "Are you going to eat with us?" he asked Kamilah.

She nodded. "Is that okay, or is this a men-only club?" She sat next to Liam.

"If it were, Ben wouldn't be here, since he's been doing nothing but acting like a baby." Dev reached over and grabbed a wrapped brick.

"That's a whiskey-and-peach barbecue pulled-pork sandwich," she told Dev. "There are some yuca chips in here too." She pulled out a large paper bag and handed it to him.

"Thank you," Dev said. "It sounds delicious."

Liam nodded at the same time a voice from behind them

said, "It certainly does. Did you make it using Kane Whiskey?"

The four of them jumped and spun in their seats.

A woman stood by the open door surrounded by the early-evening sunlight, and for a split second she looked so much like his mom that his heart stopped. Then she moved farther into the distillery, and he realized it was only because of her height, long dark hair, and pale skin.

"Sorry," the middle-aged woman said. "I didn't mean to startle you. I'm Amanda McGuire with American Spirit Distillers. I'm looking for Killian or Liam Kane."

Liam hopped up. "I'm Liam Kane."

"Oh great." She strode toward him.

Liam met her in front of the closed garage door, and they shook hands.

"I'm here with my photographer, Danny." She motioned to a man in the parking lot taking pictures of the building. "We're here to do a preliminary walk-through of the distillery for the contest. Get a feel for it, take some pictures, and create a plan before the judges come. Is this a good time?" She eyed Kamilah, Dev, and Ben over his shoulder. Her tone was pleasant enough, but he got the feeling that she didn't really care if it was a good time or not. She was there to do a job, and she would do it.

"This is a great time," Kamilah said. "Please come in."

Oh right. Liam should probably say something besides his name. "Yes, welcome to Kane Distillery, Ms. McGuire. Let me show you around."

She smiled, revealing a small gap between her two front teeth and a crooked grin. It made her look younger. More approachable. "Please, call me Mandy, and give me a minute to collect Danny. He's obsessed with the decorative brick-work on the outside of the building."

"The building used to be a brick works and smithy," he told her.

"Both?" Mandy made a *hmm* sound. "Interesting." She looked at Liam and then at the rest of them. "I'll be right back." She strutted back out the door with purpose.

As soon as it closed behind Mandy, Kamilah was up out of her seat and rushing over to him. "Oh my God, this is so exciting!"

"Are you kidding? This is terrible," Liam whispered. "Granda is supposed to be here to show them around." He had no idea what to do. He'd probably say or do the wrong thing as usual, and then they would get dropped from the contest or something.

Kamilah reached over and grabbed his hands. "Liam, relax. They aren't the judges. They're just here to see everything before they come with a camera crew." She paused and let that sink in. "We knew this was a possibility, which is why you prepared and practiced."

That was true. Liam had been running a tour in his mind all day for weeks. He even gave tours in his dreams. "Yeah, but—"

"But nothing," she said, cutting him off. "You know what to do: give them a bit about the building, about the founding of the distillery and Killian's background, hit up the grandfather-and-grandson angle, and then talk about what you know best, which is how your distillery makes the best damn whiskey and has the coolest product branding."

"Right." Liam nodded. "Or," he said and held up a finger as if he just had an idea, "you could give the tour."

Kamilah smiled and shook her head. "I can't, because I

have another plan to help you out and end this whole thing with a bang. I'm going to feed them bomb-ass food with your whiskey in it."

"Is that considered bribery?"

She scoffed. "No. It's just like a more detailed kind of tasting." She sounded sure of the fact, but the way she looked away spoke volumes. "Anyway, you kick ass, like I know you will, and those two—" she pointed at Ben and Dev "—are going to help me get everything else set up."

Liam glanced out the window and saw Mandy coming back in with Danny in tow. He blew out a breath and tried to calm his racing heart. He could feel beads of sweat rolling down the back of his neck. "Are you sure I can do this?" He felt a hand on his cheek.

Kamilah pulled his face around. "Listen to me, Liam Kane." She waited until he looked her in the eye. "There is no one on this earth who can do this better than you. You are Kane Distillery, and you've got this." She put her other palm on his cheek. "Do you understand me?"

He nodded as best as he could with his face sandwiched between her hands.

She placed a quick but hard kiss on his lips. "I believe in you, and I've got your back." Then she dropped her hands, spun on her heels, and called to Dev and Ben. "You two, come with me."

Dev stood.

Ben, who'd just shoved a handful of chips into his mouth, looked up in surprise. "Us? But what about our food?"

"There's no time for that now," Kamilah said as she marched to the condo door like a sergeant leading her troops. "Let's go. And grab that cooler bag."

Dev gave Liam a nod of support, picked up the bag, and followed Kamilah.

Ben huffed in displeasure but stood up anyway. He turned to Liam and said, "Break a leg, bro," before stealing Liam's uneaten sandwich off his plate and leaving.

"All right, Liam," Mandy said from the entryway. "We're ready for you."

Liam closed his eyes, took a deep breath, and remembered what Kamilah had just said. *You are Kane Distillery, and you've got this.* He opened his eyes, pasted a smile on his face, and turned to Mandy. "Let me show you everything Kane has to offer." And then he started talking.

For the next hour, he led Mandy and Danny around the distillery, giving explanations, answering questions, and allowing them to take pictures of anything and everything. He sort of noticed Kamilah and his friends trekking in and out the space, cleaning up the mess from dinner and setting up her tasting idea, but he didn't let that distract him.

"And now we get to everyone's favorite part, the tasting," Liam eventually said. He motioned over to where Kamilah was standing behind the tasting table. His friends were nowhere in sight. They must've left.

"Hi," Mandy said, reaching the table and leaning over it to shake Kamilah's hand. "I didn't catch your name before."

"I'm Kamilah. My family has owned the Puerto Rican restaurant in the front of the building for as long as the Kanes have owned the distillery. Liam and I grew up together."

"She's my fiancée," Liam added. He pointed to her left hand. "That's my grandmother's ring." His brows crinkled slightly before he fixed his face. *What the fuck was that?* There was no reason to say any of that, so then why had he felt the need to proudly claim her as his fiancée? Their engagement wasn't even real.

"I love that," Mandy exclaimed. "The deep family connection here is just amazing. You can feel it in the air."

"Just wait until you meet Killian," Kamilah said. "He is a force to be reckoned with, for sure, but everyone loves him."

"I'm looking forward to it. I hope he is feeling better by the seventeenth."

That caught Liam's attention. "The seventeenth of November? Is that when the judges are coming?"

"Yes, I'll be back with a camera crew and the judges on Saturday the seventeenth." She looked at the table, which was full of small covered plates sitting next to custom whiskey tasting glasses and different bottles of Kane Whiskey. "Now, tell me about all this."

Liam looked to Kamilah, but she just smiled at him and gave him an encouraging nod. "Kamilah is a highly trained chef, so she thought it would be cool to make some food with our whiskey instead of just tasting it by itself." He sounded so unsure by the end of his explanation that it sounded more like a question than a statement.

Kamilah sighed and shook her head. "Men, am I right?"

Mandy chuckled and nodded.

"I am a trained chef and a bit hyperactive, so I'm frequently experimenting with ingredients that catch my attention. Lately, that attention-grabbing ingredient has been Kane Whiskey. Ask anyone in my family. I've been obsessed to the point of annoyance."

Mandy laughed. "I get that. My husband and kids feel the same way about me and black licorice lately. Hot flashes suck, by the way." She fanned herself with her hand.

"Well, then," Kamilah said with a cheeky smile, "I guess

we should start with my frozen treat." She reached into a cooler and pulled out one of those plastic Popsicle-making contraptions.

"Oh yes," Mandy enthused. "Let's start there."

Kamilah motioned him over to stand by her. "Liam can tell you a little bit about this whiskey while you try it, and then I'll tell you about this treat."

Liam went around the table to his usual spot for tastings.

As he passed her, Kamilah leaned in and whispered, "Talk up the name and how it goes with the flavor profile."

Liam picked up the bottle featuring a crone-like woman with ghostly pale skin, pitch-black eyes, and long tangled hair, screaming in distress. The banshee's windblown hair flew above her head to form the words *Bean Sídhe*. "As I said during the tour, I get the inspiration for the names from the stories of Irish folklore that my grandmother used to tell me." He pointed to the bottle in his hand. "This isn't her."

Everyone laughed, and Liam puffed out his chest a little bit. *Look at me, telling jokes.*

"This whiskey got its name because, like the wail of a banshee, the powerful woodsy nose catches your attention from afar, the sharp sour notes freeze you in your tracks, and the long finish lingers in your mouth, reminding you that you just made contact with something dangerously otherworldly. This whiskey is a warning and not for the faint of heart." He handed off the sampling glasses and waited until everyone had tried it.

"Wow," Mandy said. "I see what you mean. That's intense, but delicious."

Kamilah stepped forward. "It's interesting because you get this earthy smell that is reflected in this bitterness of the taste, but there are also some definite citrus-fruit smells and flavors coming through." She started popping the frozen treats out of the mold and handing them out. "I wanted to play up those sour flavors, so I used it to make a limber de tamarindo, which is basically a tamarind-flavored Puerto Rican Popsicle." She handed one to Liam and gave him a wink. "Tamarind, if you aren't familiar, is this sweet and tangy pulp that surrounds seeds in a pod-like tropical fruit. It's used all around the world, but in Puerto Rico we love to use it to make juice and limber." She held one up, so Danny could take a picture of it.

"Oh my God, I am in love with this," Mandy said around a bite. "It's the perfect blend of sweet, sour, and bitter."

Liam had to agree. Throughout his life, he'd had limber of all flavors, from peanut butter to passion fruit, thanks to it being the Vegas' favorite summer treat. Somehow they'd never thought to add his whiskey to it. Rum, certainly, but his whiskey gave it an all-around different flavor.

"More, more." Mandy clapped like a kid at a candy store. "I want to eat all the things."

Liam and Kamilah continued feeding her. Liam would give a brief description and tasting of his whiskey, and Kamilah would talk about why she used it to make a dish and then give them a sample. They worked perfectly together, just like the flavors of whiskey and the food. By the time they were done, another hour later, Mandy had tried five whiskeys and five dishes and asked five hundred more questions.

"I'm going to need to be wheeled out of here," she said as she watched Kamilah carry the dirty plates out of the distillery.

"I'm glad you enjoyed yourself," Liam told her. He eyed Danny, who was over on the other side of the distillery, taking more pictures of their copper still.

"Enjoyed myself? This was seriously one of the best experiences I've ever had at a distillery or a brewery or even a restaurant. This is genius." She leaned forward and motioned for Liam to do the same. "Look, I am just one of the organizers of this thing. My job is to make sure it goes off without a hitch. I have no control over the results at this point. That's up to the judges and the public votes once the segments go up. But I was raised in the business, and I ran it like a badass during my time. I have a really good feeling about this place and about you. If you win this thing, Kane Distillery will explode to new heights, and I want to help you make sure that you can take full advantage of that."

"What do you mean?"

"I mean you and your grandfather know how to do this the right way on a small scale, but what about once you start really growing? You're going to need to amp up production big-time, which means employees running more machinery in a bigger place. You need someone to help you with that. Someone who will appreciate your craftsmanship and your ideas and doesn't want to change you or take over but can help you keep up the momentum."

She was absolutely right. Liam worried about how they could manage Kane if they grew. He'd especially been thinking about it since Granda got sick. There was no way they could do it, just the two of them. It would be impossible for him to do it on his own.

"Unfortunately, knowledgeable benefactors who don't want to take control aren't easy to come by."

"I know someone," she said. "She has been looking for a young, ambitious, talented, and capable entrepreneur to mentor, but she's not going to take just anyone. However, she would definitely consider the winner of Best Craft Whiskey Distillery someone worthy of her partnership."

"You're saying that if we win, you'll partner with Kane and mentor me."

"I'm saying that you need to make sure your charming grandpa and your bubbly fiancée are here on the seventeenth. After the winners are announced, you and I will see if we need to discuss the particulars more." She put her card on the table, stood, and then yelled to Danny that it was time to go.

Liam walked her to the door. "Oh shit. It's pouring," he observed. He looked around in panic for something to cover their heads.

Mandy waved him off and pulled some keys out of her pocket. "Don't worry about it. We aren't made out of sugar." She hit the start/unlock button on a key fob, and a kick-ass Benz started right in the first row. She took off running with Danny right on her heels. Liam waved as they pulled out. The parking lot was empty aside from Valeria's Toyota, which meant that all of Kamilah's family members must've gone home. He wasn't surprised. It was nasty out.

Lightning flashed, and thunder rumbled a second later.

Liam had just closed and locked the door when the lights flickered and went out. "Shit." Barely a minute had passed before he heard pounding footsteps, and the door to the condo was thrown open.

Kamilah barreled through the door, cell phone in hand with its flashlight bright. She ran and took a flying leap at him.

At the last second, Liam braced himself and caught her. "Umph."

She wrapped her arms and legs around him like an orangutan.

The light of her phone was beaming directly into his eye, so he turned his head. "I see you're still scared of thunderstorms," he said nonchalantly. He tucked his hands under her thighs and hauled her up into a more comfortable position. Comfortable for her. He was already getting hard. *Stop that*, he ordered his dick. She was scared and didn't need him fantasizing about how supple and warm her inner thighs felt against his sides.

"You try almost dying of hypothermia because your idiot brother locked you out on the roof right before a thunderstorm and didn't tell anyone where you were because he didn't want to get in trouble."

Fucking Leo. That asswipe. "I should beat Leo's ass for that," he said.

"I don't want that," she said. "He already feels extremely guilty. Trust me when I say no one could make him feel more horrible about it than he already does."

"I don't believe it. I've hardly known Leo to show remorse for anything he says or does to you."

"No, seriously. One night after I got out of the hospital, it stormed again. I ended up in the tub, shaking, crying, and scared out of my mind. Leo found me there, crawled into the tub with me, and held me close. Every storm after, he'd make his way to me. He would sleep on my floor and hold my hand. He even used to get in trouble in school for pulling me out of class and sitting with me in the storage room." Her phone buzzed in her hand. She looked at it and then held it up for him to read. "See?"

Leo: Heard the power is out. U good?

It was the very least he should do, but Liam knew how defensive Kamilah got when anyone bad-mouthed her brothers. "I guess I can let it slide for now." At the end of the day, he was just grateful that she'd been found and that, beyond a bad case of pneumonia, she was fine. Relatively speaking. There was still the issue of freaking out during bad thunderstorms.

Lightning lit up the distillery, and thunder boomed directly overhead.

Kamilah gasped and buried her face in his neck. "I'm usually not this bad, but I guess I'm still not used to being in your house instead of my own."

Liam felt for her, he really did, but he also couldn't ignore the way her ass filled his hands or her breasts pressed against his chest. She smelled amazing: like the coconut oil she used in her hair, the sweet but spicy smell of her homemade body butter, and the tang of her sweat. His mouth began to water. "What helps you when you get like this?"

"I need a distraction." She lifted her head and looked at him. Her eyes were large and dark in the shadowy space.

He swallowed hard and thought that maybe he could hold back, but then she said the words that would completely derail his good intentions.

"Distract me. Please. I need you, Liam."

16

Kamilah saw a change come over Liam. One minute he was concerned and sympathetic, the next his eyes went dark and he gazed at her with intent. She would've been a bit scared by the way he looked ready to take her apart with his bare hands if it weren't for the ridge she felt against her inner thigh. She licked her lips, and he zeroed in on her mouth. Every part of her came to attention, but particularly the part between her legs.

"You want me to distract you?" he asked in a low, rough voice. His gaze tracked from her lips down to her chest and back up.

Unable to speak, Kamilah nodded her head.

"Don't say yes when you don't know what I'm talking about."

She opened her mouth to say that she didn't care what he was talking about, but he lifted his hand and held a finger to her lips.

"Listen first." He waited until it was clear that she wasn't going to say anything, and then he dropped his hand and palmed her ass again. Her skin was on fire under his touch. "I want to strip you bare," he whispered. "And once you're naked, I'm going to sit you down on my tasting table and do exactly what its name dictates I do."

Kamilah inhaled shakily.

"That's right. I'm going to taste you. I'm going to savor you like one of my whiskeys, and I'm not going to stop until I'm drunk on you."

Oh my God.

Who in their right mind would've ever suspected Liam—practically nonverbal Liam—of being the best at dirty talk?

Her body was going haywire switching between fear and nervousness and pure lust. She could barely breathe. She couldn't swallow, so she gulped. Her clothes suddenly felt three sizes too small. She longed to rip them off.

"What do you say? Is that enough of a distraction for you?" His voice was soft and sultry against her ear.

Kamilah couldn't talk, so she did the next best thing. She grabbed him by the back of the neck, turned her head, and yanked his mouth to hers. She kissed him like she'd been longing to kiss him for weeks: deeply.

He met her stroke for stroke, and while she was still a bit shocked that she and Liam were making out in his distillery, she wasn't at all surprised by how good it was. Despite their differences, they'd always complemented each other perfectly. Like honey and sriracha, salt and watermelon, chilis and chocolate. She gave his bottom lip a nibble, thoroughly enjoying his taste.

He gave her lip a bite and tug in response.

Her legs clenched around his waist.

He pulled his mouth away and pushed their foreheads together. "I need to hear you say it out loud," he told her. "I need you to say yes. I need you to tell me that I'm not fucking everything up like I did at your prom."

He just had to bring that up, didn't he?

"Liam," she panted, "I swear by all that is holy, if you stop like you did back then, I am going to hurt you."

"Is that a yes? I need to hear it."

She pressed a kiss on his lips and pulled back. "Yes." Another kiss. "Yes." One more kiss. "Yes to everything."

He turned with her in his arms and started walking toward the tasting table.

Kamilah huffed out a breath and trembled in relief. Goose bumps pebbled her arms, but not with fear of the storm. With anticipation. With need. She unwound her arms from his neck and reached down to the edge of her tank top. His voice stopped her.

"No," he bit out. "I do that. Not you."

"But—"

He nipped her earlobe and then gave it a suck. "I have been waiting to undress you for fifteen years."

The warmth in her belly and other places threatened to ignite into a raging inferno. She gulped and nodded at him.

His eyes blazed. "I plan to enjoy the fuck out of it, and not even you are going to take that pleasure from me." He suddenly let her go.

She landed on the table with a smack of her bare thighs against the cold metal. Before she could adjust, he was there between her legs.

His mouth was on hers, and his hands were everywhere else. His palms slid up the inside of her top along her stomach and over her chest.

She took that as her invite to do the same to him. His skin was so soft. Everything about him was familiar, yet alien at the same time.

He groaned and pulled back after a minute. He grabbed the bottom of her shirt and ripped it over her head. He attacked the front zipper of her sports bra. He made a sound of frustration when he saw the clasp that held the inner cups together. Then it was opened, and her bra was tossed away somewhere with her shirt. He stared down at her and let out a breath. "Shit," he whispered. He bent his head and put his mouth on her while his hands went to the button and zipper of her shorts.

"Hurry up," she ordered, using her hands to lift herself off the table.

He grabbed her shorts and panties and pulled them both down at the same time. He got them over one boot, but they got caught on the other. They both left them there. He put a hand in the middle of her chest and pushed her back.

She shivered from the cold metal against her back and from anticipation. She looked up at him.

Still fully dressed, he stood between her thighs as he took in every inch of her from the top of her head to where her knees bent at the edge of the table. "Fuck. You're better than I ever imagined. My dreams don't even come close."

Kamilah felt her body flush. "You can't even see anything," she said. "It's almost pitch-black in here." Of course, that was the exact moment lightning flashed and illuminated the entire distillery.

He licked his bottom lip, and then his mouth curled in one corner. "I can see enough."

"Liam," she begged. She didn't know if she was begging him to spare her embarrassment or get on with it.

He leaned over her, put both hands on the table by her shoulders, and then kissed her deeply.

She wrapped her limbs around him to hold him close, but it didn't last long.

He broke her hold and started making his way from her mouth to her neck, from her neck to her breasts, and after spending some time there, he dragged his mouth lower, over her stomach, to her hips, to her thighs, and then between.

Finally.

At that point she wasn't sure what she was saying. She didn't know if she was speaking in English, Spanish, or some mix of the two. She didn't even know if she was saying words. She could've very well just been communicating via moans, grunts, and breathy sighs as she stared at the ceiling and grabbed pointlessly at the table beneath her. All she was aware of was Liam's hands and mouth. That was it. Nothing else in the world existed at the moment but him. He was the beginning and end of her consciousness.

His tongue hit a particularly good spot, and she cried out. She looked down and wished she could see more than a dark head and a large pale hand on her stomach. She wanted to see his face. She wanted to look into his eyes. She wanted that connection with him.

As if it had heard her vehement wishes, lightning flared again brighter and longer than before, right when Liam happened to look up at her. His blue eyes flashed white-hot like the lightning. He sucked one more time, hard.

Kamilah was propelled out of her body into the surrounding storm. It beat at her from all sides like it had years ago, but unlike then, she wasn't scared. There was too much heat, too much pleasure, for her to be scared. She simply let it take her, twisting and catapulting her through the electric sky.

Through it all, Liam was there with her, urging her higher and deeper into the storm.

After some time she came back down into herself. She should've been exhausted, satisfied, by her trip, but she wasn't. It was as if the electricity from the storm was inside her now, demanding a conduit to escape. She sat up quickly, grabbed Liam by the face with both hands, and pulled his mouth to hers in a kiss made of pure static and currents. "I need you," she said between kisses. "Inside me." More kisses. Rougher and wetter. "Now."

He groaned, and she felt it deep in his chest where it was pressed against her own. His fist came down on the table and the vibration reverberated up her body. "I don't have condoms."

"What?" she panted. Her brain still wasn't working right.

"I haven't needed them." His tone was a touch defensive, but more frustrated than anything.

"I have some," Kamilah informed him. "They are upstairs in the drawer of the nightstand on my side."

He shot her a look of surprise.

"What, you don't think I can have casual sex sometimes?" She didn't tell him that she'd bought them less than a month ago in a moment of horny hope.

He straightened, his face blank. "Is that what this is for you, casual sex?"

Kamilah's head jerked back. "Fuck, no. There's nothing casual about this." She was having a difficult time with the thought that this was Liam, the same Liam who'd once hidden her in one of his father's empty whiskey barrels in an attempt to get her parents to forget her at his house so she could sleep over. Then again, he wasn't that Liam at all. He was completely different in body and in temperament. This Liam was large and hard and dark. The only people he showed his soft underbelly to were his grandfather and her. Some primal part of her loved that, loved that she got a piece of him that no one else did. She leaned in and put her mouth to his neck like she did when they slept—the other time he showed vulnerability with her.

"Damn right there's not." He turned his head and gave her a hard kiss. "This is *not* casual." A sucking kiss on her neck. "This is years' worth of anticipation, expectation, desire." He worked his way down to her nipple.

She nodded. It was all of that and more. It was two magnets finally getting close enough to snap together. It was the last two pieces of a thousand-piece puzzle finally clicking into place. It was two hearts beating in time, finally.

I love you. I loved the boy you were, and I love the man you are.

There was no more denying it. No more acting like she cared about him solely as a friend. No more excusing her pull to him as an attraction birthed of close contact. She loved him.

She loved that he was adorably awkward when he had to do anything outside of his wheelhouse. She loved that while he seemed gruff and antisocial, he was deep and sensitive. He had the personality of a cranky old man, but the soul of an artist, and she adored that she was one of the only people who knew that. She loved that he never expected her to be at his beck and call, but he went out of his way to be there for her. It hadn't always been that way, but it was that way now, and that was really all that mattered.

Although he'd deny it, Liam had grown into the potential of his youth. He was sweet and caring, loyal and dependable, strong but vulnerable, and insecure but so incredibly gifted. And she loved him.

"Take me to bed," she told him. She used the same phrase that had spurred him into action before. "Please. I need you, Liam."

★ ★ ★

Liam was unable to deny her anything she asked for, especially when she asked him like that: breathy, needy, and naked.

He briefly contemplated running up the stairs to grab a condom and running back down, but that would take too long. Instead, he grabbed her wrist, dipped, and used his grip to pull her over his shoulder like one of his seventy-gallon barrels.

"Liam!" She wiggled. "What are— Put me down. I can walk."

"Stop wriggling. I don't want to drop you." He put a hand high on her thigh to steady her. He could feel her moisture with his thumb. He licked his lips in an attempt to taste her once again. She was exactly as delicious as he'd imagined. Better.

In his mind, she'd been tentative. He'd had to coax and seduce her by degrees. In real life, she was bold, demanding, and dived in headfirst. He didn't know why he'd ever thought she'd be anything else. She was bold and fearless in everything she did. She was like holding on to a live wire.

He pulled the door to the condo open and picked up his pace as soon as the door closed behind him.

"My blood is rushing to my head," Kamilah complained. "I can't think."

"That's fine. You don't have to think." Liam grabbed on to the railing and started taking the stairs two at a time.

She squealed and grabbed on to the waistband of his pants with both hands. "Cuidado. Me vas a dejar caer."

"I'm not going to drop you," he told her. He reached the top of the stairs, turned, and quickly made his way down the hall to their room. He threw the door open, strode over to the bed, and flipped her onto the mattress. He didn't even pause to enjoy watching her body, highlighted by the flashes of lightning, bounce on the mattress. "Take your boots off," he commanded as he stalked to the nightstand while he pulled his shirt over his head. He tossed his shirt aside and yanked the drawer open.

He paused and stared at the sight in front of him. He'd expected a few loose and probably old condoms tossed in the drawer without a care. That was not what he saw in her drawer. "Umm. Why is there a brand-new, bulk-size variety box of condoms in here?" His tone revealed surprise, confusion, and more than a little amusement.

Her response was hesitant. "I was hopeful?"

Liam bit his lip and looked at everything in the room but her. He made a choking sound and tried to cover it with a cough.

Her highly aggrieved voice came from the bed. "Are you laughing right now?"

Liam shook his head and held his breath in an attempt to stifle his laugh. A bulk box of condoms ranging from small to double XL...because she was hopeful. He squeaked and covered his mouth.

"You *are* laughing," she accused. "I don't know what's so funny about me being prepared. I mean, I know you're almost six-five and as bulky as a winter sweater, so I figured everything else was built to match, but I don't exactly have firsthand knowledge. For all I know, you could have a little squeaker."

Liam lost it. He couldn't help it.

A boot hit him in the back.

He laughed harder.

"Fuck this," she said. "I don't have to deal with bullshit.

I have a perfectly good vibrator hidden in the closet, and it's charged."

Liam was going to die. He couldn't breathe.

Only her. Seriously, only Kamilah could have him as hard as the ironwork in his apartment but dying of hysterical laughter at the same time. Out of the corner of his eye, he saw her stand and start tugging at the sheet. She was going to stalk away.

He moved quickly despite his laughs. He snatched the box and then tackled her to the bed before she could get the sheet free.

She wheezed out a hard breath when he fell on her. She made to push him off, but he settled deeply into the cradle she'd instinctively made with her legs. Her bandanna had come off at some point, and her scrunchie was barely hanging on. A chunk of hair had flopped into her face when she fell.

He pulled a few curls away from her eyes and let them fall back. The eyes he revealed glared at him.

God, he adored her.

"Get off me. I'm no longer interested."

"I'm sorry," he said, doing his best to stifle his amusement. "I wasn't laughing at you. I was just caught off guard."

Her light brown eyes narrowed on him, but he could see the uncertainty behind her anger. She thought he was going to push her away like he had when they were young.

As if that were possible.

He was more willing and capable of chopping off his own hands with a rusty saw than he was of pushing her away now. Not after he'd felt her soft skin. Not after he'd tasted her. "Don't you get it?" He lifted a finger and drew it lightly from her hairline down her nose. "Everything about you delights me." He outlined her lips. "I've spent so long acting like it doesn't." He trailed the finger to her chin and along her jaw. "But I don't have to do that anymore." His finger swooped down the side of her neck and stopped at the thrum of her pulse. "The freedom is making me a bit giddy."

She huffed and rolled her eyes, but her lips curved in a pleased smile.

He was forgiven. He leaned down and started placing kisses along her collarbone in gratitude.

She squirmed.

He knew he was working her up again, but he wanted her wild like during their time downstairs. He started making his way down her body. Shit, he wished the electricity wasn't out. She was exquisite in the darkness; he could only imagine what she would be like in the light. He wanted to look at her in bright light. He wanted to trace every line, highlight, and shadow of her like one of his labels.

He used his tongue to outline her belly button, and then he placed a sucking kiss on her lower belly. He was about to go lower when she grabbed a fistful of his hair and yanked him up.

"I need you," she said again.

It was a phrase he could get entirely too used to hearing. "I'm right here," he told her. "I'm going to take care of you." He tried to pull back and down, but she gripped harder.

"No," she told him. "Inside."

He didn't have to be told twice. He stood and shucked his shoes, pants, and boxer briefs in record time.

On the bed, Kamilah ripped the box open. She eyed his erection like a tailor examining the fit of a suit, looked back down and dug around in the box, and then pulled out a string of extra-large condoms.

Liam made a Herculean effort to not react.

She tore one foil package off the string and ripped it open. "Come here," she commanded in a low, husky voice. "I need you now."

At the sound of her voice, rough and full of need, all amusement fled. He felt the same way. He needed her. He needed her so much it scared the ever-living shit out of him. He didn't tell her that, though. Instead, he joined her on the bed, let her roll the condom on him, spread her legs, and then joined their bodies together.

He tried his very best to ignore the part of him telling him that their hearts were also joining.

17

Kamilah awoke late the next morning to fingers playing in her hair. She loved that feeling so much. It was one of the greatest sensations in the world. It made her feel pampered and cherished. Now it also made her want to purr like a cat. She opened her eyes and watched Liam twirl one of her curls around his fingers.

His face was severe, but she knew him now. He wasn't brooding or indifferent. He was absorbed in his task. He coiled each spiral perfectly around his index finger as if it were a matter of life and death. Every few seconds he would stop to smooth the hair with his thumb. He didn't even notice she was awake until his hand finally reached the side of her face.

"Buenos días," Liam murmured, and Kamilah felt her body warm.

God, she loved when he spoke Spanish. It made her glow like a lightning bug.

"Buenos días," she whispered, feeling shy. She'd come to

the realization that she loved him last night. She couldn't even pinpoint when she'd fallen. She didn't think there was an exact moment. It had happened slowly and over time, like one of those extravagant domed desserts that you pour a warm sauce over until the dome disintegrates and reveals a rich and luxurious treat. She wanted to tell him. She wanted to just blurt it out, but for once in her life she was going to be circumspect. "You seem to really like my hair," she observed instead.

"I do. It's like you, determined but soft and just a tiny bit of a mess. Plus, it smells like coconut." He leaned in to smell it. A sound of satisfaction rumbled all the way to his chest.

It reminded Kamilah of the sounds he'd made last night, and her body instantly heated. She turned her head until they were face-to-face and then leaned in for a kiss. She loved kissing Liam. He kissed like he was trying to commit every single second of it to memory. Like he gloried in her lips, worshipped at her tongue, and savored the intricacies of her flavor. Liam kissed her like she was sustenance, like he needed her kisses to live.

When they finally broke apart, Kamilah found herself lying on his bare chest. She took a moment to simply enjoy his face with his strong jaw, sharp nose, and piercing eyes. "What have you been thinking about while playing with my nappy hair?"

"Besides you and everything we did last night," he said and shrugged, "the contest, mostly. Mandy said something yesterday that got me thinking."

"Was it that you're awesome and going to win?"

He chuckled. "She did say that she liked our odds, especially if Granda is there and you are there with your whiskey-inspired food."

"I'm in. I'm totally in for that. I have so many more ideas."

He was shaking his head. "I don't want to ask that of you. You have your own stuff going on."

Kamilah tilted her head to the side, but her *Really?* look was ruined by the tangle of curls flopping over her face. "You're not asking me." She tried to blow them out of her face without success. "I'm offering. Anyway, our tour-stop date is the tenth." She tossed her head to the other side, but more hair fell in her face. "I'll be done with the Foodie Tour before your big day." She felt Liam's hands in her hair.

He used his hand and forearm to gently brush it up to the top of her head, just like she did. "If you're absolutely sure it isn't too much." He pulled a hot-pink silk scrunchie off his wrist and over her bushel of curls. He didn't loop it around another time, just like she didn't.

Kamilah practically melted. He paid such close attention to her that he'd picked up how she handled her hair. "I'm positive. I want to support you, and if playing around with fun food flavors is the way I get to do that, then even better."

"Okay, thank you. I appreciate it. Hopefully, this will make everything easier."

"What do you mean?"

"Mandy is offering me a partnership. She wants to help me take Kane to the next level, which is perfect. It's getting too difficult running everything, just Granda and I. We need a staff and a more efficient way to produce and sell."

A partnership? Kamilah didn't necessarily like the sound of that. It sounded a lot like selling out. Killian was dead set against anyone other than him or Liam running Kane.

He smiled at her. "Do you have to work in the restaurant today?"

Kamilah shook her head. "They told me I was working them like I was a pharaoh in ancient Egypt and threatened to revolt if I didn't leave them alone today." She smiled at the memory of her papi demanding a day of rest. *Even God took a day off, mamita.*

"Good," Liam said. "Then it will be a lot easier for me to convince you to play hooky with me today."

Kamilah's jaw dropped before she let out a delighted chuckle. "Doth mine ears deceive me? Did Liam Kane just say the words *play hooky with me*?" She sat up, straddling his waist, and lifted her hand to place it on his forehead.

He caught her wrist.

"Come here." She lifted her other hand only for him to catch that one too. "I have to check you for fever." She giggled, and she continued to try to reach his head, and he kept deflecting. "You're obviously sick or something."

"That's not where I want your hands," he told her as he ogled her chest under the thin nightshirt she'd slipped on in the early-morning hours.

She felt the beginnings of an erection against her ass.

"Oh no," she said. She freed her hands and rolled off him quickly. "Don't even think about it." She kept rolling in an attempt to escape the bed. "We aren't starting that again." She'd almost made it to the edge when a large, heavy body landed right on her back. "Umph." She wiggled underneath him, but there was no going anywhere.

"It's your fault," he murmured in her ear. "You're the one who bought a Costco-size box of condoms."

"It wasn't a challenge to see how many we could use in one night!" She put her hands flat on the mattress and pushed. She tried to gain some leverage with her knees, but it didn't work. She just ended up grinding her ass against his groin.

"Look at you, teasing me even now," he chided in her ear. "You know how I feel about this ass." He rocked into her.

A certain part of her went hot and wet at that, but that same part needed to calm the fuck down. There would be no more sex for a few days…a day…a few hours, at least. "I'm sore as hell," she told him.

His weight was gone off of her in an instant. He dropped on the bed next to her. "You're sore?"

She turned her head to look at him.

His forehead was furrowed. He was greatly displeased by this information.

"I don't know what else I could be," she grumbled. "You worked me over like a double batch of sourdough."

The furrow deepened, and his shoulders tightened. "Did I hurt you?" He radiated concern.

Everything in her went soft and mushy. "No," she said, reaching up for him and pulling his head down until it was flat on the mattress right next to hers. She stared into his eyes. "You'd never hurt me." She kissed him on the tip of his nose. "No seas tonto."

"It's not dumb." His tone and face were serious. "I hurt you before."

She knew he was referring to their past and how his rejections had wounded her. "That was then. This is now."

He smiled. "You're right. Everything is different now." He leaned in and kissed her forehead. "Come on. Let's shower and get ready. I have somewhere to take you." He tossed the sheet to the side and made to get up.

Kamilah eyed his impressive and very primed package. "About that," she began, only for him to cut her off.

"Don't you worry about that." He stood and gestured to his erection. "He will just need to keep his shit together until you're ready."

That was what he thought, but he didn't know what she

had in mind for their shower. The rest of her body might have been sore, but her mouth certainly wasn't.

An hour and a half later, a smug Kamilah sashayed out of the front door with a very happy Liam on her tail. She walked up to his big black pickup truck. "Where are we going?"

Liam pulled his keys out of his pocket and hit the button to unlock. "I'm not telling you."

Kamilah stopped right at the front of his truck. "Then I'm not going."

"Oh you're going, even if I have to shove you in the car."

She pointed at him. "That's called kidnapping, and it's exactly why women don't just go with guys to surprise locations."

He gave her a look. "Really? You think I'm going to lock you in my secret lair? Or is it that you don't like surprises unless you're the one delivering them?"

Definitely option two. Growing up with four older brothers taught her to be very wary of males promising fun surprises. Such situations had ended up with her grossed out, scared, embarrassed, angry, or some mixture of the previously stated. But Liam had never been like them. He'd always been too serious for those types of pranks. "Fine," she said. "But the next time I spring some activity on you, you don't get to be all pissy about it."

"Can't wait," he said in a dry tone. "Now, let's go."

Twenty minutes later, Kamilah sat up in her seat. "We're leaving the city?" she asked as she watched Liam take the exit toward Milwaukee.

"Yeah."

She turned to him with puppy-dog eyes. "Can you please tell me where we're going?"

Liam shook his head once. "Nope."

She huffed and plopped back in her seat. "Can I at least put some music on, since it seems we are going all the way to Wisconsin?"

"We aren't going that far north, but sure." Liam used his free hand to push up the sleeve of his dark gray Henley and then switched to push up the other sleeve.

Kamilah nearly whimpered at the sight. *Seriously, it should be illegal for men with corded forearms to wear their long sleeves like that.* To cover her leering, she leaned forward and hit the button to turn on the radio. The sounds of Radiohead's "Creep" poured out of the speakers, and she laughed. "Seriously? We were like ten when this music was cool." She laughed again.

"I like nineties alternative rock, no big deal. I mean, it's no Aventura or Daddy Yankee, but it does the trick."

"Hey, don't pigeonhole me. I listen to all kinds of music from all different decades. I probably know the songs they play on here." To prove her point, when "Basket Case" played next, she sang along with Green Day.

They drove along in silence for a while, listening to music and watching the city disappear into the suburbs and eventually into sparsely populated farmlands. The silence wasn't awkward at all. It felt wonderfully normal.

When Liam exited the freeway, Kamilah stopped singing Red Hot Chili Peppers and looked around in interest. "Liam?"

"Yes?"

"I have two theories. You're either going to murder me and bury my body in a field, or we're going to a pumpkin farm."

"Well, there is a wheelbarrow, some rope, and a shovel in the bed of my truck. I hope you enjoyed your life."

Completely unconcerned about being murdered, Kamilah smiled and clapped. "I love pumpkin farms." She turned in her seat and began talking a mile a minute while gesturing wildly with her hands. "How did you find it? Is this like a *farm* farm or one of those pimped-out farms with hayrides, corn mazes, and haunted houses and stuff? I hope it's a pimped-out one. I love doing all the Halloween stuff."

"I drove past it the other day when I was picking up some barrels from a winery. And considering you were supposed to be born on Halloween, your preoccupation with the holiday is understandable."

October 31 was Kamilah's original due date, but Mami hadn't wanted her daughter to be born on the devil's day. She'd fussed until she convinced the doctor to do an early C-section under the guise of also wanting to get her tubes tied. Yes, her mother was *that* extra.

However, not being born on All Hallows' Eve never negatively impacted her love of the season. "Sofi always tells me I turn into a Basic Becky as soon as fall rolls around."

Liam laughed. "You have been drinking a lot of pumpkin-spice lattes, and you do own a lot of leggings, boots, flannels, and circle scarves."

She was, in fact, wearing leggings, boots, a flannel button-down, and an infinity scarf at that very moment. Not to mention slouchy socks and a puffy vest. If it weren't for the fact that she'd just washed and styled her curls, she would probably also be wearing a beanie. She was pretty much #BasicBitchFallEdition. "I don't care. Fall is the best. Scarves and boots are awesome. I live for anything pumpkin-spice, and if that makes me basic, then so be it. Also, you're basic too, because whose flannels do you think I've been wearing?"

"You've been wearing my clothes?" Liam gave her a thorough once-over, before jerking his gaze away and putting it back on the road where it belonged. "Are you wearing my shirt right now?"

She was. It was a green, blue, and black flannel she'd seen him wear numerous times. She loved seeing it on him because it highlighted his pecs. But she couldn't tell how he felt about her borrowing his stuff. She replied hesitantly. "Yes?" She rushed to explain. "Your shirts are longer and thus better for wearing with leggings. Also, for some reason they're softer, and they smell like you, which means I get to smell you even when you aren't around."

He was quiet for a moment. "Come here." His voice was low and gruff but firm.

"Huh? Why?"

Liam didn't bother repeating himself. Instead, he reached over and pulled her in for a deep but too-brief kiss. He pulled back and looked her in the eyes. "I fucking love that you wear my clothes because you want to smell me wherever you are."

I love you.

There they went again. Those three little words trying to jump out of her mouth without her permission. She bit them back. Instead, she murmured, "Well, wait until you find out that I wore your boxer briefs the other day because I forgot to put my wash in the dryer, and now I have no intention of giving them back."

"Don't make me pull this car over."

She pushed him back into his seat. "You better not. You promised me a kick-ass pumpkin farm, and I expect you to deliver. Although," she said, as she read various yard signs and billboards, "I wish you would've told me we were coming to the boonies. I would've straightened my hair and left my jewelry at home." She looked down at her Timberlands. "I would've worn different shoes too."

Liam didn't pretend to misunderstand her concerns over being a brown woman—with big curly hair, even bigger gold hoops, and a nameplate necklace featuring her unusual name—out in an area of the state where the people might not be happy to see her. "Shit. I'm sorry. I was so focused on the surprise, I didn't think. You can use my hat if you want, and I can lock your jewelry up in the glove compartment." He paused. "Of course, turning around is always an option."

They turned on a bend in the road, and the pumpkin farm came into view.

Kamilah couldn't see everything, but this place seemed to check off every fall favorite on her list.

"Do you want to turn around?" Liam asked. "Shit, we're only a few miles from Wisconsin. We can go to Milwaukee if you want. There are some pretty cool distilleries and microbreweries up there."

There were plenty of cars already parked in the small parking lot and along the road. Kamilah could see tons of people meandering around. Her apprehension was greatly reduced when she noted the diverse crowd. Of course, that didn't mean nothing would happen, but at least she wouldn't be the only person of color there.

"No," Kamilah told him. "It's a sunny Saturday afternoon in October, you planned an awesome surprise for me, and I'm going to enjoy it exactly as I am. Let's go."

Liam saluted her. "As you wish." He pulled into the parking lot and paid five dollars for a space.

Enthusiasm firmly back in place, Kamilah barely waited for them to park before she hopped out of his truck. "Ave Maria, I love this." She was bouncing on her toes and knew she was grinning like a fool.

Liam eyed the hordes of families and children with reservation. "God, I hope this place serves alcohol."

Kamilah chuckled. "Let's see." She reached out a hand.

Liam took her hand, interlocked their fingers, and let her lead him to the main entrance.

As they waited in line, Kamilah took in the features she could see. There were various pavilions—some enclosed but many open—as well as a large farmhouse, a small store, and two huge barns. In between the buildings were smaller kiosks and animal enclosures. There was an empty field with a bunch of carnival rides set up on it. Surrounding the main areas were acres of land that appeared to house a large apple orchard, a number of pumpkin patches, and extensive cornfields. It was hard to believe that this mini town was hidden only a few miles from the freeway and only about an hour away from one of the biggest cities in the US.

They made it up to the cash register and chose their entry package, which included two large bags for apple picking, one special sticker for their choice of pumpkin, a punch card for rides, and a roll of food and drink tickets. "It's like if a farm, a state fair, and Six Flags had a baby," Kamilah crowed.

"And almost as expensive." Liam was looking at the small map they'd been given. "They have pig races. Why?" He didn't seem to really want a response because he followed that immediately with "Where to first?"

Did he even know her? "Rides, obviously, then food, then apple- and pumpkin-picking, then more food, then animals, then the farmers' market, and then more food for the road."

Liam pulled his sunglasses from his collar and put them on. "Yeah, I don't do rides, but you have fun with that. I'll drink a beer and watch."

"Since when? We used to go on rides together all the time."

"Since I was eleven," he responded in a monotone.

The accident. Right. Kamilah looked down at their ride punch cards and looked at a family with two older kids sitting a few feet away eating corn on the cob. She walked up to them. "Hi. Do you want these two punch cards? We aren't going to use them."

The woman reached for them gratefully. "Sure. Thank you."

"No problem." Kamilah turned and almost ran smack into Liam.

"You didn't have to give them away," he murmured to her. "I wouldn't have been upset if you went on rides without me."

"I know, but I want to spend time with you, so you pick something."

"Let's hit the orchard and pumpkin patch while everyone else is preoccupied with lunch."

"Sounds good."

A few minutes later, they were seated in a wooden hayride wagon, making their way out to the apple orchard while a worker explained how to find the ripe varieties on the map they were given. Kamilah studied the map and read the descriptions of the different types of apples. "I definitely want to get some Pink Ladies," she told Liam. "They're great for making galettes."

"What's a galette?" Liam leaned closer and looked at her map as if searching for the answer. The arm he had resting along the edge of the wagon fell onto her shoulders.

Kamilah snuggled closer. "It's like a rustic, free-form tart. I'm thinking the judges would love an apple galette with homemade ice cream flavored with your yet-unnamed whiskey and topped with a salted caramel."

"That sounds delicious, but use one of our other whiskeys. That one isn't for public consumption. That's mine alone."

Kamilah's smile faltered. She really thought the flavor profile of that specific whiskey would go best with the galette, but she would figure something else out. She went back to planning her apple-picking strategy.

Liam quickly became a hot commodity in the lanes of apple trees. His height made him the perfect person to reach the biggest apples at the tops of the trees or help someone smaller reach those apples. After a few kids saw Kamilah on his back grabbing a Honeycrisp the size of Liam's fist, it was over. His retrieval or lifting services were requested left and right, but he picked up kids or dug around between branches without complaint. In the end, Kamilah was forced to save him by grabbing his hand while the kids were distracted and quickly ducking between the trees in the middle of the lanes until they found one completely devoid of people. It was devoid of apples too, but she didn't care.

"I think we're safe," she said.

Liam was giving her a funny look. "But at what cost?"

"Huh?"

He smiled. "You have a bunch of twigs and leaves in your hair."

Her hands flew up to her head. "Get them out."

He reached out a hand, snagged her wrist, and pulled her close. Then he started meticulously grooming her. "Tilt your head."

"I feel like a baboon," she grumbled, looking at her feet as he pulled something from the crown of her head. "Stupid trees and nature." She felt his silent chuckle as his chest bumped her head. She wished she could look at him, but he was still pulling stuff from her curls. She could see the small leaves falling to the ground where he released them.

"Are you done picking apples?"

"Yes. I filled both of our bags while you were busy playing Johnny Appleseed."

"Let's go get a pumpkin, then."

"My favorite part!"

"I know." He took the bags with one hand and reached for her free hand with the other.

They decided to just walk to the pumpkin patch instead of waiting for one of the hayride wagons to come back around. A breeze blew through the rows and stirred the fragrant air. It was sweet and sour like the fallen apples coating the ground beneath the trees. In the distance Kamilah could see bright yellow, red, and orange leaves getting blown away from the tall maple trees surrounding the farm. The sunshine was warm on her face, but lovely. Almost as lovely as holding Liam's hand.

She loved that they were there together after so many years.

She didn't want to bring it up, but it was his parents who'd always taken them to the pumpkin farm when they'd been kids. While Kamilah and Liam searched the entire patch for the perfect pumpkin, Connor would stand behind Lori with his chin on her shoulder and watch her sketch the landscape. Then Connor would buy them all the apple cider they wanted and chase them through the corn maze while Lori would laugh and tell them all to be careful. After she and Liam were hopped up on apple cider and cotton candy, they'd pile in Connor's Jeep and drive back to the city. Kamilah and Liam would be giggling in the back seat while Lori and Connor held hands up front.

Kamilah wondered briefly if Lori did the same thing with

her second husband and their daughters. She also wondered if Liam ever regretted their estrangement and not having a relationship with his half sisters. She knew things had got really bad between them during Liam's early teens, but a lot of time had passed since then. Maybe one day she'd ask him, but today wasn't that day. All she wanted to do today was stroll hand in hand with her fiancé and create some new memories, just the two of them.

18

"How much longer?" Liam readjusted the enormous pumpkin in his arms for the fiftieth time. "This thing is heavy."

"I've seen you lift whiskey-filled barrels like they were a gallon of milk," Kamilah said, swinging the bags of apples in her hands. "You can carry my pumpkin for a few more minutes."

That gave Liam an idea. He lifted the pumpkin and rested it on his right shoulder. Much better. Liam heard a dreamy sigh and turned to look at Kamilah.

"It wasn't me," she said, trying to contain the smile that clearly wanted out. "You've gained a fan club." She pushed her sunglasses onto the top of her head and looked to their left.

Liam followed her gaze and saw a group of four young moms with strollers and wagons sneaking glances at him. Actually, only three were sneaking. The fourth one was brazenly looking him up and down. She leaned in and started whispering to her friends, who giggled and nodded along.

Liam felt his face heat. He knew from experience how red his cheeks had gone.

"Oh my God, would you look at those arms. He can carry me around on those broad shoulders anytime. That man is a whole damn snack."

It took him a second to register those words weren't coming from the moms, but from the smart-ass, frizzy-headed woman beside him. He turned toward her with a glare.

Her eyes were wide with mock innocence. "What? I'm just saying what they're thinking."

"If I weren't carrying this pumpkin, I'd push you right into that blueberry bush."

At that, Kamilah lost her ability to keep a straight face. "Poor Liam," she laughed. "Unable to handle a little appreciation from the ladies."

He felt his face flame hotter. "You are seriously asking for it," he rumbled.

She licked her lips as if she liked the sound of that. "What are you gonna do, spank me?"

Oh yes. That. "Don't tempt me."

She moved close enough for her breasts to brush against his chest. "What if I like tempting you?"

Liam bit back a groan. "I'm about two seconds away from dropping this pumpkin, grabbing you, and disappearing into one of these rows of trees. Are you sure you want to continue this game?"

She tilted her head to the side as if she were considering it.

Dear God. If she didn't cut it out, he was going to be sporting some wood of his own in the middle of a family-friendly pumpkin farm. "Kamilah," he growled.

She shot him a cheeky smile and stepped back just as the tractor toting the passenger wagon came around the bend.

They loaded up and made their way back to the main part of the mini fall-themed amusement park. Thankfully Liam was still wearing his sunglasses, because as they bumped along, Liam couldn't help watching Kamilah's boobs bounce.

Back at the pumpkin patch she'd unbuttoned the top half of *his* stolen flannel to reveal a low-cut white tank top.

He could see right down the front of it, and the sight only served to remind him of how he'd had his mouth and hands all over her last night. He found it equal parts unbelievable and predestined.

On the one hand, he couldn't fully comprehend that he and Kamilah had finally had sex. It seemed like another dream from which he'd awaken alone and frustrated. On the other, he knew on a gut level that their getting together was inevitable. Something that fate had in store for them from the beginning. It was like one of those fantasy stories where two people found each other in endless lives throughout time. It couldn't be stopped or changed. But what did that mean? That they were soul mates? *Impossible.*

"Why are you mean-mugging that guy like he owes you money?" Kamilah whispered in his ear.

Liam blinked and gave his head a tiny shake. He looked around and noted that they were almost back at the loading station. "I'm not mean-mugging him. I'm just thinking."

"About what? That you have a mortal enemy to disembowel with your bare hands later?"

He let her see how unamusing he found her. "No, smart-ass. I'm getting hungry." It wasn't a lie per se. The smell of meat grilling and corn roasting was, indeed, making him hungry.

They came to a stop behind another tractor.

"I forgot how hangry you get." Kamilah gathered their

bags of apples. "Let's eat. I'd hate for you to make some poor kid cry with that scowl."

Liam picked up the pumpkin that was between his feet and put it back on his shoulder. He followed Kamilah off the wagon and through the crowd. Someone squeezed past Liam so close he felt the back of his shirt move. He threw a disgruntled look over his shoulder. This place was way too crowded. "Can we get drinks now?"

Kamilah reached into a penned-in storage area and grabbed the scratched handle of a beat-up and faded red Radio Flyer wagon. "Yes, Mr. Antisocial, we can go get your peopling medicine now." She placed the bags of apples into the wagon, and Liam placed the pumpkin next to them.

The café was right around the corner and included simple fare like roasted corn, burgers, hot dogs, and sausages. Kamilah ordered a hot dog, fall sangria, and a six-pack of warm apple cider doughnuts, while Liam opted for a bison burger, a bag of jalapeño kettle chips, and beer. They went outside and sat on some conveniently placed haystacks to eat.

"I can't believe that I bring you to a place with fresh bison burgers and you eat a hot dog." Liam shook his head in mock sadness.

Kamilah swallowed a sip of sangria. "I didn't want to get a lot, because I plan on eating all of these award-winning apple cider doughnuts."

"Well, let's see if these doughnuts live up to the hype." He reached over and snagged one out of the paper tray.

"Hey, I didn't say you could have one!" She made to snatch it out of his hand.

He popped the entire thing in his mouth.

"You're supposed to savor it, not swallow it whole, you Hungry Hungry Hippo."

"Meh. It's okay," he said around a mouthful.

She glared at him and turned her back to him. "Then eat your own food."

"It's more fun to eat yours."

"Not if you want to continue living," she shot over her shoulder.

Liam chuckled. "And you called me hangry." But he kept his hands on his own food.

When they were done, they disposed of their trash and made their way toward the farmers' market.

He spent the next hour trailing Kamilah as she wandered from stall to stall scooping up butternut squash, acorn squash, spaghetti squash, eggplant, pepper jelly, regular jelly, yams, veggies, and just about every variation of honey. He listened as she chatted in Spanish with the only Latinx vendor there and they made plans to meet and discuss a possible partnership with El Coquí.

Once they moved on, Liam took a look around to make sure no one was paying them any mind. "Can I ask you something?"

"Okay. Sure." She picked up a burlap-sack couch pillow with *Pumpkin-Spice Everything* embroidered on it in glittery thread and put it in the wagon.

"Why have you never left El Coquí?"

She spun to face him. She didn't speak. She just looked at him in surprise and a little confusion.

"I know you want to keep the family tradition going, but I always felt like there was more to it than that," he explained. "I mean, why else put up with so much shit from your family when you could've easily gotten a job in a kitchen somewhere else?"

Kamilah pulled some cash from her pocket and handed it

to the vendor. She waved away the offer of change, and they started walking toward the exit. "I don't know if you remember this, but I wanted to leave. I planned to go to school in France."

"I remember. When you didn't get in, you decided to stay at home and go to Kennedy-King."

They walked out the exit of the farmers' market with a wagon overfull of goodies. Kamilah turned and led him in the direction of the parking lot. She wouldn't meet his gaze. Eventually, she let out a deep sigh. "Yeah. I've never told *anyone* this, but that's not really true."

Liam stopped walking. "What do you mean?"

Kamilah stopped as well. She turned in his direction but still wouldn't look at him. "I was accepted. I even won the Julia Child Scholarship. I rejected the offer because Abuela's cancer was back, and I was needed at home."

Hold on. What? "You gave up a full-ride scholarship to your dream school?"

"What else was I supposed to do? Just leave? It was bad enough that I—" She cut herself off.

"That you what?"

She was quiet for so long that he didn't think she was going to answer. Finally, she threw her shoulders back and faced him. "It's bad enough that I was mad at her for being sick." She stared at him in a challenge, as if daring him to say something.

Liam wasn't going to say anything. He was all too familiar with being mad at someone for dying.

"Did you know she constantly forgot to take her meds?" Kamilah continued. "I was always finding them still in her pill case after I would spend an hour organizing them all for her. And when it was time to go get a checkup scan, she'd say, 'Estoy bien y hay demasiado que hacer.'" She mimicked her grandmother's voice perfectly. She crossed her arms and held on to her biceps as if hugging herself, "When it came back worse than before, I was mad at her. When I sent that email to Le Cordon Bleu in Paris rejecting their offer, I was pissed. When she asked me to promise that I would do everything in my power to keep El Coquí going after she was gone, I was seething." Kamilah shook her head and let out a bark of unamused laughter. "How messed up is that? My grandmother, the woman who taught me everything I knew, the woman I idolized, was dying, and I was mad at her as if she'd done it on purpose."

"Kamilah, you were eighteen years old."

"Exactly!" She threw up her hands. "I was an adult, and I was basically having a temper tantrum that I wasn't getting my way. It was wrong, and it was selfish." Her voice broke on the last word. "*Familia primero.* I cut my teeth on that saying. I did my best to uphold it, but I failed when it mattered most. When I was supposed to really prove that I knew the meaning, I proved that I was more worried about myself." She worked her lips and closed her eyes.

Liam could see the unshed tears when she opened them again.

"You want to know why I'm dedicated to El Coquí? It's because I remember how horrible it felt to be truly ashamed of myself, to not be who my family raised me to be, and I never want to feel that way again. I promised her that I would do whatever it took, and I won't fail her. Not this time."

Liam could only stare at her, completely dumbfounded. Of all the things she could've said, this was the least expected. "Mila." He walked over to her and tilted her chin up with his forefinger. "Of course you were upset about giving up on your dream. That doesn't make you selfish. That makes you human. You don't have to be a magnanimous superhero to deserve your family's love and respect. You just have to be yourself."

"I know that's how it should be, but it doesn't feel that way. I feel like I let everyone down so much more than anyone else when I stumble. Like my mistakes are remembered more and judged harder. I feel like I can't say no and have that be enough."

He pulled her into his arms. He didn't know what to tell her, because he'd seen the family dynamic in action. He knew what she meant, but he also thought a lot of it was because of the position she'd put herself in. That didn't seem like a helpful thing to say, though. She'd just opened up to him and told him her deepest, darkest secret. He wasn't about to repay that by belittling her feelings. Instead, he shared a secret of his own. "I'm still pissed at my dad. It's been twenty years, and I'm still fucking mad at him."

"For dying?"

"For killing himself. He took off his life vest. He couldn't swim. But he took it off anyway."

Kamilah looked at him as if she could see right into his very soul. "Oh, Liam." She dropped a kiss on his chest, right over his heart. "I'm so sorry."

Thankfully she left it at that.

"Have you ever regretted giving up the scholarship and the opportunity to leave?" he asked after a few moments of just holding her.

"In the beginning I was mad and disappointed and hurt. I think that was one of the reasons I got in so deep and fast with Chase, even though I knew he wasn't the one for me. I just wanted a dream to replace the one I'd given up. But now

I can honestly say that I don't regret it. Do I sometimes fanta-
size about what might have been? Sure. Especially when Leo
is really pissing me off, my parents refuse to listen to me, or
they talk about selling El Coquí to the highest bidder. I just
think *Ah, if I were in Paris, I wouldn't have to deal with this shit*."

"But?"

"But if I had gone, I'd have missed out on those last months
with Abuela, which are the hardest yet most rewarding memories I have of her. If I'd gone, I wouldn't have been able to
build the relationship I now have with Abuelo. I wouldn't
have been here when Saint lost his wife and brought Rosie
home because he needed our help. I wouldn't have been here
to get to know your grandfather in a deeper way. I wouldn't
have reconnected with you. There are so many moments
that I treasure that I would never have experienced. I choose
to focus on that. On what is here and real. Not what might
have been."

That was a good motto. Something he wished he could
follow but didn't think he could. "You are an incredible person, do you know that?"

She looked up at him.

"I mean it," he told her. "Your optimism and your dedication to the people you love is unlike that of anyone else
I've ever met."

She lifted up and pecked him on the mouth. "Thank you.
I think you're incredible too."

"Tell Granda that for me, will you? He's been on my ass
about not doing things right while he's recovering."

Kamilah laughed.

The reaction he'd been looking for.

"I will tell him when we drop off these maple bacon cup-
cakes for him and Abuelo."

They packed all of Kamilah's spoils into the back seat of his truck and then returned the wagon to the designated area. Kamilah picked up a bunch of Halloween cookies for her nieces and nephews and some caramel apples for her friends and family. Then they climbed into Liam's truck and pulled out of the parking lot.

In between feeding them both bites of caramel apple and singing Incubus, Kamilah kept giving him these intense looks he couldn't decipher. "What?" he eventually asked her. "You keep staring at me like I have something on my face."

"I'm sort of annoyed with you."

He frowned. "Why?"

"For being sweet and sexy and considerate and all-around amazing. I wasn't supposed to think these things about you. I wasn't supposed to feel this way. That wasn't part of the deal." She paused. "It was unfair of you to make me fall in love with you."

Fall in love with him? Kamilah loved him? Liam's chest squeezed so hard that he couldn't tell if it was pleasure or pain. He didn't know what to say to her confession, especially because she didn't sound very happy about it. She said she was annoyed with him. Did that mean that she didn't want to feel that way about him? He opened his mouth to ask her if she meant it, but then a piano started playing the familiar intro to a famous power ballad.

Just like that, he was plunged into numbing cold.

Liam hated this fucking song—his dad's favorite. Da would tell Liam to play the air drums while he played the air guitar and belted out, "I would do anything for love, but I won't do that."

It was the very song that had played when a drunken idiot on a Jet Ski capsized their skiff. It was the same fucking song that had continued to play from his dad's brand-new water-proof portable stereo while he'd been crying and begging his dad not to leave.

Liam's hands tightened so hard on the wheel he worried he'd snap it right off like a Matchbox car. Whenever Liam heard this song, he was tossed right back into the past.

"Do you see Nana?" Da asked.

Liam shook his head.

"Stay here," Da told him, while fiddling with the buckles on his life jacket.

"What are you doing?" Liam cried. "Put that back on." He knew Da couldn't swim. It was supposed to be a secret, but Liam knew.

"I won't be able to go under with this thing on. Don't worry. I'm just going to take a quick look."

"No," Liam cried. He knew his eyes were wet from tears and not water.

"I will be right back. I pro—" Da stopped. He must have decided not to insult them both with more lies.

"Please," Liam whispered. "Please, Da…don't go."

Da wiped a big hand over his face. "I have to. When I send Nana up, I'm going to send her up right here. I want you to grab her, but I don't want you to get off the boat."

"Da—"

"Promise me, Liam."

"But—"

"Promise me," he shouted at Liam.

"Okay," Liam was startled into replying.

"Be ready to grab her," he said. Then he grabbed Liam hard by the back of his neck and placed a cold wet kiss on his forehead. "I love you, son. So much." He pushed off the side of the boat and went under.

"Da!" Liam screamed. "Da!" He rolled off the side of the boat

and back into the water. Liam tried and tried to go under after him, but the life jacket wouldn't let him. He grabbed on to the straps and tried to undo the buckles, but his frozen fingers wouldn't work. "Come on," Liam gritted out. "Come on. Come on."

He heard a splash behind him and spun around. He immediately recognized Nana's gray hair and blue jacket. "Nana," Liam exclaimed, swimming over to her. She was facedown in the water. He turned her over. Her face was white, but her lips were blue. He lifted Nana's head and put it on his shoulder, hoping that it might help her breathe.

Liam began to frantically look around. He was looking for anything. Any sign of where Da might be—a flash of his green jacket, a splash of water, air bubbles, anything.

There was nothing.

The ironic part was, after Liam was rescued, the coast guard said only eleven and a half minutes had passed from the time their boat capsized to when the guard arrived. They said it as if they couldn't understand how so much had gone wrong in such a small amount of time—Liam in shock, Nana brain-dead, Da just dead.

Eleven and a half minutes.

This stupid fucking bullshit love song was a full thirty seconds longer.

Whenever Liam heard it, he took that extra thirty seconds to remind himself of how his dad left on a suicide mission after claiming to love him, how Nana didn't come back despite loving him, and how his mother abandoned him after saying she loved him so much she would do anything for him. At the end of the day, none of them had loved him enough.

Unable to take another second of the torture, Liam reached over and shut off the stereo. Kamilah shot him a questioning look, but Liam ignored her. He continued to do so for the rest of the drive home, because love was bullshite, and Liam couldn't trust it.

19

Abuelo looked around and gave a subtle nod. "I like how this is turning out."

Kamilah had to agree. In just two weeks they'd managed to completely overhaul the dining area, and it was all due to her cousins' genius.

Gabi and Alex had come up with a design that was cheap, relatively simple, and brought the feeling of Viejo San Juan right into the middle of Humboldt Park, Chicago. The hammocks that hung from the ceiling were removed. Gone were the tiki huts over the bar, stage, and booths. Even the booths were gone. In their place Saint and Alex had made a long padded wooden bench. Those changes alone opened the space immeasurably.

Her cousins had come up with the idea of making the interior reflect the exterior of the historical homes in Old San Juan, so they'd painted the walls a warm terra-cotta, while all the molding received a fresh coat of white paint. The old blinds and curtains had been removed from the arched windows to install custom-made (by Saint and Alex) walnut shutters that matched the bar, which had been sanded and refinished along with the rest of the wooden surfaces.

They'd run into the issue of some large cracks and chunks of missing wall, thanks to the removal of the tiki hut behind the stage. It would've meant a complete demo and rebuild of the wall, but then Saint had the idea to fill the spots with concrete for safety, cover them with Spackle, and then create fake shuttered windows to cover the places their repairs were still visible. All they'd had to do was purchase more molding to outline the faux windows and hang the shutters. It looked so cool they'd decided to do the same thing on the other side of the restaurant where they'd removed the booths.

Kamilah had to hand it to her oldest brother: he might not have agreed with her insistence on trying to save the restaurant, but he was the first one to show up ready to work when it came time to get things done. He'd added input and know-how that solidified Kamilah's vision and an authoritative approach for issuing instructions that made the whole endeavor go smoothly.

Kamilah stretched long and hard. Her arms and lower back seized in pain. *Shit.* The long hours of renovations had her feeling like an old woman. She looked around to see if anyone else seemed to be having the same problem. Leo, Sofi, and Alex seemed fine. So did Mami and Papi. The only two people who looked as weary as she felt were Abuelo and Rosie. *Well, damn.* Kamilah apparently had the same amount of stamina as an eighty-year-old and a four-year-old.

Then again, she'd spent most of the night having vigorous sex. That certainly had to play a role in how exhausted she was. But Liam had been right there with her, and she didn't see any lag in his stride when he entered the restaurant via the tall repurposed wooden shutters they'd made into the new swinging doors of the kitchen.

He and Saint were carrying a large thin box. "It's here," he told her.

Kamilah squealed, all traces of pain and exhaustion gone. She rushed over to where they were carefully lowering the box onto the huge island table that had undergone a make-over of its own. It too had been stripped, sanded, stained, and finished so it was no longer painted like the flag but matched the bar and the shutters. "Open it. Open it." She shook Saint's arm in emphasis.

"¿Qué es?" Mami asked, coming up behind her and look-ing over her shoulder. It had taken a few days for her to come around, but Kamilah could safely say that Mami was cau-tiously on board.

At least with the redesign. The food part was still a tug-of-war.

"It's the art I was telling you about." She'd been putzing around on Etsy while sitting on the toilet—as one did—when she'd come across this gorgeous tile mosaic from an artist in Puerto Rico. She'd bought it in a heartbeat. "I want to put it behind the bar where the mirror was."

"That wasn't my fault," Leo grumbled.

Sofi scoffed.

It had totally been his fault for flipping the hammer around like a baton twirler, but Kamilah didn't care anymore because she had the perfect thing to replace it. This piece would be the first thing anyone saw when they walked in the door.

Everyone crowded around the table as Saint pulled out his box cutter and sliced through the tape. Then he stepped aside and motioned for Kamilah to do the honors.

She pulled back the flaps of the box and then removed the thick slab of Styrofoam that covered it. After that she peeled back a thin sheet of foam.

The piece was a large rectangle made up of green-blue tiles of different shades to represent the water. In the middle, the main island and the smaller ones surrounding it were made with pieces of tiles in shades of tan, beige, and taupe. The words *Yo soy de aquí como el coquí* were in the upper-right corner of the island with black tile. The middle and bottom-right were covered with the beautiful tile rendering of a coquí sitting on a Flor de Maga, the cousin to the hibiscus and the official flower of Puerto Rico.

Kamilah put a hand to her chest, Mami gasped, and other appreciative noises sounded all around her.

"It's perfect."

Kamilah startled a bit to hear her own thoughts reflected out loud. She looked up and met Papi's gaze across the table.

"It's perfect," he repeated. His eyes were suspiciously shimmering.

Kamilah's own eyes became wet. It was the first truly positive thing he'd said. He'd been mostly going along with the plan silently but with a definite lack of enthusiasm. "You like it?" she asked. She wasn't just asking about the artwork.

Papi nodded. "It's different, but it's still us."

A tear almost escaped out of the corner of her eye, but Liam's thumb caught it. She turned so her cheek was cupped in his hand.

He was looking at her with pride and affection, like she'd just accomplished the most incredible feat. As if she'd just painted his name on the sun.

Kamilah's own pride and happiness were dampened a bit as her continued confusion flared. She just didn't get him.

Everything pointed to the fact that he loved her. The way

he looked at her, talked to her, touched her. He couldn't keep his hands off her, really. Yet he didn't say the words. Hell, he still hadn't even acknowledged her declaration.

What did that mean? Was it fake to him? Still?

"I never thought I would say this, but I really like it, princesita," Leo blurted loudly. He slapped Kamilah on the back so hard she jerked forward.

She broke her eye contact with Liam and spun to punch him in the chest in retaliation.

Leo shot her a disgruntled look and rubbed his pec. "I mean it," he continued. "I think it looks classy. Maybe now more of the hot hipster girls moving in the neighborhood will stop by, and you know what that means." He rubbed his hands together and waggled his eyebrows.

"Cochino." Mami smacked him upside the head.

"Oww, Ma. I meant more customers." He paused and smirked. "And if one of them looks good enough, maybe she'll provide you with another grandbaby," he joked before leaping out of her immediate range.

Mami grabbed the rag from her shoulder and swiped at him. "Mira, no seas atrevido porque te meto una pela."

Kamilah couldn't remember how many times she'd heard Mami threaten Leo to stop being bold before he caught a beatdown. Yet Leo still loved to push buttons. Apparently, beating the boldness out of him didn't work.

"God help the woman you ever get pregnant," Sofi told him. "She'll end up dealing with two babies."

"Please, women beg me for my—"

"Leo." Saint cut him off and gave a purposeful nod in Rosie's direction.

Her four-year-old niece was soaking everything in like an enthusiastic sponge.

"I'm just saying," Leo continued. "Who wouldn't want a baby with these eyes?" He put the back of his fingers under his chin and fluttered his eyelashes like an old-timey coquette.

"There is no guarantee that your kid would inherit your eyes, idiot," Sofi said. "But I wouldn't expect the dude who failed biology three times to understand genetics."

"You only passed because you seduced Jesus Rios into being your lab partner and doing all your work for you."

"False, sir. I passed because I didn't skip class to smoke Black & Milds in the parking lot and make out with Jessica Rodriguez in the girls' locker room."

"Correct me if I'm wrong, but weren't you the one who was always getting detentions for—and I quote—" Leo held up his hands to make air quotes "—*excessive and inappropriate public displays of affection* with your boo, Raul Baez?"

Kamilah felt a tap on her shoulder.

"I have to get back to the distillery," Liam told her. "I left Granda unsupervised."

As expected, Killian was a terrible patient who kept trying to rush his recovery. Just the other day she had caught him trying to lift a crate of full bottles while Liam's back was turned. He wasn't even supposed to lift a gallon of milk.

"Go, go," she said, shooing him out.

He placed a kiss on her forehead and disappeared through the swinging doors.

In her back pocket her phone started to vibrate. She pulled it out and saw her call was coming from the office of the Fall Foodie Tour coordinators. She dipped out the front door while everyone was still distracted by Sofi and Leo's ongoing argument.

"Kamilah, it's Samantha. I'm glad I got a hold of you right away." Samantha was one of the coordinators of the tour.

Every time Kamilah talked to her, she was equal parts friendly and perky.

Kamilah's pulse picked up. "Why? Is something wrong?" *Dear Sweet Baby Jesus, please let nothing be wrong.* She had just made some major headway with her family. She didn't want to have to go give them some bad news.

"Nothing is wrong per se," Samantha drawled. "In fact, this may be good news for you, since I noticed you're doing some renovations. That's why we thought it best to pick El Coquí."

"Pick El Coquí for what?"

"Some things came up, and we had to do some shuffling around. A lot of the other businesses have already started promoting their tour date, so it didn't seem right to move theirs."

"We aren't kicked off the tour, are we?"

"Oh it's nothing like that," Samantha said quickly. "We just have to push back your tour-stop date."

That could work to their benefit. "That shouldn't be a problem," Kamilah assured her. "We'll make any date work. We're happy to accommodate."

"I love when people are flexible," Samantha said. "Your new date is November seventeenth."

Kamilah's stomach dropped. She prayed she'd heard wrong. "Saturday, November seventeenth?"

"Yes." There was a pause. "That's not going to be a problem, is it?"

Kamilah tried to think of a way to say that yes, there was a problem with that date because she'd promised her fake fiancé, who she was in very real love with, that she would help him wow the judges at his own very important event taking place on the same day.

"Look." Samantha's voice was no longer friendly and perky. "The truth is that your family restaurant is lucky to be included. You didn't submit your paperwork on time, and you're technically not even open right now, which very nearly violates our policy. If this date change is going to be a problem, then maybe you should hold off on entering El Coquí until next year."

In other words, you do it when we say or not at all.

"There's no problem," Kamilah blurted out. "Like you said, this works in our favor, and we're very grateful for how flexible you all have been."

Samantha's voice was back to perky. "Great! I'm glad to hear that. We'll see you on the seventeenth, then."

"Yup. The seventeenth." Kamilah gave a half-hearted goodbye, spun around, and proceeded to bang her head on the small bit of brick between two of the restaurant's windows. She said every curse word she could think of in both English and Spanish.

What was she going to do?

There was no way she would pull El Coquí from the tour now. Not after all the work she'd done and not after finally getting Papi on board. He'd be pissed and would demand that Abuelo sell.

But she'd promised Liam she would help him. She'd been adamant about wanting to support him. She knew how difficult it was for him to trust anyone, but he was giving her the chance to prove that he could trust her. Their relationship was already a clusterfuck of contradictions; she couldn't back out on him. He would completely shut down on her if she did.

Her mind raced so hard and fast that it was impossible to think of any solution at all. She needed time. That was all. She would come up with something. She just had to give herself the chance to sort it out. Until then, she would keep quiet, because she wouldn't be able to concentrate with her family's opinions in her ears, and she couldn't risk Liam pushing her away.

20

"Leo." Giggle. "Cut it out." Giggle, giggle. Gasp.

Liam grimaced but kept his eyes firmly on the shitty action movie playing on his TV. He had no idea what was going on in the plot or if there was even a plot to begin with. All he knew was that he absolutely did not want to know what Drogon the dragon was doing with Daenerys Targaryen at the other end of Liam's brand-new couch. He took another large swallow of whiskey from his glass. The night hadn't even truly begun, and it was already a pain in his ass.

The only thing he could imagine that was worse than clubbing was clubbing in a fucking Halloween costume. He had to suck it up, though, because it was Kamilah's birthday and that was what she wanted to do. According to Sofi, it was tradition. As was showing up at ten in the morning to kidnap Kamilah for a day of pampering and day drinking, thus ruining all of Liam's plans. But hey, he'd been welcome to join them for dinner before coming back to his place to get ready and pregame. That was good enough, right?

Wrong.

For days Liam had known that there was something wrong with Kamilah, and he'd planned to use the day to find out what it was. It wasn't just that Liam hadn't said anything when she'd claimed to love him.

He knew he'd fucked up by not responding to her declaration. He should've said something. *Anything.* He shouldn't have shut down after hearing Da's favorite song, but sometimes he couldn't help it. The past would just creep up on him and drag him back. It always took him a few days to return to the present, to be able to look at things through a healthier lens. By the time that had happened, she'd already been in the thick of the most strenuous renovations and acting like she'd never said anything. They still talked, kissed, touched, fucked as if that whole car ride had never happened. And because he was a coward, he let it continue.

But something else had happened after that, because she'd started avoiding him. He hadn't spent fifteen years avoiding things without learning to recognize the signs. She had gone back to leaving before he woke up and was asleep by the time he came to bed. Her many random, rambling text messages throughout the day had trickled down to a few sparsely worded texts and sometimes just an emoji or GIF. Whenever they spoke, she was preoccupied or cagey.

Liam wanted to get to the bottom of it. He wanted to talk to her. To apologize for his response. To tell her that it wasn't that he didn't love her back, it was that love wasn't reliable. It didn't last, but that didn't mean he didn't want her. He did. He wanted her more than he wanted his next breath. He always would.

"Oh my God, Leo," Daenerys whispered. "I can't believe you just said that to me. Dirty boy." Giggle, giggle.

Leo whispered something back that sounded like "You like me dirty."

Son of a bitch.

Before he could fix things with Kamilah, Liam had to pretend like everything was fine for the next few hours and that spending the foreseeable future squished in a loud, smelly club among drunk strangers didn't make him want to hide out on the roof.

The unmistakable sound of kissing was cut off by the doorbell.

Liam never thought he'd be excited by his doorbell ringing, but it was the godsend he didn't know he'd been waiting for. He jumped up eagerly from his spot, squeezed past Leo and his date, and swung his door open with glee. Then he saw who was standing there. "Of all the things you could've picked, you chose a leprechaun?" he asked Ben.

Ben looked Liam up and down and smirked. "Look at you. Ready for your Grecian bondage party, Zeus? I bet you're happy I never let you skip leg day. You look swole, bro." He brushed past Liam.

"I'm Odysseus," he corrected his friend, but Ben wasn't listening.

"Oh by the way, I found these two outside. I figured I should probably invite the vampire in, otherwise he'd be stuck outside." Ben motioned behind him to where Dev and Rome were standing.

They obviously hadn't given much thought to Kamilah's mythical-creature theme. Rome was dressed as Scorpion from *Mortal Kombat*, and Dev, the vampire, was wearing regular street clothes.

"You look like you normally do," Liam told him.

Dev smiled and showed off some of those fake fangs that stuck on with wax.

Liam was standing there in a toga and sandals, and all this guy had on were some fake teeth? "Really, dude?"

Dev shrugged. "My sister told me to do this. She said I look like some actor from that *Originals* show, so people would know who I am."

Liam had no idea what Dev was talking about. "And you?" he asked Rome. "Scorpion is not really a mythical creature."

Rome removed the yellow half mask that covered the bottom half of his face. "I needed something that covered my face but wouldn't get hot."

Liam guessed he could understand that, considering Rome's celebrity.

"Where's the birthday girl?" Ben asked Liam.

He pointed to the second floor, where Beyoncé's *Homecoming* album could be heard blaring. "She's upstairs getting ready with her friends."

"Babe," Ben called. He was rubbing his hands together and smiling mischievously. "Come down here! I have a surprise for you!"

Besides stopping over multiple times a week for dinner at Kamilah's invitation (another way she was avoiding spending alone time with Liam) and proceeding to pick on Liam, Ben had started calling Kamilah *babe*, and she'd reciprocated. *Nails on a chalkboard.*

"Stop fucking calling her *babe*," he growled at his best friend, who just looked at him with an idiotic expression of fake innocence.

"I'm sorry, bro. I had no idea you were so possessive," he said loud enough for everyone to hear, especially Kamilah, who stood at the top of the stairs in an outfit that sucker punched Liam right in the gut. Or perhaps lower. He'd known she was dressing as a siren, matching his Odysseus costume, but he didn't realize he'd need to be tied down to keep his hands off her.

Shouldn't have thought about being tied up.

She wore a pair of mermaid-print leggings with dark tutu-type fabric from the shins down to look like fins. At first glance, the leggings were black, but when she moved, the light hit the pants in such a way they looked like an oil slick with purple, blue, green, pink, yellow, and orange scales. She wore a black corset decorated with netting and what looked like actual seashells, dark pearls, and plastic aquarium plants. It ended at her waist and seemed to only be held up by the generous cleavage threatening to spill out of the top.

Her long curls hung down in thick heavy ropes that still looked wet. She wore a big seashell, coral, and starfish head-band like a crown. Sofi had managed to transform the soft, tan skin on her forehead and cheekbones into iridescent scales that matched the colors of her leggings and her eye makeup. They had glued dark pearls, gems, and even a small starfish to her eyebrow and temple area. Her succulent lips were painted a dark purple that brought to mind juicy plums.

She looked naughty and alluring. The ultimate bad girl.

Liam shifted on his feet, suddenly wishing he weren't wearing a fucking lightweight toga.

"Where's my surprise?" she asked Ben as she clicked down the stairs in a pair of sky-high heels.

He held out his arms. "It's a birthday kiss from yours truly."

Liam was tempted to punch his friend in the junk. "You're a dick," he murmured to him right before Kamilah reached the bottom and threw her arms around Ben.

She kissed Ben's cheek, not leaving a mark by some sort of dark makeup magic. "That's the only kiss you'll get from me."

"You're breaking my heart, babe," Ben told her.

"Babe, I'm one hundred percent sure that you'll get over it." Kamilah turned to Dev and Rome to greet them with cheek kisses and questions about whether they were hungry. "Are you sure? I can whip something up really quick."

"Ain't nobody got time for you to be making meals, Giada." Sofi made her way down the stairs while fixing the foot-long gold glitter unicorn horn on the top of her head. Her unicorn costume consisted of a tight white holographic bodysuit with a big fluffy tail made out of pastel rainbow tutu fabric. Her tail matched her wig and the shiny makeup on her face. Her white platform boots made her almost as tall as him.

Liam saw Rome's eyes nearly fall out of his head.

Poor kid. He had no idea that Kamilah's best friend was a certified man-eater who was more likely to break his heart than hand over her own.

Kamilah stuck her tongue out at her best friend, and Sofi made a grab for it with her clawlike nails. Kamilah moved her head away. "Sofi, meet Liam's friends. Ben, the leprechaun, Devon, the CW vampire, and Roman, the best video-game character of my childhood. Guys, this rude hoochiecorn is Sofia." A lizard-like alien creature walked down behind Sofi. "And this is my cousin Lucia."

"Can I ask something?" Dev asked Lucy after the introductions were made.

Lucy sidled up next to Dev and fluttered her eyelashes at him, which looked creepy, considering her blackout contacts. "You can ask me whatever you want, Marcel."

Dev gave a small side smile but didn't comment. "What are you?"

"I am a pleasantly plump, bisexual, Puerto Rican woman," she said, putting a strong emphasis on the word *bisexual.* "But if you're asking about my costume—" she struck a pose with her hip out "—I'm the Chupacabra."

Dev gave a somewhat nervous laugh. "What is a Chupacabra?"

"The Chupacabra is a Puerto Rican mythical creature that kills livestock," Lucy told him. She walked her blackish-green clawlike fingers up his arm. "Oddly enough, it's kind of like a vampire because it drains their blood."

"Which is how it got the name *Goat Sucker,*" Eliza finished. She stood at the top of the stairs with a large drink in her hand. "And don't let my wife fool you with her outrageous flirting. She's crazy in love with me, the goat." She gestured to her outfit, which was basically a pair of footie pajamas with a cartoon goat face, floppy ears, and small curved horns on the hood. She looked both cute and comfortable, and Liam was jealous he couldn't have worn pajamas.

Lucy toasted her wife with her drink and blew her a kiss before turning back to Dev. "As soon as Kamilah decided on the mythical-creature theme, I knew what I wanted to do. I have to rep my people, you know." She turned and showed him the hand-sized Puerto Rican flag on the right butt cheek of her skintight bodysuit.

"Okay, well, that's enough of that." Kamilah grabbed Lucy's arm, muttered something about too many edibles, and started dragging her toward the couch. "Let's order these Ubers and get out of here."

Liam started to emit a put-out groan but stopped as soon as she looked at him. He brought his glass to his mouth and took a deep swallow.

"No need," Ben said. "Since I figured you wouldn't run

away with me tonight, I got us a way to travel in a large stylish group. That's your real birthday surprise."

Ben made bank as a sports agent who represented not only his wide-receiver cousin but a bunch of other top athletes, including a highly decorated Olympic gymnast and one of the best pitchers in the MLB. As such, he liked to throw his money around. It was all part of the suave, flirtatious, and confident GQ-model persona.

Please don't let it be a limo. Anything but a limo.

It was worse. It was a party bus complete with a fully stocked bar, strobe lights, and a stripper pole.

"Aw, shit," Lucy said. "We are about to party like Paris Hilton and Nicole Richie circa 2003."

They piled into the bus. Shots of tequila were distributed.

Liam accepted his with a grimace. He and tequila were not friends.

"To Kamilah's Dirty Thirty," Sofi toasted.

Dirty Thirty! was cheered, shots were slammed, and the party began in earnest.

The collective group was about three or four shots in by the time they pulled up to the club where Kamilah's youngest uncle, a DJ of international renown, was throwing his annual Halloween bash. They joined Gio and more of Kamilah's cousins in the elevated VIP section next to the DJ booth.

"You made it just in time," he told them after all the greetings were given. "I go on in twenty minutes." He was shouting to be heard over the hip-hop bumping so loud Liam could feel the bass in his bones.

"You're gonna do it up right for the birthday girl, right, Gio?" Sofi shouted.

He smiled. "Just be ready to get turnt." At only thirty-seven, Giovante was more like one of the cousins than an uncle, and it showed in the way he was always ready to participate in his nieces' and nephews' wildness instead of curbing it.

Liam watched everyone yell conversation at each other as they mixed drinks from the juices, sodas, and bottles of high-end liquor at the table. He spotted a bottle of Four Roses Single Barrel and snatched it before anyone else could claim it, since it was the only passable alcohol present. He decanted an extremely generous pour into a tall glass and dropped in a few pieces of ice. He took a drink and savored the bourbon. Maybe this wouldn't be as bad as her prom. He would just sit back, sip on his drink, and watch everyone else make asses of themselves.

Taking the bottle with him, he made his way over to the empty velvet high-backed chair next to where Rome sat on the low backless couch chatting with Kamilah's cousin Ricky and his girlfriend. He did a quick scan of the area but didn't see Kamilah. His eyes quickly found Leo and Daenerys—Liam really should've remembered her real name—grinding in the corner. As a matter of fact, everywhere he looked couples were grinding. Ben had already found a vintage pinup girl to dance on, and Dev was making flirty conversation with a sexy Disney princess. Still no Kamilah. He looked down into the sea of bodies on the dance floor and found her instantly.

Sofi held Kamilah's hand up in the air as she maneuvered them through the crowd. The rest of the crew followed behind them, their drinks in the air to prevent getting them spilled. They made their way to the front, where some club employees were dancing on a short stage while Gio stood a few feet above mixing pop, hip-hop, reggaeton, and dancehall. A triple air-horn blast announced the beginning of a new song, and Kamilah's Dirty Thirty crew let out a scream of excitement and immediately started rapping along in Spanish. Kamilah slammed the rest of her drink, passed the empty cup to someone, and then started dancing.

Liam immediately understood that this wasn't going to be anything like Kamilah's prom. It was going to be much worse. As wild as things had got at her prom, it had still been a school-sanctioned event with chaperones making sure things didn't go too far. At the club, there was no one to tell the birthday girl not to have a twenty-minute twerk off with her best friend while a bunch of horny, barely legal idiots looked on.

Kamilah bent forward, put her hands on her knees, and rolled her hips to the floor and back up.

Liam chugged the rest of his drink and then refilled it. He took another gulp and tried to find anything else in the club to focus on, but it didn't work. His eyes would go back to Kamilah after only a few seconds, because he lived for the moments when her eyes would meet his and she'd give him a small smile, a saucy wink, or a sexy lip bite.

Liam was unaware of how many times he'd emptied and refilled his glass.

When she and her friends climbed on the stage with the dancers, he could've sworn he could see the beads of sweat rolling down her neck to her cleavage under the flashing lights, even though he knew he was too far away. He wanted to follow the trail with his tongue. He wanted to do more than that. He wanted her alone, so he could tear everything off her and make that ass bounce on his lap for his pleasure instead of the pleasure of everyone in the fucking club.

He was barely conscious of Gio announcing the end of his set and bringing up another DJ. He really didn't pay attention to anything but Kamilah until her head swung around in his direction, her face lit with excitement.

She started rushing toward where he was sitting by himself, everyone else having found something better to do than sit in the VIP. "Liam, do you remember this song?" she shouted as she hustled over.

He forced himself to focus on the music for the first time in hours. He did remember the song. He remembered it all too well. It was that fucking heart song by Aventura that she'd made him dance to in front of everyone at her prom, even though she knew he couldn't dance and hated being the center of attention. Sure, she'd repaid him with a kiss that had led to a hot make-out session, but that didn't drown out the memory of her ex and his friends pointing and laughing at Liam's uncoordinated attempts.

She stood in front of him, panting from her hours-long workout and sprint to his side.

He watched her chest heave above her corset. He had to. It was right in his line of sight.

Kamilah wrapped a hand around his wrist and tugged his arm. "Come on," she said.

Liam's eyes shot to her face. "What?"

"Come dance with me!"

He shook his head. Just like he had all those years ago.

And just like back then, she ignored his answer and kept tugging. "Ven. Baila conmigo."

"No. I don't like dancing."

"I know you know how. I taught you myself."

"I said I don't like it, not that I can't." Although, he really couldn't. Despite her efforts, he hadn't picked it up.

"Please." She blinked those big brown eyes at him, and he could see her disappointment.

Suddenly, Liam was pissed. Some part of his brain told him

it was irrational, but he couldn't help it. He was tired of people trying to push him to be something he wasn't.

To make her happy, he'd attended her party. Even though he sat in the corner all night, like an idiot, while she'd virtually ignored him. Actually, she'd ignored him for days while he sat like a fucking idiot waiting for her to give him a moment of her time. But she thought she was the one who got to be disappointed? She always did that shit to him. She used her wiles to make him jump to do her bidding. She always wanted him to jump. Well, fuck that. Liam wasn't jumping.

"I said no." He yanked his wrist from her hands.

Her head jerked back, and her eyes went wide in surprise. A moment later, her forehead scrunched. "What is your problem?"

"My problem is that I already told you no, and you keep pushing me. That's all you do. Push me."

"All I want is for you to have fun."

She must've been way more drunk than he'd thought.

"Nothing about this is fun for me. Not this song, not this stupid club, not these half-dressed children running around here making me feel like a sleazy old dude at the beach, not the cheesy party bus, and not this stupid fucking costume. I only did this because this is what you wanted to do."

She just stared at him with those doe eyes filled with hurt.

Liam sighed. He shouldn't have said any of that. He was ruining her birthday like a complete asshole. "Look, I'm gonna go home, so—"

"Of course," she scoffed. "Of course you're going to leave."

"What does that mean?"

"That's what you do to me all the time, Liam. It's been like that since we were preteens. You turned your back on me because I didn't fit into your world anymore. You were everything to me, and you just tossed me aside like I was nothing. I had to be fine with you hurting me, because you were hurting. I get that for back then, but you keep doing it. I reach out to you, you walk away from me, and I keep reaching out to you anyway, even though I'm hurt."

"Kami—"

"But you know what? I refuse to be hurt today. It's my birthday, and I'm going to have fun with the people who want to have fun with me. Since you're not one of those people, you should go home." She snatched the bottle of bourbon off the table next to him and walked away before he could even get a word out.

Not that he knew what to say. She'd been right to kick him out.

Liam slipped through the crowd without anyone seeing him, ordered an Uber, and went home. When he got there he shed his costume and lay on the couch in nothing but a pair of gym shorts. He tried to sleep, but his mind kept replaying Kamilah's aching words and the pain on her face. The pain he'd caused but had no idea how to make right or even if he could.

21

Kamilah was dead. There was no way she could still be alive, considering the pain pounding in her brain and radiating to her stomach.

Fucking Dirty Thirty.

"I'm never drinking again." She waited for the scoff of disbelief or other such smart-ass comment. Nothing. She reached out her hand to feel the bed next to her. She reached and reached and hit...a boob?

"Hands off the merchandise," a scratchy voice grumbled. A hand half-heartedly swatted at her own.

Kamilah slowly turned her head and creaked one eye open a sliver.

Sofi lay in the bed next to her, still in her holographic bodysuit. She had a pillow over her face to block out the sun.

"What the...?" Kamilah trailed off, too miserable to even finish her sentence. Where the hell was Liam? *Oh right.*

When she and Sofi had stumbled through the door in the

wee hours of the morning, he had been asleep on the couch. She'd made extra noise in an attempt to be petty, but he'd been wearing a pair of noise-canceling headphones. The jerk.

A jab of pain radiated from her brain to her eye. She was going to stay in bed. All day. *A perfect way to avoid Liam.*

Her bladder quickly shot down that plan. *Shit.*

Okay. Time to get up. One, two, three.

Puñeta. Instant pain.

Kamilah stumbled to the bathroom. It took her a minute to realize she was virtually naked. She was in nothing but her lacy peekaboo cheeky panties and a baggy tank top. One that looked suspiciously like Liam's. Kamilah took a peek in the mirror and gasped. She looked like a chalk picture on the sidewalk after it rained. Her badass-siren makeup was nothing but a smeared memory.

After half-heartedly scrubbing her face with a makeup wipe, Kamilah brushed her teeth and checked out her hair. *Dear God.* She was still wearing her mermaid crown and her hair had claimed it like evil alien tentacles catching their prey and squeezing the life out of it. Yeah. It was just going to have to stay that way. She was not about to touch her tender head.

She grabbed the packet of wipes and walked back into the bedroom, where Sofi was moaning in pain and claiming over and over to hate her life. "I blame you for this. You and your Dirty Thirty shots." She threw the pack of makeup removers at Sofi and hit her right in the stomach.

Sofi grabbed her stomach and rolled to the side. "Oh you asshole," she panted. "You're gonna make me puke."

"You better not," Kamilah warned. "If you puke, I'm gonna puke, and then I'm going to kick your ass."

Sofi lifted her hand and motioned Kamilah to bring it.

Kamilah plopped her butt onto the bed instead. "I think we're dying."

Sofi tossed the pillow to the side and revealed that at some point she'd lost her pastel-rainbow wig and unicorn horn. Her low bun was still intact, but her baby hairs created a cloud of frizz around her still-done-up face. "We just need to drink some water and eat." She pushed herself into a sitting position and let out a sobbing groan.

"Fuck water," Kamilah told her. "We need Bloodys."

"You're right. But first we have to leave the house." There was a distinct pout in her second sentence.

Less than twenty minutes later, they emerged from Liam's place like vampire zombies setting foot in the light.

"Ah. Hellfire." Sofi pulled the string of the light blue hoodie Kamilah had given her. All that Kamilah could see of her face was her nose and a pair of big sunglasses. She looked like the guy from *Mean Girls* who shouted, "She doesn't even go here." Because they'd stupidly sewn her tail to the back of her fanny pack (so she didn't have to carry a purse), she was shooting rainbow tulle out of the back of her borrowed leggings. She shuffled forward in Kamilah's fuzzy slippers.

Kamilah, ever the fashion icon, was rocking a baggy pair of Liam's sweatpants, the same tank top she'd woken up in, Nike slides with mismatched socks, a denim jacket, her own pair of large sunglasses, and, of course, her mermaid crown. "I hate the sun." She turned left to go toward where she'd parked.

"Where are you going?" Sofi asked.

"To my car?"

"Hell, no, I'm not getting in your raggedy-ass car." She pulled her keys out of her fanny pack and turned right to where she'd left her car in the parking lot.

Kamilah really did not want to go past the distillery. They'd been lucky enough so far to not run into Liam. She didn't want to chance it now. She needed a plan before she faced him. "Hey, don't talk about Doña like that. She is a classic beauty."

"She's a busted old bitch, and you should've replaced her a long time ago." Sofi kept walking, forcing Kamilah to follow.

"I don't have the money." Kamilah shot a furtive glance in the windows of the distillery. She didn't see Liam, but that didn't mean he wasn't in there. She kept her head down, rushed past them, and over to the passenger side of Sofi's car.

Sofi paused in the act of opening her car door. "You do have the money. You just keep funneling it into El Coquí."

"Ugh. Don't yell at me." Kamilah opened the car door and slid into the passenger seat. "I'm too hungover right now." Sofi was forever trying to convince Kamilah to set boundaries with her family and to leave El Coquí to strike out on her own. She didn't get why Kamilah stayed, but that was because Kamilah had never told her about giving up her scholarship. She couldn't tell her, because by doing it, she'd forced Sofi to change her plans too. From the day they'd met in middle-school French class, they'd planned to study in France together. But when Kamilah hadn't gone, Sofi's mother had refused to let her go. Instead, Sofi'd studied at Northwestern before getting a bomb-ass internship that had turned into a sweet job.

Many times Kamilah had tried to confess her sin to her best friend, but she'd ultimately kept silent. She glanced over at Sofi as she maneuvered her way through traffic and wondered for the millionth time what her best friend would say if she knew that they didn't know everything about each other.

In her pocket her phone vibrated. She pulled it out and

saw her uncle's face, almost identical to her father's, on her screen. "Bendiciones, Tío," she said as soon as she answered.

"Mila, you will never believe what I just did." Her uncle was never one to waste time with pleasantries when it came to his family. He did that enough at work.

"You finally convinced local lawmakers to do something about the landlords in District Twenty-Six arbitrarily raising rents?"

"No. I'm good, but I'm not Jesus."

Kamilah chuckled.

"What I did do was convince Mayor Johnson that it would be good for him to be seen participating in a foodie tour designed to bring attention to community restaurants. Specifically one long-standing community restaurant that represents the perfect mix of traditional Humboldt Park and innovative change."

She froze. "What?" she whispered.

"The mayor is coming to El Coquí for the Foodie Tour and he's bringing cameras."

Kamilah screamed in glee, causing both her and Sofi to wince and groan afterward. But she didn't care. This was huge. If the mayor came to El Coquí with journalists during the tour, when the restaurant was sure to be packed, it would make them look like the hottest ticket in town. They'd drum up so many more customers that there was no way her plan would fail. Her parents would have to admit that she knew what she was doing. "Tío, this is amazing! Mil gracias."

"It's nothing. It took me a while to admit it, but I don't want to lose El Coquí either." He paused and took a deep breath. She wondered if he was thinking about Abuela. "Anyway, I have to confirm with his office, so when is the tour?"

"It's November seventeenth."

"All right, I'll confirm the date with them, but be fore-warned that his schedule could change at any time, so they may give a time only to change it later. You're going to have to be prepared for anything."

Fuck. She'd hoped to get a set time for his visit. She'd finally come up with a plan in regard to her double-booked problem. She'd planned to do them both, be at the restaurant but slip away when it was time for the distillery judging. She had no idea how she could slip away if the mayor was coming to El Coquí.

She said a distracted goodbye to her uncle, pressed her forehead against the passenger-side window, and groaned. God, she wished she could call Liam. He would know exactly what to do. Of course, he was also the very last person she could call. Especially after kicking him out of her birthday party.

She still didn't exactly understand what had happened. One minute she was having a blast and wanting to share the moment with the man she loved. The next he was snapping at her about the whole party and calling her pushy. Then again, he'd been moody and irritated since the moment Sofi had shown up to sweep her away for their annual b-day tradition. *Oh shit.* What if he'd had something planned, even though he said he didn't? What if he'd wanted to tell her that he loved her, and she'd ruined it all by going off with her friends all day? To make matters worse, she'd dragged him along on a night that she knew he'd hate. Why had she done that? It was as if she was testing him to see how much shit he'd put up with for her, and then she got mad that it wasn't enough. Why did she always do that?

"On my life, if you throw up in my car, I'm going to murder you."

"It's not that." Her stomach did feel like trash, but she didn't feel sick. Yet.

Sofi spotted an empty space in the tiny parking lot of their favorite breakfast spot. She quickly entered through the exit to cut off another car and snag it before they could.

Kamilah gave her a look at the dickish move. "I know you're hungover, but really?"

Sofi nodded once. "Yup." She took the keys out of the ignition and opened her door. She stared at the car of angry people as they passed, daring them to stop and say something. When they didn't, she turned on her heel and strode to the door, her unicorn tail swishing in time with her hips. The place was busy as usual, but they snatched two seats at the diner counter and ordered their Bloodys before even touching the menu.

Kamilah propped her elbows on the counter, closed her eyes, and started rubbing her temples. Between the aftereffects of at least ten Dirty Thirty shots, the heavy crown that listed to the side and pulled her hair, and her double-booking problem, she had the mother of all headaches.

Something made a clink right in front of her, and she opened her eyes to see her drink get pushed toward her. She grabbed it and took a deep pull from her straw. She and Sofi sat in silence for a few minutes, just sucking down their hangover cures.

Finally Sofi sighed in relief and turned on her stool to face Kamilah. "Okay. Now tell me what's up, starting with what your tío just told you that made you almost yak in my car."

Kamilah opened her mouth and spilled everything about Liam's contest judging and El Coquí's tour stop being on the same day.

Sofi just continued to sip her Bloody and look pensive.

"I can tell you have an idea." Kamilah wiggled in excitement. Sofi always had an idea, and hers were usually much better than Kamilah's.

"I was just thinking of how much I could get from Televisa if I sold them your story."

"Bitch." Kamilah grimaced at her best friend, even though she had a point. Her life had become very telenovelaish. "Sometimes I can't stand you."

"You love me," Sofi replied breezily. "If we weren't straight, you'd be my happy little housewife."

"You forget that I was almost forced to fulfill that role in college. That's why I jumped on moving in with Chase so fast."

"Malcriada," she retorted.

"Ha," Kamilah barked. "If anyone is rude and spoiled it's you."

"It's not spoiled if you do it for yourself. It's called *self-care*."

"I can't help but note that you didn't say anything about being rude."

Sofi stuck up her middle finger and used the tip of her long rainbow nail to scratch the bridge of her nose.

"You're not being mature or helpful right now."

Sofi placed her free hand over her heart. "Oh. I didn't know I was supposed to be helpful right now. I thought you just wanted to vent, because the solution is so simple that even your hungover ass could figure it out." She pulled the celery stick out of her glass and took a bite.

Kamilah didn't respond.

Sofi set her glass down and took off her sunglasses so Kamilah could see her roll her eyes. "Have your family take over for you while you help Liam."

Kamilah started laughing despite her lingering headache.

"Can you imagine trying to tell my parents that they have to take over the tour that I forced on them and they still don't want to do?"

Sofi grimaced. "Yeah. I don't even know why I suggested that. They will kill you, serve you to the mayor like in *Sweeney Todd*, and then sell the restaurant." She took a long drink of her Bloody and then gave a one-shoulder shrug. "Well, then you'll have to tell Liam you can't cook for the judging because they changed the date of the tour stop and the mayor is coming."

"I can't," Kamilah said quickly. Especially not after she'd just railed at him for turning his back on her. "I'm fucking up," she told her friend.

"What did you do?"

"Like a complete idiot, I blurted out that I'm in love with him."

"Good for you," Sofi said. "Way to be proactive."

"Right. Except that was weeks ago, and he still hasn't mentioned it at all. He's been acting like he didn't hear it, which I know is a lie because he froze as soon as the words came out of my mouth. Now I have to act like I never said anything because he's two seconds away from completely bailing on me instead of just walking away from me on my birthday."

"Ouch," Sofi replied.

"Exactly," Kamilah exclaimed.

Sofi motioned the server over and ordered two more Bloody Marys. When she was done, she gave Kamilah her attention once more. "Mira, you already know how I am. I'm allergic to pendejadas, so I say, tell him that you can't do it. The sooner, the better. It's not like he and Killian are going to be left with nothing. They've been planning this oppor-

tunity for years. They can make it work without your appe-
tizers or whatever."

"But what if he gets mad and pushes me away?"

"Then you'll know for sure that you were the only one to
catch real feelings in your fake engagement."

That's exactly what I'm scared of.

"You got this, Mila," Sofi told her from the driver's seat.
"Just go in there, tell him that you two have to talk, explain
everything, and see what his reaction is."

Kamilah nodded. *Go talk to him. Be honest and straightforward.*
She'd been telling herself that the entire time they finished up
their second Bloodys and enjoyed some cheesy hash browns.
Now she was back at home and had to actually do it.

She swung the door open and stepped out. "I got this,"
she said aloud.

"You got this."

She saw Liam's truck sitting in its normal spot and swung
back to Sofi. "Are you sure I got this?"

"Yes."

Kamilah exhaled. She closed the door and shook out her
arms like a boxer getting ready to step in the ring. She kept
repeating Sofi's chant as she walked up to the door, stuck her
key in the lock, and let herself in.

She found Liam, Killian, and Abuelo sitting on the couch.
It was hardly the first time she'd walked in to find them all in
there, but unlike the other times when they joked and talked,
they now sat silently.

Abuelo glanced over at her and gave her a thorough once-
over while zooming in on her crown. His eyebrows went up.

Kamilah knew then that the Bloody had made her feel
better on the inside, but on the outside she still looked a

hot mess. The thick tension in the room caused the magical Bloody Mary powers to fade from her system. "What's going on?" she asked.

Killian turned to look at her. "Oh good. You're back." He too spent time eyeing her crown. "Well, lass, you look like you had a great time at your birthday party."

Liam didn't look at her.

"I did," she replied to Killian. *Why won't Liam look at me? Is he that mad?*

"Come." Killian patted the seat between him and Liam. "We have some things to discuss."

That can't be good. It was a little too reminiscent of their conversation in the distillery. The one that had started this whole thing. Kamilah slowly made her way to the couch. The entire time she looked between the three of them, trying her best to decipher anything from their expressions. All she got was that they all looked serious. That was hardly anything new for Liam, but there was no mischievousness in Killian's or Abuelo's faces. That worried her. She sat.

"Lass, I'm not going to beat around the bush and drag this out. The procedure didn't work."

She felt Liam stiffen at her side. She glanced out of the corner of her eye and saw his hands balling into fists where they hung between his legs.

"What are they going to do now? What's the next step?"

Killian shook his head. "There is no next step."

Kamilah gasped. Without thinking, she grabbed on to Liam's thigh. After a moment, she felt his hand on top of hers. She flipped her hand and threaded their fingers together. She squeezed, and he returned it. "Killian—"

He cut her off. "It's not just me being stubborn this time, lass."

Kamilah looked around wildly, waiting for any of them to say something else. To explain.

"Anything more will be too risky," Abuelo intoned in Spanish. "He's too old for extensive surgery, and his kidneys are failing. There's nothing more to be done."

Eyes wet, Kamilah grabbed Killian's hand with her free one.

He gave her a sad smile and raised her hand to his lips for a kiss, then pulled it to his chest and rested his other one on top of it, the same way she had with Liam so many times.

She could tell her tears were killing him. She swallowed her emotions with difficulty and turned to Liam.

He held every muscle in his body still. His head was facing the kitchen to hide his expression from them, but he was gulping repeatedly.

She knew that he was doing his best to choke back his emotions. She wanted so badly to wrap her arms around him and pull him close, but she knew he wouldn't want her to. Not right now.

"We have to focus on the contest," he said after a minute. His voice was rough as if he'd just swallowed a pack of straight razors. He rotated his head back in their direction. His eyes were bloodshot but dry. "Winning is more important now than ever."

Killian waved that off. "With Mila here on our side, we've got that contest in the bag."

It became startlingly clear to her that she wouldn't be telling Liam anything about her being double-booked. She couldn't fail him. Not now. She was just going to have to figure out a way to do both.

"We have more important things to discuss," Killian said.

"Sí." Abuelo nodded. "It's time for us to talk about your wedding."

22

Liam stared at himself in the bathroom mirror and wondered how the hell he'd got to this point: wearing a navy blue three-piece suit and an emerald green tie to match Kamilah's dress.

In the mirror next to him, she leaned forward to paint her lips a glossy nude color. Her curls piled on top of her head in a waterfall-like bun held in place by a massive number of bobby pins. He knew because he'd watched her strategically stab them into place. A few curls framed her face and trailed down the nape of her neck. His eyes followed one perfect coil from behind her ear to the edge of her dress. Then he followed that edge down her neckline to the shadowy valley of her cleavage. Her hand passed in front of his view, breaking his fixed stare.

He blinked and looked back at his own reflection. "What are we going to do?" he asked her as he needlessly straightened his tie.

"I don't know." She sighed.

It'd been a week since they'd got the marriage bomb dropped on them for the second time, and their grandfathers still refused to be put off. As far as they were concerned, Kamilah and Liam would be getting married and soon. But first was the engagement party they'd planned in cahoots with Valeria and Kamilah's sisters-in-law.

Liam huffed. "Calling this thing off seemed much simpler before." Before they'd rebuilt their friendship, before they'd made it into something more, before it had become clear that everyone they loved was seriously invested in their relationship, especially his dying grandfather.

She made a noncommittal noise and brushed past him.

He turned to watch her walk away, thoroughly enjoying the way the green velvet hugged all of her curves before falling to the ground like a slick curtain of greenery covering the entrance to an enchanted cave.

She turned and sat on the edge of the bed. The dress parted to reveal a dangerously high slit. She bent to slip on her gold strappy heels and buckle them at the ankle.

Liam stared at that expanse of soft, silky leg and felt himself start to respond. He couldn't help it. Everything about her was his deepest fantasy come to life, and he hadn't put his hands or mouth on her in far too long.

Kamilah was slipping away from him.

All of his instincts were screaming at him to do something. To make it better somehow. "I'm sorry," he blurted.

She paused and looked up at him.

"I'm sorry for hurting your feelings on your birthday." It poured out of him in a thoughtless rush. "I'm sorry for rejecting all your overtures over the years. I'm sorry for abandoning you when we were kids. I'm sorry for hurting you. I hate that I did that. I don't want to hurt you. I—" *I love you.*

Come on. Just say it. He took in her too-familiar, cautiously hopeful expression. She made it right before he inevitably hurt her. Every time. Because that was all he was capable of. "I'm sorry."

Her face fell for a split second, before she shook it off. "Thank you for apologizing. I'm sorry for pushing you. I won't do it anymore." She broke eye contact with him and grabbed the little gold purse sitting next to her. "We better get going before we're late." She stood, concealing both her perfect leg and face from him.

Fuck. He'd just made everything worse. He closed his eyes on a rough exhalation. "Right." He followed her out of the room, down the stairs, and around the front of the building.

The open shutters on the inside of the restaurant windows revealed friends and family members inside. The tinkle of laughter and music trickled from the restaurant. They were having a great time celebrating him and Kamilah.

The icy chill of premonition crept over the back of his neck. He stopped.

Kamilah turned and gave him a questioning glance. Understanding dawned. "I'll figure something out," she told him. "I just need a little more time." She reached out a hand to him. "Trust me."

He nodded and took her hand.

They were greeted with cheers and confetti cannons the minute they stepped through the doors.

Kamilah laughed in delight, and even Liam had to crack a smile.

He had the brief impression of green streamers and large pictures of them, the happy fake couple, before they were swept into the large mass of people wanting to greet and congratulate them. Before long, the music was cranked up, the drinks were poured, and delicious food was served. It was a very Vega party—unlike any other. Usually, he stood on the sidelines, watching the family interact with a perplexed otherness. He didn't understand how they enjoyed the loud laughing, constant touching, and obnoxious prying.

But now that he was in the middle of it? The feeling was completely different. Their joy in being there with each other was invigorating. It felt like warmth and belonging.

When the second generation of Los Rumberos—Papo's old band now consisting of Leo and the other original members' sons or grandsons—began their performance on the tiny stage, Liam leaned against the bar and watched Kamilah dance with various family members. A smile curved his lips at her joy, until he remembered.

It was fake.

Sofi dragged Ben out onto the dance floor, much to Dev's amusement as he held his cell phone up to no doubt get a video for Rome, who was at an away game. Meanwhile, Lucy and Liza did little more than sway to the rhythm together and gaze into each other's eyes in a way that made Liam feel like a creeper for watching.

A hand fell on his shoulder, and Liam turned his head. For a split second, he thought it was Santiago, but Kamilah's dad spun her mom around like they were competing on *Dancing with the Stars.*

No, it was Rico, Santiago's identical twin.

"How's it going, Liam?"

"Good." Liam took a sip out of his drink.

"I just wanted to tell you that I'm really happy for you both."

"Thank you." The song ended, and over Rico's shoulder, Liam watched the band put their instruments down and leave the stage.

"You and Kamilah are making power-couple moves. You with the contest, and Kamilah with the amazing work here. Once the tour comes, it will blow up even more. I mean, I had to call in almost every favor I had to get the mayor to agree, but it will be worth it."

The mayor was going to the Foodie Tour? Since when? Liam tilted his head and leaned forward. "I'm sorry?"

"Yeah. He originally had some meetings scheduled for the seventeenth, but I was able to convince him that it would be good for him to be seen here that day. It is an election year, so taking part in a community-organized foodie tour is good publicity. It's a win-win."

"Did you say the seventeenth?"

"Yeah. November seventeenth. The date of the tour." He gave Liam a weird look.

The Foodie Tour was the same day as the distillery-contest judging, and Kamilah hadn't said anything to him about it. As a matter of fact, she'd told him that it was a week earlier. Why would she do that? They'd just been discussing the judging a few days ago. She'd assured him that everything was good. What the fuck was she up to? "Excuse me," he told Rico. "I have to go take care of something."

Kamilah was standing by the food table lifting a toothpick with white cheese, guava paste, and summer sausage on it. She'd just put it in her mouth when Liam reached her.

"We need to talk," he whispered in her ear. He grabbed her arm and led her through the tables. He pushed open the swinging doors to the kitchen, and once he determined it was empty, he swung around to face her. "Do you have something you need to tell me?"

Her forehead scrunched. "About what?"

"About the fact that the date of the Foodie Tour is actually the seventeenth. The same day as the contest judging you promised to help with."

Her guilt was written all over her face. "Liam—"

"You lied to me."

"I didn't!" She rushed on. "It was originally the tenth, but then they called me to change it."

"When?"

She paused. "When what?"

Liam glared. She knew exactly what he was asking, but he clarified anyway. "When did they call you?"

She scrunched up her face.

"Kamilah," Liam intoned.

Her eyes shot back to him and then dropped to the floor. "Umm… I think it was…" She mumbled the rest, and he couldn't make it out.

"What?"

"It was…" *Mumble, mumble, mumble.*

He took a few steps forward to hear better. "Huh?"

She huffed. "I said, 'It was about three weeks ago.'"

"Three weeks ago?" Liam yelled.

"I was going to tell you," she said by way of explanation. "I just needed time to figure out what to do."

I'll figure something out. I just need a little more time. Trust me. My plan will work. Trust me. I promise to be honest and up-front. Trust me.

Trust me. Trust me. Trust me. She was always telling him to trust her, but she continued to withhold things from him. She kept using secrets and lies to manipulate him into doing what she wanted. Just like she was doing to her family. His throat constricted, a searing pain in his chest.

"What you mean is that you withheld this information

from me, so you could plot how to get what you want, because otherwise you would've told me about this. So what is your new plan? What scheme did you come up with?"

Her lips thinned. "Don't make it sound like I'm some comic-book villain plotting to take over the world. I was trying to figure out a way to tell you that I couldn't be at the judging anymore. But—"

"Stop. Stop right there. Don't say 'but.' There is no *but*. You were wrong. You withheld information from me to manipulate me. Again. After promising me that you wouldn't."

"Manipulate you? I wanted to help you." Her voice was higher now, louder. Upset. But he couldn't stop himself.

He shook his head. "No. No, you didn't. You wanted to help yourself. Because you *thought* that I would be mad at you for backing out after *you* adamantly incorporated yourself into my plans. Instead of being honest with me, the man you claim to love, you lied to me in order to buy yourself some time in order to figure out a way for you to save face."

"I didn't say anything because I knew you would do exactly this. You would throw my love for you back in my face and then push me away, because that's what you do. Over and over and over."

"Right," he said. "I should be more like you, the great Kamilah Vega, who lies, manipulates, and hides things for love, and you act like that makes it all okay, because you're doing it to help. But really you're just a selfish, manipulative control freak."

Kamilah's head snapped back as if he'd struck her. "I'm not," she whispered.

"No? Then why don't you go in there and tell your family everything? Tell them about how this whole thing is a setup by our grandfathers that you happily took advantage of, because you saw the opportunity to finally get your hands on the restaurant that you care about more than the people in your life. Tell them about Paris. About how you got into that school and got a full-ride scholarship but turned it down and never said a word to anyone about it. Better yet, tell them the real reason you want to save this place is because you feel guilty for resenting your family."

Her expression closed off. "Why don't you go tell your dying grandfather that you've been lying to him this whole time, because this engagement is fake, and we never had any intention of following through with their blackmail." She took a step closer, shoulders back like a prizefighter. "And while you're at it, tell him that the reason you're determined to win this contest isn't to honor your father, because you're still pissed at him. It's because you plan to sell out at the first opportunity and turn his distillery into a corporate machine despite his wishes."

Liam felt a hot rush of anger, indignation, and more than a bit of guilt. The guilt making him even more angry. How dare she try to deflect like this? "I was an idiot for going along with *your* plan—I'll readily admit it. But I was trying to save my grandfather's life. You *act* like you're doing all of this for your family, but really you're so terrified of going out on your own and failing that you prefer to hide behind your martyrdom." As soon as the words left his mouth, he regretted it.

"And you're a coward who is so terrified of being happy that you lock yourself away in your miserable past."

The kitchen doors swung open to reveal Ben.

They both snapped their attention to him.

"What?" they said in unison, then scowled.

"Uh, just an FYI." Ben swallowed. "Leo accidentally left his mic in here...and it's still on." He pointed to the object sitting right next to them on the table. "Everyone in there can hear you."

★ ★ ★

Fucking Leo.

Kamilah stared in horror at the flashing green light at the bottom of the microphone. She couldn't think, couldn't breathe. It was exactly how she'd felt when she'd been stuck on the roof in the middle of a thunderstorm. The storm had raged at her until she slid to the ground and curled her body around her drawn-up knees. Her eyes squeezed shut, so the lightning could no longer burn them. Her hands had covered her ears, trying to stop the thunder from exploding through her head. The wind had whipped through her body, causing every part of her to tremble. And through it all, her brain shouted *This is it. This is the end.*

She pulled her gaze away from the light and looked at Liam.

He stared back at her with cold indifference.

This is it. This is the end.

She knew exactly what was going to happen now. She'd lived it so many times throughout her life. With shaking hands, Kamilah slid Eimear's ring off her finger and handed it to Liam.

His fingers snapped closed around it like a bear trap. He eyed his clenched hand and swallowed hard.

Kamilah flexed her left hand, which somehow felt much heavier without the ring on it.

Liam looked up at her, and she looked back.

Ben put a hand on Liam's shoulder and gave him a bit of a shove.

Liam barely budged.

"Just leave me alone," she told him. "It's what you do best."

Ben gave Liam's shoulder another tug, and this time he listened.

He followed Ben out the back door without looking back.

Kamilah reached a hand out, lifted the microphone, and flipped the switch to Off. Then she lowered her head. She felt the tears run down to the tip of her nose, where she watched them fall to the steel tabletop. She wasn't sure how long she stood in the kitchen, but she heard the dull roar in the dining room fade to mumbled comments and then silence.

The kitchen door opened again, and Kamilah spun to face whoever it was.

Sofi stood in the door.

"Hey," Kamilah said.

"Your parents sent everyone home. Your brothers are still here, but not their wives or the kids."

Kamilah sighed. "Yeah, I figured it's time for a reckoning." She started to make her way to the door. She expected Sofi to turn and lead the way, but instead she started toward the back door. "You aren't staying? I may need your help."

"No." Sofi shook her head. "I'm done helping you."

"What?"

"I've always had your back, but you lied to me for twelve years, Kamilah, and not some tiny bullshit lie. We were supposed to go to Paris together. We had firm plans, and then you said you didn't get in, and everything fell through. Your lie changed my whole life. It affected my future, and you didn't see fit to tell me about it. I know you too well to think that you would ever have owned up to it on your own. So yeah. I'm done helping you. I'm done having your back. I'm done with you." Sofi made her way out to the alley much the same way Liam had, without turning back.

Everything inside of Kamilah from her tight chest and spasming lungs to her shaking limbs told her not to reenter the dining area, to run away and hide instead. Except she had nowhere to hide, and even if she did, they would only track her down. This conversation was long overdue.

She slowly made her way through the kitchen doors to the front room. As suspected, her family was waiting for her. They sat at the island-shaped table surrounded by the remains of her ill-fated engagement party. It was clear that people had simply got up and left after her and Liam's fight was broadcast through the room. There were half-eaten plates of food and nearly empty cups littering almost every surface, the band's instruments were still on the stage, and the food was still out in the warming trays.

"Let's start with this," Cristian said, drawing her attention back to her stern-faced family. "How much of what we overheard is true?"

"All of it," she choked out. "It's all true. Abuelo and Killian came up with this scheme to blackmail Liam and me."

"He'd give you El Coquí if you pretended to be engaged to Liam."

"Not exactly. It was more that he'd support me in making changes and entering the Foodie Tour." She was going to be sick.

"And Liam?"

"Liam wanted a chance to convince Killian to get treatment because at first he refused."

"So you both agreed to get what you wanted."

"Yes, because they threatened to sell the building if we didn't."

Cristian continued. "You decided to lie to all of us instead of telling us what was going on."

"I tried to talk to you all before any of this ever happened, but you guys never listen to me. You never take anything I say seriously. You treat me like a child."

"Maybe because you do childish things—like this," Papi snapped. "You want us to take you seriously? Take yourself seriously. Grow up, Kamilah, because this immature *nobody understands me or listens to me* bullshit is old."

"Papi—"

"No. I'm done listening to your lies because, apparently, I've been listening to them for years." He shook his head. "You lied to us about being engaged. You lied to us about your college. Every time you told us 'Sure, no problem,' it was another lie. All you do is lie. I don't even know who you are anymore, because you certainly aren't my daughter. I taught my daughter better than that."

The tears in Kamilah's eyes spilled over. She tried to open her mouth, to explain, but all that came out were choked sobs.

"You want this place so bad, you can have it," he said. "But I'm not sticking around to hear more of your lies." He pushed back from his chair and left.

Mami, who wouldn't even look at her, did the same.

Simultaneously, Cristian and Eddie stood. They looked like they wanted to say something but glanced at each other, nodded, and left instead.

Leaving only Saint and Leo.

Leo stood.

"Let me guess," she told Leo between sobs. "You're going to yell at me some more before you leave too."

"Nah, I think you've had quite enough sucker punches for the night. I'm not going to kick you while you're down. That would just be fucked up."

"Thanks."

"I'm going to help you clean this place up, but consider that my last act as an employee here."

A fresh set of tears blurred her vision. "You quit too?"

"I'm helping you, but I'm still pissed that you lied about literally everything. You did us dirty, Mila, and I can't just overlook it."

Kamilah nodded. It made sense. It still felt like being kicked while she was down, but it made sense. She felt a presence at her side and looked over to see Saint.

He looked at her the same way he did the time he'd found her crying in the pantry because America Bustos had pinched her and put gum in her hair. "Why didn't you tell me?" Saint said. "If you'd told me you were this unhappy, I would've done something about it."

Kamilah shrugged.

She, Saint, and Leo cleaned up the restaurant in silence. Well, not silence, since she continued to sob loudly while taking down all the pictures of her and Liam throughout their lives that were taped everywhere. Saint stepped in and took the pictures from her hands while guiding her to the food trays. Yeah, that was a better idea to have the woman leaking all over the place put away food. She ended up just tossing it all in the trash. When they were finally done, Leo and Saint carried all the bags to the garbage and watched her while she locked up.

Kamilah stood in the alley for a second, realizing that she had nowhere to go. The tears started all over again.

"Oh God. Don't start that again, Sideshow Bob," Leo said, using the cruel childhood nickname he'd given her on account of her hair. But he also walked up to her and wrapped her in a hug.

Kamilah buried her face in his chest.

"Do you want me to kill him for you?" he murmured. "Because I will, and I'm sure Saint will help me. I bet he knows tons of ways to make it hurt too."

Kamilah shook her head.

"Did you just wipe your nose on my shirt?" He sounded so put out that Kamilah couldn't help her chuckle.

She wiped her eyes and stepped back. "Thank you, Leo. I'm sorry for always calling you the worst."

"Okay, let's not get overly emotional here. I only talk about feelings when it will get me laid."

Really? He'd been doing so well. Kamilah just shook her head again.

"Come on, Mila," Saint said. "You're staying with me." He put a hand between her shoulder blades and led her to his car.

Kamilah tried not to look back, but she couldn't help herself. She craned her neck to look at the building behind her. The one that had watched her grow up. The one that represented so much to her. The one she was going to lose as surely as she'd just lost everyone she loved. A sharp pain tore through her chest. "Perdóname, Abuela. Te fallé."

23

"You know, if you add a little lemon juice and zest to that sautéed spinach, it would really brighten the flavor," Kamilah said from her spot at the peninsula separating the kitchen from the dining room. "Pine nuts would be good in it too."

Saint stopped stirring with his wooden spoon long enough to give Kamilah a look over his shoulder. "You want to do it?" he asked.

Kamilah quickly returned her gaze to the alphabet-matching memory game in front of her. "No, thanks. I'm busy helping Rosie with her homework."

"Oh really?"

"Yes." Kamilah flipped over a small laminate square at the bottom left corner to reveal capital *L*. Yes! She was pretty sure she knew where its lowercase counterpart was. "We are very busy." She flipped over a square in the middle. Damn.

"Where is *she*, then?"

Kamilah looked to her left to find the stool next to her empty and her cell phone gone. "Hey!"

The sounds of a familiar game floated through the open space from the living room.

Kamilah spun around on her stool to see a little navy-skirt-covered tush and a skinny pair of light brown legs hanging over the ottoman while kicking bare feet. "You sneaky little mouse, how did you unlock my phone?" she yelled.

"Your password is my birthday," her four-year-old niece yelled back.

"How did she know that?" Kamilah asked her brother.

He gave a helpless shrug in response. "Witchcraft?"

"'Cause I'm your favorite" was Rosie's confident reply.

Saint's smirk said *She's got you there.*

"I don't have favorites. I love you all the same. Now, gimme my phone back, and get your little booty in here so we can practice your letters."

"I already know all the letters."

"Oh really? Then what is the first letter of the word *wasting* as in *You're wasting time*?"

"*P!*"

Kamilah made a buzzer sound. "Nope. It's the letter *W*, which means you need to come over here and study."

"I don't want to learn my letters, because I don't want to go to school. I hate school."

Kamilah looked to Saint, who shook his head sadly.

"She's still not talking in class?" she asked.

"Nope," he replied. "And I can see why Rosie doesn't want to talk to her teacher. The woman is really starting to piss me off."

Kamilah raised her brows in surprise. It was seldom if ever her steady and even-keeled brother said someone was pissing him off. She'd met the friendly blonde and had a few conversations with her in the mornings when she dropped Rosie off—aka pulled a sobbing Rosie off her leg and then escaped to her car to cry.

She'd been doing a lot of crying in her car lately, and not just because she hated leaving an upset Rosie in the doorway to her classroom. Mostly it was because she did a lot of driving around and thinking. As a matter of fact, she was due for a good, long drive. "Hey, I'll be back in a little bit."

After wrestling her phone away from Rosie, she walked to her car and took off.

She didn't even really know why she grabbed her phone. It wasn't like anyone was going to call her. In the last few days, the only people she'd talked to were Saint and Rosie. She couldn't recall the last time that had happened. She was pretty sure it had never happened before. In her deepest fantasies, she'd dreamed of it: no nagging parents, no idiot brothers forcing her to do their chores, no one expecting her to be at their beck and call, just silence and peace. Now that she had peace, she could say that it sucked. Not seeing her family was the worst thing that she'd experienced in a long time. Well, second-worst thing. Number one was Liam throwing her love back in her face, calling her manipulative and selfish, and then leaving her standing in the rubble of her broken heart in the midst of her shocked and pissed-off family.

She understood that she'd played a huge role in getting herself to that spot, but it still didn't change the fact that she was without friends, family, the restaurant, or Liam. She was completely alone. All in all, her life was a raging dumpster fire, and she wasn't exactly sure what to do about it.

If the world were any kind of fair, it would at least be a sunny day outside, but it wasn't. It was a miserable, cold day with snow in the forecast. As if to prove how terrible the world really was, Kamilah had just turned onto North Avenue, when Doña began to sputter and shake like an old lady with a pneumonic cough.

Kamilah immediately pulled over and turned her car off as she'd learned to do when Doña acted up. She counted to forty-five in her head and then turned the key. Nothing happened. Shit. She looked around and suddenly realized where she was. She was sitting right outside of Swig. Oh hell, no. She tried the key again. Nothing. "You can't do this to me. Not after all we've been through together. Remember yesterday we went to Leone Beach Park and just sat there watching the sunset? It was beautiful. We can do that again. I promise. Just don't do this," Kamilah pleaded. "Not now."

She tried the key one more time and listened as her car gave another wheeze, only to be strangled silent by the unfriendly hands of fate. "Seriously, Doña?"

When Doña stayed eerily quiet, Kamilah hung her head and had a moment of silence, but it didn't last long. She had to get out of here. Kamilah mentally scrolled through the list of people she could call for help. Considering her exiled status, there weren't many. She knew she could always call Saint, but he was in the middle of making lunch for Rosie. Plus, he'd already done so much for her. Maybe Leo would help. He'd helped her after the party from hell.

The side door of Swig started to open. She knew exactly who would step out without even having to look, because her luck was shit and she looked like the Pigeon Lady from *Home Alone 2*.

Kamilah frantically tried the key again. "Come on. Start." Nothing. She watched in the rearview mirror as Chase got closer and closer. "I swear to God, Doña. If you don't start right now, I will take you to an empty parking lot and set you on fire *Waiting to Exhale*-style." Still nothing.

Kamilah banged her head on the steering wheel a few times. Maybe if she knocked herself unconscious this whole thing would be less painful.

Knock, knock.

"I'm going to enjoy watching you burn, you prickly old bitch," she told her crappy car before slowly turning her head to look out her driver's-side window.

Chase was bracing his hand on the top of her car as he leaned over to peer at her through the window. There was an unruly lock of blond hair falling into his amused eyes. "Are you stalking me?" he asked with the quirk of his mouth.

The self-absorbed jackass. Of course he'd think that. Kamilah stared at him as she locked the door, then turned back to her phone. Maybe she should call Leo, anyway.

"Kamilah, I was kidding. Open the door."

She ignored him and instead addressed Siri.

"Call Leo." As the phone rang, Chase knocked on the window again. She continued to ignore him. Mostly because, surprisingly, being petty felt sort of awesome.

"What?" a gruff voice called from her phone, startling her out of her reverie.

"Hey," she chirped, reaching for her phone on her thigh and nearly knocking it onto the floor. She made a mad scramble for it and almost hung up on him. "I need you to come help me with my car." When she didn't hear the whining she'd expected, she pulled the phone away from her ear to check the screen. From her unlocked screen her nephews and nieces smiled back at her. It took a second, but it finally clicked. "No. He did not just hang up on me."

"Kamilah, let me help you."

Ignore him.

She called back. It rang and rang and went to voice mail. She called again. Same thing. She immediately called again. She'd do it all day if she had to. Leo knew that. Which was most likely why he picked up the fourth time.

"Are you serious right now?" he growled over the receiver. "I wasn't answering for a reason."

"I know, but my car is dead, and I need you to come help me."

"No."

"Leo."

"I don't know why you didn't already get rid of that dumb car a long time ago. It's never been dependable, and now look, you're stranded…" And off he went.

"Kamilah." That was Chase.

She interrupted her brother's lecture. "Leo, I need you to get out here. There is a creepy man staring at me through the window," she said loudly.

"Ask him for a ride."

"Seriously, Leo? He could be a murderer."

"That's a chance I'm willing to take."

"Hey," she said. "Too far."

Leo exhaled a rough breath. "Kamilah, I've had you on the Find My Friends app since 2012. I know exactly where you are right now, and if you got caught stalking your ex like a psycho, that's your problem." He hung up again, and Kamilah didn't even try to call him back.

Mustering all the dignity one could when stranded in front of their first ex-fiancé's restaurant looking like a Dickensian street urchin, Kamilah gathered her things and exited her car. "I'm not stalking you," she told Chase. "My car is just an asshole."

"Yeah, okay." He nodded, taking in her frizzy, messy bun, grease-stained El Coquí shirt, holey sweatpants, and ratty chanclas. She really was the height of fashion these days. "You look...great."

She snorted.

"Why don't you come in, and we'll call Triple A or something?" He gestured to the front door of Swig.

"Triple A," she laughed. "We should just call the junkers, because that's basically what she is now." But she followed him anyway.

Chase held the door open for her, and she stepped into the bustling kitchen. "We can go to the dining area or my office." He pointed to the closed door in the corner.

Kamilah immediately said, "Office." There was no way she was showing herself in the dining room.

He led her to the office and over to the desk. "You look like you could use a drink. Can I get you something?"

She shook her head. "I shouldn't. I feel like if I start, I probably won't stop." Plus, smelling any kind of alcohol made her think about whiskey, which made her think about Liam, and then she'd start to cry.

Chase leaned on the desk looking fresh and clean and handsome and not at all like a ragamuffin. "Do you want to talk about it?"

"No offense, but with you? No."

"I'm guessing this has something to do with Liam."

Kamilah startled at the sound of his name. "How would you know that?"

Chase shrugged. "You aren't wearing your engagement ring, so..." He trailed off, looking at her bare left ring finger.

"Yeah we broke up, but no sympathetic comments necessary."

"Hmm," he said. That was it. Just *Hmm*.

She hated when he did that, acted like he knew something she didn't. It was as irritating as it was patronizing. "Don't do that," she told him. "I'm not trying to play this game with you."

"What game?"

"The game where I ask you 'What?' and you play coy for a while, but really you're dying to impart your wisdom on poor, ignorant me. It was the story of our relationship."

"That's interesting, because I remember the story of our relationship being me trying to get through to you, and you using every possible excuse in the book to push me away. You didn't love me the way I loved you."

"You didn't love me, Chase," she countered. "Because not only did you audition without me, you stole my recipes. I heard nothing else from you until you showed back up in *my* neighborhood—one you hated before but obviously have no problem with now that it's being whitewashed."

His chest puffed in the way guys' chests did whenever they were offended. Next he would say something douchey. A girl learned the pattern quickly when she had four older brothers.

"Is that what you think?"

"It's what I know. You think I wouldn't recognize my own recipes on national television, especially when my journals went missing after you moved out?"

He rolled his eyes. "I'm sorry you think that, but I hardly needed your amateur scribblings to win."

Kamilah's head snapped back. "Really, 'amateur scribblings'? Is that why I was at the top of our class, and you wouldn't even have graduated without me?"

"And yet I own three successful restaurants, and you don't own any." Chase raised his brows.

He couldn't even raise a single brow. What a joke. If he was trying to communicate his displeasure nonverbally, he'd have to get a more expressive face. Like Liam's. With the tiniest squint of his eye or twist of the mouth, Liam conveyed entire conversations. A pang went through her chest.

"I totally would have, if you hadn't stabbed me in the back."

For the first time he actually looked mad. "I don't care that you've made me out to be the villain, but don't use me as an excuse. If you really wanted it, then you would have done everything in your power to get it. You are where you are because of your own choices."

"You don't know shit about why I am where I am."

"Oh please, I know exactly why. It's the same reason we never would've worked out. Because you use your family as a shield."

Her jaw fell. "I do not."

"Anytime I wanted to spend time with you, there was some family function you had to be at. When we made plans, you'd cancel them because of a family emergency. When they would say rude things to me, you always took their side before you took mine. It took me a long time to realize that it wasn't your family's fault. They weren't the ones who came between us. You put them there. Just like you put them between yourself and your career. It's what you do when you're scared."

You're so terrified of going out on your own and failing that you prefer to hide behind your martyrdom.

"I don't let anything stand between me and what I want. That's why we didn't work out," he continued. "We are just too different."

The problem had never been their differences. They were just two people who had great sex and appreciated the other's talent. That was about it. Somewhere along the line, they'd confused that for love and decided it meant happily-ever-after.

Now Kamilah knew what real love felt like, just like she knew what real heartbreak felt like, and she'd felt none of those things for Chase.

"It doesn't even matter anymore." Kamilah stood from her chair. "Our past was a long time ago, and it's irrelevant in the grand scheme of things." She started backing up. "You have your life, I have mine, and that's just that."

"Except you're the one who showed up here, three times now."

Again, she didn't explain how two of those times were horribly embarrassing coincidences. She didn't care enough about what he thought. "This is a great place you have here," she said. "Best of luck." She walked out of Chase's restaurant.

As she walked down the street, one thing Chase had said played in her mind over and over. Not because he'd hurt her but because it seemed to match what Liam thought. They both claimed that Kamilah used her family as an excuse to keep others at a distance and not move forward. Maybe they were both right, but that was hardly a problem anymore, since her family had pretty much disowned her.

Now she had no excuses and no distractions, just herself and her failure.

24

Liam was in the distillery stacking crates of Da's whiskey. He should really think about creating some sort of limited-edition packaging. He usually didn't package his whiskey at all, but Da's was special. Maybe he could do a wooden box of some kind with the name engraved. He pulled out his phone to search local woodworkers. A few days ago he could've walked over to the restaurant and asked any of the Vegas to put him in contact with Luís. But the restaurant was empty. He hadn't even seen Kamilah's parents around. They were probably going out of their way to avoid him. They probably all were. However, he couldn't really bring himself to care.

He couldn't seem to care about much of anything. Not even the fact that he hadn't spoken to Ben or Dev since the night of the party. Dev had told him to make it better with Kamilah. Liam had told him that there was no point. Ben had countered that Liam would regret leaving everything as messed up as it was. Liam had barked at them to mind their own fucking business for once in their overbearing, nagging, fishwife lives.

"Fine, you want to be a dick? Go ahead," Dev had said.

"But you're going to be a lonely one, because we aren't putting up with your emo bullshit," Ben had tacked on.

They'd left.

To make matters worse, he still hadn't talked to Granda. He'd been trying every day to see him, but both Granda and Papo had revoked his visitation privileges at the home and wouldn't answer any of his calls.

The only person he'd seen was Saint when he'd come to collect some of Kamilah's things. He'd looked at Liam like he was dog shit and told him it would be better if he weren't around for the rest of the move. Not a problem. Liam barely entered his house at all. He slept in his office, ate takeout from the Chinese restaurant a few blocks away, and showered quickly in the guest bathroom. He couldn't stand being in there for longer than a few minutes at a time.

Looking at his kitchen reminded him of kissing Kamilah or watching her cook. Sitting at the dining-room table made him think about the hours he spent working with her on their plans. The lack of festive fall pillows and blankets on his couch hit him like a fist to the groin every time. And forget about the bedroom. He'd gone in there one time to grab a bunch of his clothes and ended up breaking down in the half-empty closet when he realized the room didn't smell like coconuts.

He was a wreck. He knew it, but that was hardly news. He'd been a wreck for twenty years.

"As you can see, I'm not dead yet, so you can stop calling the home asking about my fecking health."

Liam nearly dropped the crate in his hands. He spun around and found Granda standing in the doorway to the distillery looking as formidable as ever. *Thank God.* "Granda," Liam croaked. "I'm so glad you came."

"We'll see how long that lasts."

"Why would you say that?"

"I've been going back and forth for days trying to figure out the best course of action." Granda walked over to him and perched on the edge of the table. "But this morning I got up and decided *Let's get this over with.*"

"Get what over with?"

"This fight that has been brewing between us for years." Granda stretched his neck and shoulders as if gearing up for a real fistfight. "Come on. Let it all out. Everything you've been wanting to say to me."

"What makes you think I have things I want to say to you that I haven't already said?" Liam lifted another crate of bottles off the table and went to stack them in the storage area.

"Because you're mad, lad. You're mad at everyone, including me."

He was right. Liam was mad. He'd been quietly seething for years. But what good would fighting with his grandfather do, now that he was dying? "I don't want to fight with you, Granda."

"I don't want to fight with you either, but I refuse to let this shite continue, so we're going to have it out. I'll start first if you want." He didn't wait for Liam to say anything. He simply continued. "I'm pissed as hell at you for making plans about my distillery without me. You didn't once think to bring up this offer to me, even though I still own more than half of this place. You just continued on making your own plans as if I were already gone. All while you were begging me to get treated."

Liam flinched and then hung his head. He rubbed both

palms over his face. "To be fair," he continued after a moment of silence, "I've been telling you that we need help with Kane for years, but you never even listen to me. So yeah, when this opportunity fell into my lap, I kept it to myself, even though I knew I shouldn't. But you have to admit that you're so stubborn that you'll cut your nose off to spite your face."

"I'm a stubborn old goat, but you're a wee whiny baby. 'Oh I'm Liam. I'm mad that life is hard, so I'm going to act like a fecking gobshite for the rest of my life.'"

"Where do you think I got it from? You've been pissed off at the world since I could remember."

Granda sighed. "You're right. I have been pissed off at the world, and I did my best to make you mad too. I sowed those seeds when you were young and vulnerable, when I should've been doing my best to help you heal. It's my fault your emotional growth was stunted, so I figured it was my responsibility to put you on the right track. It didn't work out like I thought it would."

"Is that why you did all this? You think you need to fix me?" Liam felt his rage boil over. "Why are you always trying to make me into something I'm not?" he yelled. "I'm not you, and I'm not *him*. I tried so hard to be him for your sake, but I can't because I'll never be like him, and I don't want to be. He was an idiot who went off and drowned himself instead of letting me go look for Nana."

"Why would he let you go?"

"Because I could swim, and he couldn't."

Granda staggered back. "The feck do you mean he couldn't swim?"

"I don't know why, but he never learned. When Nana didn't resurface he tried looking for her, but the life vest wouldn't let him go very far under. He started to take it off, and I begged him not to. I told him I'd go look for her instead and *he* could stay on top of the boat, but he wouldn't let me. He took it off, went under, and never came back up."

"Why did you never tell me this before, Liam? Did you think that I didn't deserve to know the truth?"

Liam let out a ragged breath. "You'd already lost so much. I didn't want you to lose your perception of him too."

Granda frowned. "Why would I— Ah. That's why you're mad at him, because you think that if he'd listened to you, he wouldn't have died."

"He wouldn't have. He chose to die. He chose to leave me. Leave us. And because of that, we lost everything."

"Especially you, right? I lost my wife and my son, but you lost everyone in some way or another. And now you're losing me."

Liam dropped his head into his hands. The thought of being completely alone was suddenly more than he could bear. He held his breath in an attempt to prevent the sob he could feel clawing its way up his throat.

He heard the soft tread of Granda's boots on the concrete floor and then felt a hand on his shoulder.

"Ah, lad. We really did a number on you." He tightened his hold. "I should've never put myself in between you and your ma, I should've never let you stop going to that shrink, and I should've never let you think that I wanted you to be like your da. If I'd been a better man, it wouldn't have taken me all this time to realize how much you're still hurting. I failed you, Liam, and I'm sorry."

"I'm so mad, Granda," Liam choked out. "I'm mad that everything in my life turned to shit when that happened, and I'm pissed that I'm not strong enough to get over it like everyone else did."

"Is that what you think? That you can get over it? There is no getting over it. There's only learning to live with it. And it's bloody hard—take it from me. But missing someone you loved for the rest of your life doesn't make you weak, Liam. It makes you strong, because you survive despite that onslaught of pain."

"Love is bullshite. Love is a lie that people use as an excuse to do shitty things to other people and be forgiven for it."

"That's where you're wrong, boyo. Love is the only thing that makes living in this shite world worth anything. Your nana used to say, 'Love is creation,' and she taught that to your da. Why do you think he created this?" He pushed a bottle of Da's whiskey into Liam's hands.

Liam stared at the bottle. "What do you mean?"

"I understand now more than ever why you'd be mad at him, but, Liam, you were his son, and he loved you more than anyone."

"Did he?" It seemed to Liam that he'd loved Nana more.

"Yes. He did. I know it's hard to think about it from his perspective, because you're not a father yet. But, Liam, no real da would put his child in harm's way to save himself. If he had done that, he wouldn't be the son I'd raised or the man we both knew. The man who loved to make whiskey with his da, sing rock ballads with his wife, take his ma on adventures, and who thought the sun rose and fell on his boy." Granda stared off into the distance as if looking into the past. He smiled softly and shook his head. "From the moment you came into this world, he thought you were the smartest baby that had ever been born. You'd shit your pants or piss in your ma's face, and the man would act like you'd just done something spectacular. You were everything to your da, and that's how I know that the only reason he did what he did was because he knew that you were safe on top of that boat in your life vest."

Liam squeezed his eyes shut at the sudden zing of pain. He bit his lip, and for the first time in over ten years, he allowed himself to think about Da outside of his final moments. To remember the man who used to call Liam his best friend, take him to the store every week to buy new art supplies, and never once made him feel like he had to be anyone other than who he was. Then he remembered something else from that day.

Before that idiot on the Jet Ski caused them to capsize, Liam had been drawing. Nana, his biggest fan, had complimented his technique. Da had asked to see his picture and was impressed by Liam's abstract interpretation of the scenery. Liam had mentioned that some of the other boys in his class laughed at him because he liked to draw instead of play football.

Da looked at him. "Don't ever let the fear of other people's judgment change you. You're a supercool and interesting kid who is going to turn into an awesome man."

"Like you?" Liam asked.

"No, not like me. I'm a simple guy with simple tastes. You're complex and a little intense, but you're innovative. Whatever you do, you'll turn it on its head and make it something new. Something never done before."

Liam turned to the back of the bottle and read the nose and flavor profile. *Lingering deep oak spice coupled with smoke, well-lively nose with dried fruit, leading to a soft vanilla, sherry nuttiness. Complex and a bit intense at first, but with a bright freshness that shines through at the finish. In the end, it balances out into something you've never tasted before.*

Holy shit, Da's whiskey was Liam. At least, how Da had

seen Liam. It was the embodiment of Connor Kane's love for his son.

I love you, son. So much.

"He made this for me," Liam whispered. Damn, Liam wished he was the man his father had hoped he would be. The type of man who deserved to have a whiskey crafted after him.

"He did."

"He did love me."

"He did. So do I. And so does Kamilah."

Because he was already off balance, Granda's mention of *her* had Liam completely thrown. He shot Granda a scowl. "I don't want to talk about her."

"Too damn bad, because I said we were putting all our cards on the table, and she is the fecking royal flush."

Liam snorted. "Royal pain in the ass, more like."

"Oh shut it, you smart-ass. You're being an eejit. You are in love with that girl. You've loved her since you were kids, and you're throwing that all away for what? Because it's not comfortable? Because it's hard, and it requires you to change and grow? Well, guess what? That's what life is. Life is a series of unexpected, uncomfortable, and usually-unwanted incidents that you can either grow or hide from. And, lad, you've been hiding for twenty years."

You're a coward who is so terrified of being happy that you lock yourself away in your miserable past.

Liam thought about his own whiskey—his favorite special blend—with its sweet softness, notes of caramel and coconut, and its spiced warmth. Everything that Kamilah embodied. It represented the love and longing he'd felt for her for almost two decades. That was the real reason the whiskey was unnamed and not for sale. It was too important, too private, and he'd never wanted anyone to know how very much she meant to him. Especially her.

I reach out to you, you walk away from me, and I keep reaching out to you anyway, even though I'm hurt.

I knew you would do exactly this. You would throw my love for you back in my face and then push me away, because that's what you do. Over and over and over.

For years he'd kept a wall between himself and everyone who cared about him. He'd isolated himself from the rest of the world. He told himself it was because he was smart enough to realize the sham of love and hope, but really it was because he didn't think he could handle any more pain. He'd pushed away the person who for him epitomized love and hope. While keeping his distance, he'd sneered at her, criticized her, and belittled her when he should've been letting her in and being honest with her.

He'd called her a hypocrite, but really he was the hypocrite, because he'd been upset about her hiding things from him, when he'd hidden his feelings for her for fifteen years. All those years he'd spent focused on the wrong things: the past, his pain, his anger, his insecurity. He'd stolen and destroyed his own opportunities for happiness when he should've been fighting for them.

"I wasted so much fucking time," he said aloud. He hadn't really been talking to Granda, but Granda answered anyway.

"You always were a little slow on the uptake, Liam, my lad."

Liam frowned at him. "Really, Granda?"

Granda let out one of his trademark crooked smiles. The scamp. "Now that you've finally seen the light, what do you plan to do about this?"

"I don't think there is anything to do now."

"The hell there isn't."

"You didn't see her face, Granda. I let her down, and she's done giving me chances. She told me to leave her alone." He had. He'd left her alone to pick up the pieces of their broken agreement and her tattered relationship with her family.

"But—"

"Granda, after this conversation, can you honestly tell me that you think I'm ready for a real relationship with her? I'm fucked up. I need to work on myself. I need to be better and do better, before I can be with anyone." He was going to fight for his happiness instead of sabotaging it. He wasn't unrealistic. He knew he still had an epic battle to fight—one he'd probably fight for the rest of his life. He didn't have the right to drag anyone else along on that journey with him.

"So you are just going to let her go? You aren't even going to try to fix this?"

Just because he couldn't see them being together didn't mean that he didn't have to try to make it right. However accidental, he'd still revealed her secrets to her family and then walked away. "I'm going to try to make it up to her, I owe her that much, but I'm not going to try to convince her to be with me. That's not fair to her. She deserves better than to put up with my shit."

"Lad, I think you're making a decision for her, just like you accused her of making them for you. I also think you're still hiding. I say that you put it all out there, everything you feel. And then let her decide if she wants to give you one more chance to get your shit together with her at your side."

Just the thought of having Kamilah in his life and in his corner made him all the more determined to fight to win. She made him *want* to be open to new people and ideas. She made him look at the positive aspects of life and think outside of the box he'd confined himself in. Through her eyes, he could see a future that might not always be bright, but it was full of possibility, and that was more than Liam had felt before.

"You're right, Granda. It's my turn to put myself out there, but I don't know what to do."

Devilry flashed in Granda's eyes. "I have an idea."

25

It was becoming more and more clear to Kamilah that if she wanted anything to get better, she was going to have to apologize. It wasn't anything she hadn't already known, but there was a pretty big part of her that had hoped her family would sweep the whole thing under the rug and ignore it— like they did with so many other problems.

Alas, they still weren't talking to her. She had to change that. She walked up the back stairs that led to the apartment she'd been raised in and knocked on the door. A few moments later, it opened to reveal her mother. She didn't say anything to Kamilah. She just stood there.

"Bendiciones, Mami. I was hoping we could talk."

Mami gave a curt nod and backed away so she could enter. Kamilah went to the kitchen, and she followed. The most delicious smell in the world filled the air.

"Are you making carne guisada?" That was Kamilah's favorite. She wasn't picky about her Puerto Rican beef stew, but no one made it better than Mami. Not even her or Abuela.

Mami's masterpiece called to her from the stove. Kamilah walked over, lifted the lid, and took a big whiff. Mmm. The smell of the tomato sauce, spices, sofrito, garlic, carrots, potato, and beef married in perfect balance made Kamilah's mouth water.

"Baja eso," Mami scolded from behind her. She rushed over. "You're letting out all the steam, and then the meat won't be tender."

Kamilah dropped the lid as directed and refrained from reminding her mom that the caldero wasn't a pressure cooker. "Pero huele tan rico," she whined playfully.

Mami's lips quirked. She recognized Kamilah's childhood refrain. She would always snap at Kamilah to stop sniffing everything like a dog, and Kamilah would reply, "But it smells so good." Mami would laugh.

Today Mami just shook her head and lifted the lid to stir the stew before replacing it. "Loca," she said. There was more fondness than accusation in the word.

Kamilah sensed a softening in attitude. Tentatively she reached out and wrapped her arms around her mother's shoulders from behind. Mami's hands came up to grab on to Kamilah's. She lifted them to her mouth for a kiss before resting them back on her sternum. It was a peace offering. One Kamilah gratefully jumped on and reciprocated with a kiss to Mami's cheek. Kamilah put her chin on Mami's shoulder and leaned her head against Mami's. Mami leaned her head deeper against Kamilah's. They stayed like that for a while, neither speaking a word.

"I'm sorry, Mami," Kamilah eventually said. "I've done so much wrong, and not just in the last few months but for years. I just felt, I don't know, stuck and scared, and so I lied. All I wanted was to make you proud of me."

Mami was quiet for a while, but finally she said, "I've been too hard on you. I pushed and criticized and broke you down when I should have been building you up. Pero todo lo que hago, lo hago por tu bien." It was another familiar refrain: "Everything I do, I do it for your own good."

Kamilah knew that. "Lo se y todo lo que yo hago, lo hago por amor." Kamilah really wanted her mom to realize that Kamilah was acting out of love, not ambition.

Mami nodded. "Lo se y te perdono."

Kamilah tightened her arms around her mom and held on for another moment.

Behind them someone cleared their throat. There was only one person it could be. She turned to face Papi, unsure of what she should do. It was a weird and distinctly unpleasant feeling, being unsure of what to do in the house she was raised in.

Papi walked into the kitchen and took a seat, so Kamilah did too. She fiddled around with the embroidered place mat in front of her and crossed and uncrossed her legs. All the while Papi just stared at her.

"I'm sorry," she forced out and then promptly burst into tears. Her father had always been the one she went to when she needed comfort. He was the one who picked her up when she fell off her bike. He was the one who put Band-Aids on her cuts. He was the one who sat with her in his lap during Connor's funeral when she was scared and confused and so terribly sad. He was her rock, and she'd hurt him.

"I'm so sorry that I lied to you and kept secrets from you." She continued through her sobs. "I was wrong and so stupid, and I thought I was helping, but I wasn't. I made everything worse, and I betrayed your trust." She put her face in her hands and tried to get herself together. There was more she had to say. But the tears wouldn't stop, and a lump clogged her throat.

Kamilah heard the legs of the wooden chair scrape across the linoleum floor. Then she was hauled out of her chair and into her father's arms. "Shh. Ya." He murmured over and over while rubbing her back like he used to when she was a little girl. "Ya, mi amor."

"I'm sorry," Kamilah kept repeating.

"I know," he said.

Eventually, Kamilah's sobs turned to hiccups and her hiccups waned. She stayed in her father's arms until he put his hands on her shoulders and pushed her back a little. He looked down at her, and Kamilah noted that his eyes were also a bit wet and red.

"Better?" he asked.

Kamilah nodded. "I just love you all so much, and I wanted the best for you. I wanted you all to be happy."

"I know."

"Somehow it all got away from me. I got lost in *Familia primero*. I thought that in order to prove your love to someone, you had to be willing to sacrifice for them, so that's what I started doing, and at first it felt great. I loved it when I was the one that was able to help get something done and figure something out. To be honest, I still do. But somewhere along the way, I made myself a martyr. It got to the point where I felt like everything fell on me and I was the only one who could fix anything, and then the little white lies started, followed by the secrets, and I figured it wasn't a big deal because I was doing it for you guys."

"Ay, Kamilah," Mami said. "I should've known you'd take

everything we ever told you to heart and then run with it. Siempre has sido un poco ingenua y muy exagerada."

Kamilah couldn't argue with that. She was naive and gullible. Especially when it came to love. She believed that the ends excused the means and that everything would work out. And she did tend to go a bit overboard...i.e., faking an engagement and lying to everyone she knew in order to hold on to the restaurant.

Papi nodded. "I understand, Kamilah. I get it."

But how could he? He'd never done anything like that.

"Ven." He motioned for her to take a seat. This time he sat in the chair next to her. Mami took the chair across from her. "Here's something only your mami and your tío Rico know. I never wanted to run the restaurant. I never even wanted to work there."

Kamilah's eyes rounded. "What?"

"Growing up, I hated that restaurant. It felt like it took all the attention away from us kids, and we worked there like indentured servants. Home from school and straight to work until close. Working from sunup to sundown on weekends. We never got to go anywhere and have fun because we weren't allowed to go anywhere without our parents, and our parents were always there."

"So how did you end up taking it over?"

"A lot like how you did, actually. Your tía Rocio had just gotten married, Rico was pursuing his community projects, Ali was babysitting and volunteering at the hospital, and Flaca, well, you know your tía Carmen. She was off rehearsing, como siempre. I was the only one around, and I felt like it was my duty to help. Like you, things got away from me, and suddenly I was in control of everything but the kitchen. Your abuelo really just wanted to hang out with his friends and play music, so he put everything on my shoulders. Because I didn't want to disappoint him or fail your abuela, I let him. When I met your mom, I decided to tell your abuelos that I didn't want to work there. Your mami and I were making other plans. Then Papi had his first heart attack, and I stayed quiet. Your mami loved me, so she didn't push. We ended up married and working at the restaurant, taking on more and more responsibility."

"And secretly resenting it," Kamilah finished for him.

"Yes. I get it. I understand how the pressure to be there for your family can get away from you, but I never wanted to put that pressure on you. I didn't want any of my kids to feel how I felt. And more than whatever nonsense Papi and Killian concocted, I'm hurt that you sacrificed your dream and never said anything about it but held it against us. When sacrifices are made in excess, out of duty, or with resentment, they cease to mean anything positive."

"I know that."

"You need to realize that *family first* doesn't mean at the expense of everything else. It means that we all look out for one another, support one another, and respect one another because the love we feel for each other is first in our hearts."

"Look, I'm here because I admit one hundred percent that I was wrong to hide how I felt and use lies to cover it up. I was wrong to try to manipulate the situation to benefit myself through dishonest means. But I think it's really important to talk about why I felt desperate enough to see that as my only option." The words made her throat tighten, and still, she choked them out, needing them out. "And that's because I felt for a long time that I put my family first, but they put me last. You mentioned love, respect, and support, and I didn't feel that. I felt pressure to prove myself as valuable because it was like every mistake I made was highlighted, but any positive was glossed over."

Papi nodded. "We've been talking about this a lot and thinking about the ways we contributed to this whole thing. Sadly, you're right. We didn't support you as we should have, and we didn't value your opinion even when we didn't agree. I accused you of acting like a child, but I also kept treating you like one and undermining your efforts when you did try to assert yourself as an adult."

"We were scared that you'd given up on your own dreams," Mami said in Spanish. "We didn't want you to be stuck at El Coquí living the life we never wanted. We tried to block your efforts so that you would decide to leave the nest, but we didn't see that in doing that, we clipped your wings."

Papi reached over and grabbed Kamilah's hand. "We were trying to give you the choice we felt like we never had, and we went about it the wrong way. All we want is for you to have the freedom to be who you are and choose your own path. We want you to do what makes you happy, but to do it openly and honestly, without secrets and lies."

Freedom. She rubbed the scarred surface of the table. It had always been there at the back of her mind. She'd felt like a wrongfully accused prisoner who'd been serving a life sentence, only to have some new evidence exonerate them. She was released from all expectations beyond doing what made her happy.

"I don't know what that is," she stated.

"What did I just say about lying?" Papi scolded. "You know exactly what that is."

She did. She wanted her own place. She wanted to make the decisions, create the menu, change things as she saw fit. She couldn't exactly envision it yet: she'd focused on El Coquí for so long that anything else was nebulous. But there was one very clear image in her imaginings of the perfect future. It was Liam. She'd never been happier than when she was with him. He always allowed her to be exactly who she was. He supported her in whatever she wanted to do and had given up his time and comfort to help her achieve it. In return, she had only pushed and pushed him to be who she wanted him to be and hadn't respected his boundaries. She didn't blame him for not believing that she loved him.

"I ruined that too," she confessed. "I pushed him too hard right when he was starting to open up to me. If I had just taken it a bit slower, Liam might have been able to reciprocate my feelings."

"Kamilah, me niego a creer que eres tan tonta."

Kamila grimaced. "Ouch, Papi."

"I'm sorry, but you are being dumb. You think Liam doesn't love you too? That man has been in love with you since he was a boy, and everyone knows it. Everyone but you, it seems."

"He has not. He could barely stand to be around me, and when he was, it was clear that I annoyed the hell out of him. When we lived together, we figured out how to be friends again." Friends and lovers, although she wasn't going to say that to her parents. "But that was it. At least, from his perspective."

"There you go again." Mami threw up her hands in exasperation. "Thinking you know what everyone thinks and wants."

"Mami, he called me a hypocrite, a manipulative liar, and a coward, and then he walked away from me."

"Sí." Mami nodded. She pointed a bony finger at Kamilah. "Y eso es lo que te pasa por pendeja."

Kamilah furrowed her brow and scrunched her nose. She'd heard that saying many times when her fooling around got her hurt, but it had never stung so much as it did now. "Dang, Mami."

Mami threw up her hands and gave Kamilah a look that said *Well, what did you expect after you lied to him and hid things from him? That's not how you treat someone you love.*

"I was scared," she told them. "I was scared he'd turn his back on me. Again."

"And he did, and it hurt you," Papi said. "But that doesn't mean that he was wrong to do it this time, and it doesn't mean that this can't be fixed."

"No, he was right to walk away from me. I messed everything up and went about it all in the wrong way. But even if I can figure out a way to fix this, that still doesn't mean that he wants to be with me. Even before the party, I told him that I loved him, and he didn't say it back."

Papi shook his head. "You know better than anyone that love is not expressed in words but in actions. Everything that he has shown you has been actions of love. He stepped in to defend you and support you. He opened his home and his life to you. To all of us. For the first time since his mom left. He didn't do that for some idiotic blackmail agreement. He did that because he wants to build a life with you. He wants to be a family with you."

Kamilah blinked, then she frowned, and then she blinked some more. It had never occurred to her that he'd acted out of anything more than partnership and perhaps a bit of lust. "Oh my God, I *am* an idiot," Kamilah exclaimed. "He wasn't ignoring my feelings. He was trying to share his own in his awkward and completely Liam way." He had offered her his heart over and over, and she'd ignored it because he hadn't done it the way she wanted. Then she'd chosen herself and her wants over his. No wonder he'd scoffed at her declaration of love.

"What are you going to do about it?" Mami asked.

"I'm going to finally be a woman of my word and be there for him." Kamilah pulled out her phone. "I'm going to text him right now and tell him that I want to support him, but I don't want to force my help on him." She spoke as she typed. "Then I'll offer to still make the food for the tasting, if he wants me to." She hit Send. "I don't know if that will be enough to fix things with him, but I do know how I can fix things with you both. I want you both to have the freedom you've always wanted." She took a deep breath. "I'm pulling El Coquí from the Fall Foodie Tour, and you both have my support to sell."

She could feel the tightening of her throat and the welling of tears. It hurt so much to tell them to sell—she felt as if she were separating her soul from her already-broken heart—but it was the right thing to do. They all deserved the freedom to choose what came next.

26

With trepidation, Liam eyed the two camera operators and the audio technician currently focusing their cameras and analyzing the acoustics. Liam tugged at the cuffs of his denim button-up shirt. "What if she doesn't like my surprise?"

"She's going to love it," Granda assured him.

"But what if she gets mad that we're taking all of the judges over there and interrupting the tour?" No one was more surprised than him to have received a text from Kamilah asking if he was okay with her still making some dishes for the tasting. He'd jumped at the opportunity to grab the olive branch and said yes before remembering that she was going to be swamped at the restaurant.

"Liam, she already said that it was fine."

"Right." Liam tugged at his sleeve again. He felt like everything he was wearing was too small.

"Stop playing around with your shirt," Ben scolded him. He'd come as soon as Liam had called for backup. Dev and

Rome had added their support as well, although they were too busy to come in person. "I worked hard to perfect your look."

"It's hot," Liam complained. He was already sweaty. He started unbuttoning the cuffs to roll his sleeves up.

"Fine. Fine." Ben brushed his hands away. "Let me do it, before you wrinkle everything."

Liam held his arm out while Ben meticulously folded the cuff over his forearm. "What if I fuck this up?"

"You won't," Granda told him. He put a hand on his shoulder. "You're ready for this."

As he cuffed Liam's other sleeve, Ben eyed Liam's already-sweaty forehead and took in his rapid breaths. "Do you need a Xanax or something? I have some in my car."

Liam shook his head. "I just want this to work."

"Relax." Granda pounded him on the back, but Liam barely felt it. "Everything is going to go according to plan."

Liam gave his grandfather a suspicious look. "Granda, why do I feel like your plan and my plan are not the same thing?"

"I came up with your plan, so your plan is my plan." Granda broke eye contact and started brushing off the front of his brand-new Kane Distillery T-shirt that read *Don't be an eejit. Drink Kane.*

He was definitely up to something.

"Granda," Liam warned.

"Kamilah's here," Ben whisper-shouted, pulling Liam's attention away from his troublemaking grandpa.

She stood in the doorway in jeans, a white chef jacket, and apron. Her hair was held back from her face with a thick bandanna headband. There were flags of red across her cheeks, and she glistened with a light sheen of perspiration. She was the most beautiful thing he'd ever seen.

"Am I interrupting?" She looked at him with those eyes of hers.

Liam wanted to drop to his knees and beg her forgiveness. Once she forgave him, he wanted to throw her over his shoulder like a caveman and disappear with her for days. A sharp elbow in his side yanked him back to the present. What had she asked? Something about interrupting? "We're still waiting for the judges."

Somebody pushed him forward. Liam followed the unspoken demand and walked to Kamilah.

"Hi," he managed.

"Hi."

They paused.

"Umm. How's it going over there?" Liam asked. He hoped she was getting all the attention she needed to put El Coquí back on the map.

She looked away and gave a small shrug. In an uncharacteristic demonstration of nervousness, she rubbed her palms on her apron. "I don't want to distract you or anything, but I got you something for good luck, and I wanted to give it to you before the judging started." She reached into the pocket of her apron, pulled out a small box, and handed it to him.

He lifted the lid to the box and sucked in a breath. He reached in and pulled out a thick steel bracelet engraved with Celtic knots. It looked old and very valuable. "Where did you get this?"

"I won an online bidding war."

He turned it in his hand and noticed the design at the front. "A claddagh?" Liam knew the story of the design well. It was his grandmother's favorite story to tell. The story of a young fisherman, captured by pirates, sold into slavery, and owned by a goldsmith. The legend said that, every day, the young man stole flecks of gold and hid them in his pockets. He believed he would one day find his way out of captivity and back to his true love. Eventually, he did. His true love had waited for him and, upon learning so, he declared himself to her and asked her to marry him. He fashioned a ring out of the stolen gold flecks he'd amassed, and he created the claddagh design.

"It reminded me of you." She took the box out of his hands and put it back in her apron pocket. "The crown for loyalty because you are the most steadfast grandson. Your life's work is an honor to your family and your legacy: dedication from your grandfather, craft from your father, history from your grandmother, and beauty from your mother. The hands for friendship because you've been my best friend since before I even knew what friendship meant. You understand me like no one else does, you support me even when it's inconvenient for you, but you also call me on my shit. Lastly, a heart for love because I don't know anyone who loves as hard as you do. You love so deeply that it pains you, and yet you still do it." She swallowed thickly. "And while you're going through this final round of judging, I want you to remember that this—" she pointed to the design "—is who you are. A loving and loyal friend who is so much more than this contest. You are more than Kane Distillery. You are...everything."

"Mila," Liam breathed. Before he could say anything else, Mandy breezed into the open garage door with a young woman, a young man, and a middle-aged man in tow. *The judges are here.*

"Today is a beautiful day for a distillery judging," Mandy said. "Let's get everyone mic'd up, and let's get this show on the road."

Liam turned to Kamilah, unsure of what he was going to

say, but she was no longer next to him. He swung his head side to side, looking for her. He caught a glimpse of her out of the corner of his eye.

She was already outside, walking past the warehouse windows. As if sensing his gaze, she looked over her shoulder and gave him a smile and thumbs-up before disappearing back into El Coquí.

"Liam, come meet the judges," Mandy called.

Liam looked down at Kamilah's gift one more time. She thought he was everything. He smiled to himself and slipped the bracelet on his arm—the point of the heart pointing toward his body, as tradition dictated. Then he went to join the others.

Mandy made brief introductions while the camera and audio guys hooked little packs onto Liam's and Granda's pants, threaded a thin wire under their shirts, and clipped tiny mics onto their collars.

"Are you nervous?" Janice, the badass whiskey connoisseur with a colorful arm sleeve, asked him.

"A little," Liam replied.

Granda licked his palm and ran it over his already-styled hair like he was in the movie *Grease*. "Don't be nervous, lad. All you have to do is sit back and make me look good."

Mandy was delighted with Granda. "Oh. This is going to be amazing."

Liam thought about the surprise he had in store. *You have no idea.*

"Nena, the tour is almost over. You'd better hurry up and finish the food."

Kamilah wiped her sweaty hairline with the sleeve of her chef's whites. "Not helpful, Abuelo." She knew she was running late, but preparing four different dishes for a pretty big group of people was a lot of work, and her so-called sous-chef wasn't very efficient.

Abuelo had spent the entire morning chatting at her or singing along to the radio while taking his sweet time cutting up anything Kamilah put in front of him.

She chanced a brief glance at him and found him dipping pieces of grilled pineapple in the whiskey glaze and then eating them, even though she'd told him to keep an eye on the fried sweet plantain cups she was making for the grilled pineapple and shrimp salad.

"Why don't you go make sure the dining area is set up and that we have the right whiskey, while I put the finishing touches on these pinchos?" She took the bowl of whiskey glaze from his hands, grabbed a new basting brush, and began adding the final layer of glaze to the beef and chicken kebabs.

He hopped off his stool. "Yes, chef." He saluted her just to be even more of a smart-ass and then moseyed out of the kitchen.

As soon as he was gone, Kamilah busted ass to get everything ready. She wanted everything to be perfect because this was her chance to prove to Liam that she could be helpful without taking over and that she really did value him as a person.

She'd just finished plating the last of the dishes when Abuelo popped his head in. "They are on their way over. I hear them."

Kamilah looked down at herself in alarm. "What? Already? But I look horrible."

Abuelo grimaced at her and nodded his head. "You do."

"Abuelo! You aren't supposed to agree with me. You're supposed to tell me that I look beautiful no matter what."

"Of course you are beautiful no matter what, but they are bringing cameras and you are really...sweaty."

"Shit," she huffed. "Shit, shit, shit."

"Mira, you go wipe yourself down, change your shirt, and fix your...self. And I'll put all the food out."

"Okay." She pointed to the plates on the table. "It's all there in order. First the plátano maduro with the shrimp and pineapple, then the pernil sandwiches with the mango slaw, after that the pinchos with the arroz con gandules, and the flan de coco with the whiskey caramel sauce is last. Got it?"

"Claro. This isn't my first rodeo. I know what to do. Vete." He waved her on.

She wished she had more confidence in his reply, but mostly she wished she had more time. She snatched her bag and the T-shirt Killian had given her off the table near the back door and then took off up the stairs to her parents' apartment. She rushed to the bathroom and almost yelped when she saw herself in the mirror. No wonder Abuelo had grimaced at her.

She was red-faced, sweaty, and frizzy-haired. She quickly rinsed her face with cool water and used a wet washcloth to wipe herself down. She reapplied her deodorant and then slipped on her new Kane Distillery–logo T-shirt that said *People are better with whiskey ~Liam Kane* on the back. Her hair was hopeless, so she pulled it into her typical pineapple. To make it look like she was wearing at least some makeup, she pulled out her trusty, long-lasting, smudge-proof red lipstick and put it on.

There. That's as good as it's going to get.

She rushed back down the stairs and into the kitchen. She was surprised to hear what sounded like a large group of people in the dining area. She streaked through the swinging doors and came to an abrupt stop. It looked like her entire family was in the dining room and they were wearing a mix of El Coquí and Kane Distillery shirts. The swinging door came back around and hit her in the ass, propelling her forward.

"What is happening?" she asked.

Three strangers and the mayor sat at the island table in the center of the room. On the table, thankfully, was everything Kamilah had asked Abuelo to set up. In the background, Mandy was pointing out features of the restaurant to one camera operator, while the other taped her family and friends smiling as they watched her reaction. In the back corner Abuelo and Killian whispered to each other. *Oh shit.* That couldn't be good. When she made eye contact with him, Killian gave her a wink and a smile. That was definitely not good.

And then there was Liam, standing tall and proud in front of the table. He turned and their eyes met. Damn, he was gorgeous.

Her hand flew to her chest as if to calm her racing heart.

Liam lifted his wrist to show off his bracelet and smiled at her. The point of the heart was pointing to his body—signifying that his heart, loyalty, and friendship were claimed.

She took what felt like the first deep breath she'd taken since the night he'd walked out the door.

He came over to her. "You have the same look on your face as you did the time your parents created that Easter scavenger hunt."

She nodded absently. "Equal parts excited and totally lost? Yeah." She made eye contact with Mami, who blew her a kiss. "I don't understand what is going on."

"I'm confused too," Liam said. "Why were we the only

people here until your parents rolled in with your whole family and the mayor?"

"You didn't invite them?"

"No. I thought you had...until I saw the look on your face."

"Abuelo," Kamilah said at the same time Liam said, "Granda."

They both turned toward the Devious Duo and found them looking extremely pleased with themselves.

"Of course," Kamilah said.

"Mila, what happened to the Foodie Tour?"

"I removed El Coquí from the Fall Foodie Tour and probably burned a lot of bridges in the process, but it was something I had to do."

Liam appeared dumbfounded. "I didn't want that, Kamilah."

Kamilah reached out and grabbed his arm but instantly let go. "No," she said quickly. "I didn't do it because of our fight. I did it because it wasn't right to go ahead with it after everything. The next time I have a plan, I'm going to go about it openly and honestly. Make or break."

"All right." Mandy clapped her hands to gain everyone's attention. "This has certainly taken an unexpected turn, but we need to keep going. I'm going to need all the audience members to be as quiet as possible while we finish shooting."

Kamilah inhaled deeply and exhaled. "You ready?" she asked Liam.

He grinned. "I was born ready." He led her to the table, and before she knew it, she was mic'd up and they were filming.

Just like the previous time, they worked in tandem to describe the profiles of the whiskey and the complementing flavors in the food. They answered questions and responded to comments. Through it all, Kamilah kept sneaking peeks at Liam. He was on fire. He was confident, funny, engaging, and drop-dead sexy. She was so fucking proud of him that she wanted to burst.

Janice, the inked judge, used her finger to swipe the last of the whiskey-caramel sauce off her plate. She licked her finger and groaned in delight. "Kamilah, I am going to kidnap you and keep you in my kitchen so that you can make me this coconut flan for every meal."

"I don't know if you should be plotting my abduction in front of the mayor," Kamilah teased.

Mayor Johnson laughed. "I'll keep my mouth shut as long as I can get more of those sandwiches and more of this Kane Whiskey."

"I'm sure we can work something out," Janice told him.

At her side, Kamilah felt Liam shift.

He bent down and grabbed a wooden box from under the table. "I have one more whiskey that I would like you all to try."

This is it. She'd wondered why his father's whiskey hadn't been included in the list of ones he wanted her to use, but now she understood. He wanted it to stand out on its own. Just like it was Liam's turn to stand on his own. Kamilah slid over to the side of the table where Killian stood. She linked their arms and rested her head on his shoulder.

Liam shot her a questioning look, but she just smiled at him and waved him on.

This was his moment.

"My grandfather started Kane Distillery before he even bought this building, but he never wanted it to be anything huge. He was content making his whiskey the way he liked it for a select group of people. It was my father who had big dreams for Kane. When he died, we thought those dreams might go unfulfilled, but after ten years of dedicated work, we're on the verge of making them come true in his honor. Twenty years ago, only a few weeks before he died, he barreled what he called his *masterpiece*. You all were supposed to taste that whiskey today, but you're not."

Kamilah swung to look at Killian.

He didn't seem alarmed at all. In fact, he was smiling like a fool. Without taking his gaze off of his grandson, he reached over with his free hand and patted her hand, letting her know that everything was okay.

The room was silent as Liam continued. "Instead, you're going to try the most important whiskey in Kane Distillery." He put the box on the table and slid the lid back. "This whiskey is the first blend I created on my own, before I could even legally drink it."

"It's his special blend," Kamilah whispered in awe. The one he'd said would never be sold or shared.

"I hadn't planned for anyone to ever drink it, besides myself." Liam lifted the bottle, unscrewed the cap, and poured the samples into the judges' and the mayor's glasses. "But that's not because it's not good."

A few people chuckled.

"It's because it meant too much to me. My dad used to say that love is creation, and when I developed this whiskey, I did it with someone very special in mind." He lifted his glass and put it to his nose. The judges followed suit. "The first thing you'll notice is the smell of coconut. That's because she's used coconut oil in her hair since we were kids."

Kamilah's breath rushed through her lungs. She felt a curious fluttering sensation in her stomach. He was talking about her.

"You'll also smell honey because her eyes turn the color of wildflower honey when she's happy. And cinnamon because she's exciting but warm."

Killian squeezed her hand, but Kamilah couldn't tear her eyes away from Liam, even though he had yet to look at her. Warmth infused her body, spreading from her chest to all of her extremities. She pressed one hand there as if to feel the heat in her palm.

He lifted the glass to his mouth and took a sip. "There are sweet notes of vanilla, caramel, and butterscotch because all those colors can be found in her curls when she's in the sun." He took another sip. "But there is also a hit of pink peppercorn and black coffee because she's more than sweetness. She has an edge and depth. The light smokiness throughout is in reference to her mysteriousness. I've known her my entire life, and there are still facets to her that I have yet to discover. All of that together is what makes *her* the most interesting person I've ever known and *this* the greatest whiskey I've ever created."

She remembered getting emotional at his reverent description and not knowing why. Now she did. This was how he saw her. Kamilah brought her other hand to her mouth to try to stifle her happy sobs. She felt so relieved, and hopeful, and truly touched. She didn't even notice that she was virtually leaning on Killian, because her knees weren't working the way they should.

"Until recently, this whiskey didn't even have a name, let alone a label, because I was afraid that somebody would find out my secret. I am no longer afraid. And I'd like to introduce this whiskey to everyone." He turned the bottle so everyone could see it.

Exclamations arose from his audience.

Kamilah leaned to the side in a desperate attempt to see the bottle, even though she could barely see out of her overflowing eyes. She wiped them with the collar of her shirt just as Liam turned to her, still holding the bottle in his hand.

"I named this whiskey Coquí, because, like the goddess to her love, my heart has always called for you." He held the dark glass bottle out for her inspection.

The label was designed to look like an ancient stone carving. Along the bottom was the name written in letters that made Kamilah think of chalk on a very gritty surface. Taking up the prominent spot in the middle of the label was the Taíno symbol for *coquí*. However, instead of its typical stick-figure appearance, Liam had added the type of embellishments usually found on larger Taíno carvings. Among the lines, curves, dots, and swirls, he'd hidden little images just for her. There was the outline of Puerto Rico, the flag arches that symbolized Humboldt Park, the profile of a woman sporting a very familiar hairdo, a chef's toque between two knives, and even a siren in a starfish crown.

Everything about this whiskey was his love letter to her. A love letter he'd started years ago.

27

Liam shifted his weight from one foot to another. He felt like there was a low hum of electricity traversing from his head to his toes. He stared at Kamilah and willed her to take the bottle from his shaking hands before he dropped it.

However, she wasn't even looking at the bottle anymore. She was gazing at him like he was someone she'd met long before but couldn't quite place.

Suddenly, his whole mouth was dry. He ran his tongue along his bottom lip. Before he could even reach his top lip, Kamilah launched herself at him.

He dropped the bottle in his hands in order to catch her, unconcerned about what happened to it. He didn't hear a crash, so he guessed it didn't break. Again, he couldn't have cared less if it had. There was plenty more Coquí whiskey where that came from, but there was only one Coquí. Only one Kamilah.

A loud roar of cheers sounded from all around them. Her family was showing their forgiveness and approval.

She wrapped her arms and legs around him. Then she pressed her mouth to his for a quick but deep kiss. She pulled away.

"I'm so sorry," she told him. "I'm sorry I didn't value you and tried to manipulate you like you weren't a human being with feelings and free will." She started raining kisses all over his face. "I'm sorry I made you think that you weren't doing or giving enough." More kisses. "I'm sorry I ever made you feel like you had to change for me." She lifted her face, cradled his between her palms, and looked fixedly into his eyes. "I don't care that you hate peopling. I don't care that you're prone to staring off into the distance and brooding instead of spilling all of your feelings. I don't care that you refuse to dance bachata with me." She rested her forehead against his while maintaining eye contact. "I appreciate everything that makes you Liam, and I love you exactly as you are."

Liam closed his eyes, completely undone. He tilted his face up until he felt the tip of her nose against his lips. He kissed it and opened his eyes. "I'm sorry I pushed you away. I was scared that you wouldn't love me enough and that you would leave me, so I left first." He sighed. "I have to remember that people are going to make mistakes. You're going to do things I don't understand or agree with, but that doesn't mean you're trying to hurt me or looking for an out." He rubbed his thumbs underneath her still-streaming eyes. "I have a lot of work to do on myself. I know I do, but I'm ready to undertake that journey. I want to be the man you deserve."

A camera operator appeared over her right shoulder, and Liam was positive that the presence at his back was the other one. He ignored them both completely. Just as he ignored the blur of blended colors that was the Vegas watching avidly from the sidelines. No one mattered but the woman in his arms.

"And I'm going to be better too. I'm not scared to be free anymore. It will hurt, but I can move on from this place." She gestured to the restaurant around them. "I can forge a new path, and I want you to know that I'm ready to dedicate myself to making this work in the best way. I'm going to make sure that everyone knows that I have a new priority—"

"Kamilah," Liam interjected. He put a finger to her lips. "I know how important your family is to you, and I don't expect you to not be the generous and selfless person you are. Your devotion to the people you love is what I love most about you. I don't want you to change either. I just want to love you. That's all I've ever wanted."

Kamilah's tears overflowed, spilling down her cheeks only to get caught in her wide smile. "We started out this life being best friends, and we're going to finish it being partners in every sense of the word. This isn't my journey. It's ours." She drew his beaming face to hers and kissed him.

Granda's voice came from next to them. "Okay. Okay. The cameras got more than enough." A hand landed on his shoulder and tugged him back. "Save the rest of that for the bedroom."

In Liam's arms Kamilah blinked a few times as if coming back to herself. Her eyes went wide, and a flush covered her cheeks.

She covered her face with her hands while repeating "Oh my God" over and over. "We just made out in front of my family, cameras, and the freaking mayor."

Liam let her slide down his body until her feet were touching the floor, but he kept his arms around her. "I don't know

what to say about those last two, but your family is going to
have to deal, because I plan to kiss you like my life depends
on it. Anywhere and anytime."

She wrinkled her nose. "Corny." She smiled. "But I love it."
Then she jerked and spun to face Granda. "Killian," she scolded.

Granda winked at her.

"What?" Liam asked.

"Your grandpa just pinched my butt."

Liam gave Granda an incredulous look, but he wasn't paying attention.

"Papo and I have one more thing we'd like to say, before
everyone leaves," Granda was saying to the room at large.
"Consider this our grand finale."

Oh fuck. What now? He and Kamilah shared a look of alarm.

"Let me start by saying, Liam, congratulations, lad. You're
no longer a dense gobshite who can't see what's right in front
of his face."

Liam shook his head, and Kamilah laughed.

"Same for Kamilah," Papo added.

"Hey!" Kamilah huffed.

"Oop," Leo said from the side of the room.

Valeria smacked him upside the head without taking her
attention off Granda.

He shot her a disgruntled look and rubbed the back of his
head.

Granda continued. "Secondly, we'd like to inform everyone that, as of this morning, this property now belongs to
Liam Kane and Santiago Vega Sr. We transferred the deed
into their names, but we did this with the understanding that
the building cannot be sold without permission from both
owners. And neither of you will even think about it unless

you want my ghost showing up in your bedroom every night to torture you."

Papo stepped forward and motioned for Kamilah to step forward as well.

Kamilah looked to Liam, but he just shrugged, clearly having no idea what was going to happen next. She frowned and wrinkled her forehead. Tons of possibilities popped into her mind at once, some good and some not so great. She wished she knew which type of surprise this was going to be.

Abuelo motioned for her again. "Ven."

With a deep breath, she let go of Liam and walked up to Abuelo.

"I am always so grateful to have such a large and smart family because that means that I have people to help me with whatever I need. In this case, I needed a lawyer, and thankfully, my oldest grandson is one. He was able to help me get everything set up." Abuelo reached into the inner breast pocket of his blazer and pulled out a folded packet of papers. "This is the selling contract for El Coquí." He unfolded the packet and put it on the table. "It includes everything from the machines in the kitchen and the chairs in the dining area to the name." He turned to her with a smile. "Kamilah is about to buy it from me."

WHAT? Kamilah's ears started ringing. She felt like she might pass out. She placed a hand on the back of the nearest chair and held on. What did he mean? She slept in Saint's guest room and didn't even own a car. How could she buy El Coquí? "Abu, I don't have the money to buy the business from you."

He grinned at her and leaned forward to whisper in her ear. "Check your back pocket."

Kamilah reached behind her, but hesitated at the last moment. "Abuelo," she murmured.

He nodded. "Hazlo."

She did it. She slid her fingers into her back pocket and felt the familiar linen-like texture of cash. *What the*— She tugged it out and found a folded hundred-dollar bill. She swung to look at Killian, who winked at her. That was why he'd pinched her ass.

Abuelo held out his hand for the money.

She shook her head and clenched the bill in her fist. "Abuelo, this is not enough to purchase the restaurant from you."

"It's more than enough," he countered. He grabbed on to the hand that held the money and pulled it to his mouth for a kiss before holding it to his chest. "Ojitos, you are the only one who loves this place as much as your abuela did. You are the one who has always seen it with eyes of hope and possibility, like her. She would want you to build yourself a new dream with this place." He pried her fingers open and took the bill. He put the money in his pocket and pulled out a pen.

Kamilah held her interlocked fingers up to her face as if in prayer. She closed her eyes and rested the bridge of her nose on her thumb. God, she wished Abuela were there to tell her what to do.

She thought about all the times she and Abuela had snuck down into the kitchen in the middle of the night to make hot chocolate and cookies. They'd talk forever. Kamilah would ask Abuela a ton of questions and share all her big ideas and bigger dreams. Every time Abuela would look at her and smile. She always said the same thing. "Lo único que le pido a Dios es que seas feliz."

In that moment Kamilah knew what her grandmother

would tell her. It was almost as if Kamilah could hear her voice say *Sign the contract and make us both happy.* She looked at her parents, who were smiling and nodding. Kamilah took the pen from Abuelo and scrawled her name on the line.

"Now, since you are the owner of the business, but your papi is the owner of the building, you will have to work out a lease agreement with your parents."

Kamilah nodded. She was already thinking of how to give them enough to pay the property taxes and still secure a profit to enjoy.

Mayor Johnson stepped forward. "As a new business owner in a historic neighborhood, there are many grants and low-interest loans available to you. Call my office, and we'll schedule a meeting to help you figure everything out."

Kamilah was awed. "Thank you."

"Now that that is all taken care of, let's talk about love and blackmail," Killian continued. "When Papo and I made this plan, we knew that not only would we have to show you both how to fall in love, but we'd have to teach you how to stay in love."

"So from now on, remember our rules of engagement." Abuelo held up a finger. "Number one. The particulars of your relationship are private. A relationship concerns only the people in it. Don't let outside forces intrude in its growth or affect its progress. Keep each other's counsel, because you need to trust one another."

Killian held up two fingers. "Number two. Be present. Loving someone is not easy. You both have to show up ready to put in the work and stay even when things get hard, and they will. But they will also be good, so enjoy each other, and enjoy the way you feel together. Life is too unexpected to waste it not living every moment to the fullest."

"Number three," Abuelo said. "Support each other. You don't always have to agree or understand each other, but you have to remember that you have a partnership. Life is full of ups and downs, but together you can not only make it through but make it through happily."

"Papo, we appreciate the life lessons and everything," Liam said. "But Kamilah and I started this life loving each other, and that's exactly how we're going to end it. The only variable left is where this journey takes us in the middle."

"I, for one, am excited to see it for myself," Kamilah said.

"I say we start here." Next to her Liam dug into his pocket. "By making this real." He pulled out Eimear's engagement ring, dropped to one knee, and held it up for Kamilah to accept or decline. "Yes?" he asked, the vulnerability in his eyes making tears form in hers.

She loved this man beyond all reason, and he knew it, but there would probably always be a part of him that would be scared it would go away in the blink of an eye. All she could do was continue to show him that it was worth the risk. "Yes," she told him. "Yes to everything."

EPILOGUE

At the corner table, Papo Vega leaned back against the padded bench. From his new favorite spot, he could see the entire dining room of El Coquí and into Kane Distillery through the newly created doorway that was always open. He let his eyes track from the fully occupied tables of the restaurant to the interior of the distillery, where Liam was giving a tour to a group of entertained customers.

Although Kane Distillery had not won first place in the contest, the footage of Kamilah and Liam had made them the most popular choice during the public voting. The video went viral on all the Caragrams and PichónChats. Since then, both businesses were busier than ever. The mayor was a frequent guest, which led to even more people around the city wanting to check them out, even in the dead of winter.

My friend, I hope you are seeing this. Killian had lost his final battle with cancer a few months ago. Papo missed him every day, but he knew that his best friend—his brother—would be happy with the way everything had turned out.

Papo wiped at his wet eyes and looked away just as his grandson and great-granddaughter walked into the restaurant. Both of them were wearing unhappy expressions.

"Hola, mi amor," he told Rosie when they approached. She was such a serious little thing, just like Saint. "Did you have a good day at school?"

She made a face and looked back at her dad.

She had not.

Papo pulled a lollipop out of his pocket and handed it to Rosie, who snatched it up, unwrapped it, put it in her mouth, and took off before Saint could object.

Saint plopped into the seat in front of Papo. He looked worn down and upset.

"¿Qué pasa, mi'jo?"

"My daughter's fucking teacher pinned a note to her back as if she's the church bulletin board and not a little kid."

"What did the note say?"

"She wants to set up another meeting. I don't know what for. I already told her that I don't know why Rosie doesn't want to talk at school." He looked over at his daughter, who was spinning on a rotating bar stool. "I've tried every damn thing she's suggested, and it doesn't work. What the fuck else does this woman want from me?"

Papo's eyebrows went up at the mini rant. It was very unlike Saint to curse and even more unlike him to display such strong emotions. He was usually calm, cool, and collected in all situations. "When is the meeting?" Papo wanted to meet this woman who had his grandson so worked up.

"When hell freezes over," Saint mumbled before getting up and going over to Rosie. He said a few words to her.

She grudgingly handed over the lollipop in her mouth, then slid off the stool. She took Saint's hand, and they walked toward the bathrooms.

An arm in a white sleeve entered Papo's line of sight. He followed it down to a small hand wearing a familiar gold-and-emerald engagement ring and holding a plate of heart-healthy pastelón. Upon first glance, it looked just like regular Puerto Rican plantain lasagna, but he knew his granddaughter, and there was no doubt that she'd managed to make it with no salt, little cheese, nothing fried, and ground turkey instead of beef. "Yo no quiero eso," he told Kamilah.

She set it down in front of him anyway. "Cuando uno tiene hambre, se come lo que hay," she shot back with a smart-ass smirk. She just loved throwing his words back in his face.

To be fair, when he used to tell her that, it was because there were a bunch of her brothers and cousins around all asking for special meals as well. Not one hungry old man who just wanted to eat some real food. "Mejor dame chicharrones y mofongo con mucho ajo." Pieces of fried pork and super-garlicky mashed plantain was his favorite dish.

She chuckled as if he'd just made a joke. "This is all you will be served here, so you'd better eat this and enjoy it."

He eyed the saltshaker sitting on the table next to his, but it was snatched away before he could even reach for it. "I liked you better before you were the owner," he grumbled.

"I liked you better before you were the freeloader who hung around all day demanding food and drink." She smiled and kissed him on the forehead.

He snorted. "You love having me here all day because you like to keep an eye on me like I am a kid in detention."

"You pretty much are."

"¿Quién yo? Yo soy un angelito."

It was her turn to snort. "An angel, my ass. The center called me and told me to keep you here because the other residents are still mad at you for throwing out all the coffee."

"That was dirt, not coffee."

"What is with your hatred of decaf?" she asked, but she wasn't really paying attention to him. From the open double doors she'd caught sight of Liam, and he of her. They stared at each other for a long moment.

Liam's face was serious and intent, but somehow he still managed to let Kamilah know what he was thinking, and it was something naughty, if the way Kamilah's cheeks reddened was a clue.

"Con permiso," she muttered before walking away from him and toward Liam.

Liam excused himself from the group and met Kamilah at the door.

She lifted her face, and he kissed her quickly.

They pulled apart at the same time and whispered things to one another.

Papo caught Liam's lips mouthing the words *Te amo.*

He was happy with the way their relationship was progressing. Shortly after the contest, they had both started counseling. They had different therapists, but whatever they were working on separately had already helped them become better partners for each other. Liam was still sad and withdrawn at times, and he was still getting used to his grandpa no longer being around.

He misses you, mi hermano. Papo looked out the window and focused his gaze on the sky, trying his best to envision Killian standing among the clouds with Connor, Eimear, and his own dear wife, Rosa Luz.

The clouds parted for a second, and a bright ray of sunshine blasted through the window to land right on the two lovebirds.

"Don't worry," Papo told the light. "I will be here for them."

The sunlight faded away as the clouds shifted in the sky, and Papo continued to think. He thought about his other grandchildren: Saint, the exhausted single dad; Leo, the reckless adrenaline junkie; Mia, the overserious surgeon; Alex, the overcompensating tomboy, et cetera, et cetera. They all needed his help.

"Abu, what are you thinking?" Kamilah was back.

He turned to glance at her. "Nothing," he said, a touch too innocently.

"Yeah, right," Kamilah scoffed. "I recognize that look, troublemaker."

"Me?" He feigned surprise. "Yo na' mas soy un viejo." He used his normal claim of simply being an old man, even though she never fell for that. "How can I be a troublemaker?" And, in truth, he wasn't a troublemaker. Why would he want to be a troublemaker when *matchmaker* sounded so much better?

★ ★ ★ ★ ★

ACKNOWLEDGMENTS

In all my years working toward being a published author, I never stopped to think about how completely nerve-racking writing the acknowledgments would be. I don't know that I have sufficient words to express my gratitude to everyone who helped make my dream a reality, but I will try my very best.

To my phenomenal agent, Patrice Caldwell. Thank you for emailing me at 3:00 a.m. to tell me how much you loved my story. You have been this book's most fierce champion from the very beginning. I'm eternally grateful for you and your badassery. I can't wait to see what else we accomplish together.

I'm grateful for Pouya, Katherine, Joanna, Meredith, and the entire New Leaf team for being in my corner and being as excited about my career as I am. New Leaf has been my dream agency since I first started exploring the possibility of being an author and I still can't believe that I get to be a Leaf!

I also give immense thanks to my editor, April Osborn, for gently and gracefully guiding me through the publication of my debut novel. I love that I can completely entrust my characters and stories to you, knowing that you will make them the best versions of themselves.

Additional thanks go to the marvelous team at MIRA and Harlequin: Ashley MacDonald in marketing, Justine Sha in publicity, Lindsey Reeder and Abi Sivanesan in digital marketing/ social media, Gigi Lau, cover art director extraordinaire, and everyone else who helped this book reach its full potential.

I must thank my amazingly talented cover artist, Andressa Meissner, for creating a gorgeous cover that completely reflects my story and is so special that I cried tears of joy when I saw it.

My journey to getting this book published has been years in the making, and it would not have happened without the kind, supportive, and special people I've met along the way.

To my Here Comes Trouble crew: Mai-Ling, Marlena, Becka, and Amanda. Thank you for being there, drinking mojitos with me from the very beginning, and for making me feel capable whenever I doubt myself.

To my WI crew: The Lizzes, Lorelie, Carla, Carrie, Jen, Tricia, and Molly. Thank you all for making me feel welcome always. A special thank-you to Liz Lincoln for always answering my chaotic texts, letting me vent, and just being the kind of friend who drops off awesome cross-stitches and waffles when I'm having a rough time.

Mil gracias to my amiga hermanas in my LatinxRom crew— Alexis, Priscilla, Mia, Adriana, Sabrina, Angelina, Liana, Diana, and Zoraida—for taking me under your wing, celebrating my milestones as if they were your own, being my biggest cheerleaders, and answering all of my dumb questions.

To all of the friends I made through Twitter: Denise, Taj, Stacey, Lisa, etc. Thanks for the words and GIFs of encouragement and celebration.

A very, very special thank-you to Author Mentor Match for

hooking me up with the greatest mentor ever, Brittany Kelley. Brittany, having you as a mentor has been one of the greatest things to happen to me. You helped me trust in myself and my voice when I was really doubting my abilities. This book would not be what it is without your support and guidance.

And, of course, I would not be here without my family and friends.

Marsh, you know at this point you are more than my best friend. You are my ride or die. Point. Blank. Period.

To my titis, tíos, and many cousins. This book would not exist without you all, simply because I wouldn't have any stories to tell. You have all surrounded me with love and laughter for my entire life, which is exactly what inspired this story. But don't go looking for yourselves in the characters, because the inspiration doesn't go that far. LOL!

Annie and Marcos, you both inspire me every day to never give up, to keep trying no matter how hard things get. Thank you both for providing me with the opportunity to be the Cool Titi to my loves Ezmi, Isaiah, Israel, and Xavier.

Mom, through your example you taught me to be strong, resilient, hardworking, forgiving, and caring. I am always in awe of you and so grateful to call you my mother.

To my abuela, who will never get to read this, everything I am is because of you. I love you and miss you with all my heart. Para Siempre.

Finally, I thank you, the reader. Thank you for picking up my book and giving it a chance. I'm so incredibly lucky to share my characters and stories with you. I hope this story was exactly what you needed it to be, whether that be a reflection of yourself and culture, a few hours of entertainment, or anything in between.